Praise for Preston Holtry and Death in Emily 3

"Engaging plot keeps the pages turning as you're effectively transported to a rugged Arizona mining town to untangle a web of deceit and murder. Masterful mix of characters and events keep your sleuthing instincts churning to the very end."—*Jack Tyrrell, Oro Valley, AZ.*

"Preston Holtry has mixed the ingredients of southwest mining history with murder and deception, added a dash of early forensic science and created a recipe sure to provide an exceptional read."—*Gary Wilde, Birch Bay, Washington.*

"*Death in Emily 3* by Preston Holtry is a murder mystery set in early Arizona mines and mining towns. You will meet strong characters you will always remember; and, you will be challenged to solve the puzzles of evidence uncovered by persistent criminal investigation. This story will introduce you to a new author. Enjoy him; he has more good stories."—*Ron Chandler, Salina, Kansas.*

"Set in a deep and dark mine in the early 1900s, with well-developed characters, the author weaves a mystery that keeps your mind and pages turning."—*Jim and Susan Campbell, La Veta, Colorado.*

"Preston Holtry's detective, Morgan Westphal, 'is a man for all seasons.' *Death in Emily 3* is a good read."—*Adrienne Eesley, Tucson, Arizona.*

"Preston Holtry's new novel, *Death in Emily 3*, introduces you to diverse people and creates an interest to follow them through to the last page. It contains a history of mining in

Arizona with suspense and surprises right to the end. A good read. I look forward to more good stories by him."—*Pamela Oldow, LaConner, Washington.*

Forthcoming Morgan Westphal Novels by Preston Holtry

A Troublesome Affair (Vol 2 in the Morgan Westphal mysteries)

Against the backdrop of the U.S. Army punitive expedition to capture Pancho Villa, *A Troublesome Affair* takes Morgan deep into Mexico in his attempt to prove the innocence of a Negro sergeant accused of the rape and attempted murder of a white officer's wife.

See the excerpt at the end of the present volume.

Look for A Troublesome Affair in 2014 from Moonshine Cove

Seal of Confession (Vol 3 in the Morgan Westphal mysteries)

Morgan is hired by a priest to clear the name of a man hanged for a murder he did not commit.

DEATH IN EMILY 3

Preston Holtry

Moonshine Cove Publishing, LLC
Abbeville, South Carolina U.S.A.

ISBN: 978-1-937327-32-3
Library of Congress Control Number: 2013951740

Book design by Cindy Guare and Moonshine Cove; cover photograph from author's collection, used with permission.

DEDICATION

For Judy, my wife and best friend.

ACKNOWLEDGEMENTS

I've taken the tour of the Copper Queen Mine in Bisbee, Arizona, several times. It's an incredibly interesting experience primarily because of the tour guides who once worked there or in other mines. By the time I completed the third visit to the mine, I knew I was going to write a mystery novel involving murder in a copper mine deep underground.

My appreciation to Moonshine Cove and all those who allowed Morgan Westphal and a storyteller to reach a wider audience.

I credit *Bisbee Queen of the Copper Camps* by Lynn R. Bailey for giving me a sense of historical background concerning the events and people for the novel's pre-WWI setting. The Douglas Museum in Jerome, AZ and the Bisbee Mining & Historical Museum in Bisbee, AZ were also invaluable resources.

My visits to Jerome were beneficial for understanding the unstable rock formations in the Emily and Imperial Mines. A number of buildings in Jerome have been displaced and destroyed because of these conditions. As for the problem of flooding in a desert land—well, the silver mines in Tombstone were eventually abandoned after attempts to drain them became a hopeless endeavor.

Adobe Wells or Mesquite Flats are figments of my imagination as are the characters. I will admit to certain resemblances Adobe Wells may have to Bisbee and Jerome. I suppose I was also thinking of Warren near Bisbee and Cottonwood below Jerome in the description of Mesquite Flats.

Prologue
Albuquerque
May, 1915

He tried to ignore the hypnotic effect of the metronomic ticking Westminster Regulator hanging on the opposite wall, but he couldn't and surrendered to the inevitable. With a jaw-cracking yawn, Morgan Westphal propped his legs on top of the desk, leaned back in the swivel chair, and closed his eyes. It looked to be a slow day for Westphal & Cosgrove Investigations, and he didn't mind a bit. He was just starting to slide down into a peaceful, dark abyss when he heard the front door of the outer office open followed by a young voice announcing, "Telegram for Mr. Morgan Westphal."

He heard Miss Clarkson tell the delivery boy to wait in case there was a reply.

Morgan barely managed to open his eyes and look reasonably alert by the time his rail-thin secretary came into the office and handed him a yellow Western Union envelope. He hesitated before tearing the envelope open, certain the telegram did not contain good news. He read the cryptic message and felt a perverse satisfaction in confirming he was correct.

> MORGAN WESTPHAL STOP FRANK IN JAIL ADOBE
> WELLS ARIZONA STOP CHARGE IS MURDER STOP
> FRANK WANTS YR HELP STOP LOOKS REAL BAD
> STOP TRUESDALE

Momentarily forgetting the secretary's presence, Morgan crumpled the telegram, stood up, and kicked the wastebasket across the office where it clanged off the far wall spilling the contents in the process. Miss Clarkson's face was a picture of stunned surprise. In the years she had known Morgan

Westphal, she had seldom seen her normally unruffled, reserved employer display so much emotion.

She hesitated before asking, "Shall I tell the messenger boy to wait for a reply?"

"Yes." Miss Clarkson nodded and started to walk to the upturned wastebasket to pick up the litter strewn across the floor, but Morgan stopped her by saying, "Miss Clarkson, don't bother in case I want to kick it again."

Wide-eyed, she quickly fled the office.

It didn't take him long to frame a reply.

"Dan, tell Frank unable to come. M. Westphal"

Morgan had just finished writing the brief message when William Cosgrove, thumbs hooked in his braces, sauntered into the office and sat down in the chair opposite Morgan's desk. Cosgrove took in the dumped wastebasket and his partner's grim face and was certain Frank Shaw, Morgan's half-brother, was somehow responsible.

Morgan picked up the crumpled message and wordlessly tossed it to Cosgrove. After reading it, Cosgrove pursed his lips and whistled softly.

"Well Morgan, I guess maybe you ought to go on down to Adobe Wells and see about this."

Morgan's response was both quick and resolute. "This time I'm not going. Will, I'm tired of picking up the pieces every time Frank gets into trouble. For once he can get himself out of whatever scrape he's in now."

"Whoa partner, hold on a minute. We're not talking about a Saturday night hoorah and a few days in the pokey. Jesus Christ, the charge is murder. "Frank's a wild one, but I can't believe the boy would murder anyone."

"The 'boy' is no longer a boy, and you know as well as I do with Frank anything's possible. Maybe over the years I did too much, and instead of helping, all I did was make him worse. I should've stopped the hand holding years ago."

"Why didn't you?"

"After my father died, mother married another miner by the name of Edmond Shaw, probably out of some mistaken belief I needed a father. The last thing I needed was a stepfather like Shaw. He was a worthless sunnuva bitch and a drunk to boot. With a father like Shaw, I suppose it isn't Frank's fault he's turned out the way he has. One day the drift Shaw was working caved in, and that was the last of him. Not long after, my mother took sick with lung fever and died. Before she died she made me promise to look after Frank. Ever since, taking care of Frank got to be a habit and a never-ending job."

Noticing Morgan's more relaxed expression, Cosgrove said, "Didn't you just say something about a promise to your mother? You could catch the late afternoon train and be in Adobe Wells tomorrow."

Morgan looked sharply at Cosgrove. A moment later, he cursed, picked up the pencil and wrote a different reply.

"Dan, will arrive Adobe Wells sometime tomorrow. M. Westphal."

Morgan walked into the outer office and handed the message to the delivery boy along with two dollars.

"Keep whatever's left." After returning to his office, he said to Cosgrove, "The last time I went to Arizona was to visit Frank in the Yuma Territorial Prison when he was serving time for aggravated assault. Considering Frank nearly killed the other man, the lawyer earned his fee for getting him off with a light sentence. It won't help him when a jury learns why he was in prison."

"It looks to me as if he's going to need another good lawyer–and maybe a good investigator."

Morgan massaged his forehead and considered the truth of his partner's last comment.

"I don't know. Could be a good lawyer and my help this time might not be enough. I've known Dan Truesdale for almost twenty years–he's the marshal in Adobe Wells. If he says it looks bad, I reckon Frank's in real trouble."

Chapter One

The all-night train ride from Albuquerque to Mesquite Flats was long and slow with frequent stops at small towns along the way or places where there was no depot at all, only a sign and a dusty road bisecting the track in the middle of nowhere. By the time the train clattered into Mesquite Flats ten hours later, Morgan regretted not paying the extra fare for a sleeper.

He looked curiously out the window. The last time he had seen Mesquite Flats was through the eyes of a young boy when he left it; he wished he was leaving it now. Apart from being larger, he thought the town was just as ugly as he remembered it. Huge mountains of mud-colored slag formed a drab backdrop to a town that appeared gray and featureless and made more so by the black smoke belching from tall smelter stacks; the largest had the initials TJ&M painted on the side. Absent were the large mule corrals, which at one time occupied much of the space on the south side of town. He wondered how the ore was now being transported to the smelters from the mines located on the escarpment two thousand feet above the town. The few horse-drawn wagons and buggies looked strangely out of place, outnumbered as they were by an abundance of motor cars rattling around on paved streets. Depending on the season, he recollected the roads had been either ankle deep in choking dust or viscous mud.

Bag in hand, Morgan stepped off the train. His nostrils immediately began to burn from the acrid, sulfuric smell pervading the air. He made his way into the depot and spotted Dan Truesdale leaning against the station wall smoking a cigarette. In spite of his small, wiry stature, he knew the aging marshal still had a reputation for being tough and uncompromising when it came to keeping the peace. He wore a white striped shirt with a cravat, vest, and a black wide-brimmed hat. Around his waist was a pistol belt and holster with the walnut butt of a revolver sticking out. His bowed legs testified to years in a saddle.

"Welcome to Slagtown," Truesdale said, his sarcasm plainly evident in word and expression.

"If I said it was a pleasure to be here, you'd know I was stretching it. Thanks for the telegram, although I confess at first I almost didn't come."

"Yeah, I didn't think you'd be too happy to get it."

"I appreciate taking the trouble to meet me, and I'm sorry the train was late."

"No trouble. I had business down here in the 'Flats', and you didn't keep me waitin' long. Everybody around here knows the train ain't ever on time. I thought by meeting you, it'd give me a chance to fill you in on what happened and why Frank's ass is in a sling–hell, might be his neck after the trial's over."

Morgan followed Truesdale out of the depot and toward an open top, black roadster parked nearby. The small badly-dented two-seater was covered in a thick coat of dust. Painted in gold on the door nearest him was a large gold star with 'Adobe Wells' above and 'Marshal' below.

"Throw your bag behind the seat, and we'll get started up the hill."

Morgan squeezed into the small automobile thinking he would have preferred hiring a buggy or a horse to get to Adobe Wells. He realized his distrust of motor cars was unreasonable and based on a fundamental ignorance of how they functioned; it was also an ignorance he had so far found no incentive to overcome. He would always prefer to be on a horse than in a motorcar.

"It looks like a few changes have taken place since the last time I was here," Morgan commented.

"I get down here a couple of times a month, and every time I do, it's bigger, more crowded. I 'spect you'll find Adobe Wells a lot different since you lived here."

Dispensing with the small talk, Morgan asked, "Tell me what happened."

Concentrating on maneuvering the roadster somewhat inexpertly around pedestrians, horse-drawn carriages, and other automobiles, Truesdale took his time replying.

"There ain't much to tell. Frank's accused of killing a fella by the name of Phillip Hardesty in a drift down in Tunnel 3 of the Emily Mine. There weren't no witnesses, and at first it looked like it was nothin' more than an accident. As Frank tells it, Hardesty must have walked from his drift through a connecting crosscut into Frank's drift after Frank had lit his charges and went back to the main tunnel to wait for the charges to go off. He claims he never saw Hardesty until after he went back to check the results of the blast thirty minutes later."

"Why thirty minutes?"

"Drillers are required to wait that long in case there's a misfire or delayed explosion. There's good reason. The dynamite most of the mines are usin' is poor stuff. Sometimes it explodes prematurely or not at all. The fuses ain't too reliable either. The muckers ain't allowed to go into the drift until the driller gives the all clear. Most times, the drillers don't wait that long 'cause they're in hurry to get back on top, and the sooner the muckers can get in and haul the ore out, the sooner they can finish the shift. Frank says he waited the required time before going back into the drift where he found Hardesty on his back with his face caved in and covered in busted rock. He figured the blast had killed him, and everybody, including Frank, assumed that's what had happened. The next day the coroner took a closer look at the body and found Hardesty had been stabbed in the back. Frank's version then started lookin' pretty thin. To make things worse, Frank and Hardesty weren't exactly the best of friends. It was common knowledge they didn't much like each other. I understand they'd had a dust-up a time or two. Under the circumstances, I didn't have any choice but to lock him up, if only for his own protection. There's hard feelings against Frank in Adobe Wells."

"Has he got a lawyer?"

"Not yet. He says he was waitin' until you got here, and maybe you'd take care of that."

"Well, that's Frank's way of getting me to pay for the lawyer." Truesdale chose not to respond well aware of Frank's past dependency on Morgan's generosity and tolerance. "Do you believe Frank's explanation of what happened?"

Truesdale hesitated before replying, his face and voice indicating uncertainty. "I don't know, Morgan. God knows I'd like to believe him, but it don't look too good. Your brother and Hardesty were the only two people in that section of the tunnel. To make matters worse, it was common knowledge there was hard feelings between them. I guess the thing that bothers me the most is that Hardesty was stabbed in the back. Frank's no saint and he has a reputation for havin' a quick temper, but to my way of thinkin' if Frank was going to kill Hardesty, he wouldn't have stuck a knife in his back. Nah, it just don't seem like somethin' Frank would do."

Morgan nodded, "I agree. Are there any good lawyers in Adobe Wells?"

Truesdale shrugged, "Samuel Spencer might do. I reckin' he's good enough, but his health ain't the best. He's got consumption, and I'm thinkin' he ain't gonna be around much longer. On the other hand, if I was on the poor side of things, Sam Spencer would be the man I'd go to, and then I'd be hopin' and prayin' he'd last long enough to do me some good. Hell, Morgan, Adobe Wells ain't Tucson or Phoenix. If you want more choices, you gotta go out of town, but if you do, better do it quick."

"What do you mean quick?"

Truesdale shifted uneasily in his seat. "You may as well know the rest of it. The judge set a trial date eight days from now."

"Eight days!" Morgan exclaimed. "Why bother with a trial? Just string him up today and be done with it. For Christ's sake, what's the rush?"

"You might say the reason is Victor LaTrobe."

"Who's Victor LaTrobe?"

"He's the local superintendent for Thurlowe, Jansen & McCormick or TJ&M. You may have noticed the initials all over the place. TJ&M owns the Emily, Pearl, and Dorothy Mines, the biggest and richest mines around Adobe Wells. The company also owns mines in Colorado and California. You might say TJ&M owns most of Adobe Wells one way or t'other which makes LaTrobe the biggest frog in this pond. Generally, whatever Victor LaTrobe wants, he gets, and right now it's no secret he wants your brother's neck in a noose."

"Why would a mine superintendent care enough one way or another if a miner is murdered or killed underground?" Morgan responded in surprise, remembering the marked lack of concern when his father was killed underground.

"Well, I'm not sure I know the answer to that. LaTrobe's eccentric and quick-tempered, but usually he'll listen to reason, leastways he did until maybe six months ago. He's done a lot for Adobe Wells. He got TJ&M to enlarge the hospital and stocked the library with a passel of books. He put up money out of his own pocket for a new wing in the school. It may be he wants to look good by showing what a good citizen he is and how much TJ&M is doing for the town, including strong support for law and order. Like I said, until recently he was a decent sort at least as much as one of them jump-upped rich bastards can be, now he changes moods faster than you can piss a couple of beers."

"I thought the law and order part was your job."

15

Truesdale shrugged and sounded defensive when he said, "I work for the mayor and the town council and …."

Morgan immediately perceived where Truesdale was heading. "And the mayor and the town council are reporting to LaTrobe, and LaTrobe wants to make an example of Frank."

"Yep, that's pretty much the way the stick floats."

"How's Frank doing?"

Truesdale frowned and shook his head. "Frank don't seem to understand the trouble he's in. His biggest concern is he's losing wages every day he's locked up. If things weren't bad enough, Judge Breen—he's the presidin' judge for the county—is gonna hear the case. Breen is fair enough, but he's tough and knows Frank only too well. About a month ago, Breen put Frank in jail for three days for drunk and disorderly. Unfortunately, it wasn't the first time Frank stood in front of Judge Breen."

The two men lapsed into gloomy silence as the roadster left the macadam behind and began to bounce on the rough and narrow dirt road tracing the sharp contours of the steep canyon wall. On the opposite side of the canyon, a small chuffing locomotive emitting clouds of black smoke pulled a long string of empty ore cars. The initials TJ&M were painted on the sides of the cars.

Truesdale pulled to a stop at the top of the hill to give Morgan a chance to take in the town of Adobe Wells. Morgan had been prepared for change, but the sheer scope of the mining operation and size of Adobe Wells was a greater shock than he could have imagined. A town once confined to the bottom of a wide canyon now sprawled up the slopes above and into several smaller and previously unoccupied side canyons and gulches. The dwellings on the steep slopes were crowded close together and perched precariously on narrow ledges. If the hills had been sparsely forested when he lived there, trees of any size were no longer evident on the largely barren rock and cactus-covered hills. Where only a few head frames had existed before, dozens of the skeletal structures supporting hoisting cables and lifting cages dotted the landscape. Above the noise of the roadster's idling engine, he heard the faint whir of the nearest cage wheels lifting ore or carrying miners down to or up from the underground depths. There was the rumble of ore cars being pushed toward long wooden drop chutes followed by the hollow roar as the ore tumbled down into collection bins below. The smelters, once located near each mine, were now gone as was the foul-smelling smoke that once covered the town like a smelly blanket. He suspected the brown pall, which had permeated the town was the principal cause of his mother's lung problems and had made the ordeal of Frank's difficult birth a major reason for his mother's declining health. Absent the smoky haze, Adobe Wells appeared on the surface a prosperous beehive of activity under a blue, cloudless afternoon sky.

"It's not quite what I remembered," Morgan said in understatement.

"You see that tall head frame over there on the left side with the long drop chute?" Truesdale said, pointing to the opposite side of the canyon. "That's the Emily where Frank was working. Next to it on the right is the Pearl, and next to it is the Dorothy. Like I said before, all three are owned by TJ&M. To the left of the Emily is the Imperial owned by the SMC, the Sandusky Mining Company. The mines on that slope have the richest deposits so far discovered. TJ&M recently bought out ten other companies and now owns most of the mines around Adobe Wells. LaTrobe keeps makin' offers for the Imperial and a few other smaller mines on that side of the canyon. So far, Sandusky and the other owners won't sell. Sandusky has the other independents convinced they shouldn't cave in for the low prices LaTrobe is offering. I'm guessin' Sandusky is just bidin' his time until he can come up with enough scratch to buy out the independents and challenge the TJ&M. There's hardly anything left down there that isn't owned by TJ&M or about to be taken over by it," Truesdale added with a sweep of his hand. "Yes, siree, Adobe Wells is fast becoming a real one-company town." Morgan wasn't able to tell if Truesdale was simply stating or lamenting the fact.

"I noticed the engine and rail cars that passed us had TJ&M painted on them. Has Latrobe and the syndicate he's working for tried to force the independents to sell by denying use of the rail, or is there another way to get their ore down to the smelters in Mesquite Flats."

"Nope, the only way to move the ore is by rail, and TJ&M sure enough owns it. TJ&M didn't build the railroad; it was built by a consortium representing all the mine owners when the ore capacity outweighed what the mule wagons were able to haul down to the smelters. When LaTrobe got here last year, he twisted the arms of the independents and bought the consortium out. He promised he wouldn't strangle the other owners by demanding an unfair price to transport the ore. So far, the arrangement seems to be working, at least for now."

Truesdale put the roadster in gear and slowly descended a gentle slope the last few hundred feet into town. Modest, one-story homes on the edge of town were replaced by two-story brick and stone buildings. Except for the roads leading into the canyons, the streets in the main part of town were paved. The wooden board walks had been replaced with brick or concrete. Electric lamp posts lined each side of the street where the store windows advertised a variety of goods and services that would have been common in Tucson or Phoenix but not the Adobe Wells Morgan recalled. There was a noticeable absence of saloon signs that before had dominated the streets.

"What happened to the saloons?" Morgan asked in surprise.

Truesdale delayed answering as he turned off the main street and was forced to brake suddenly to avoid hitting a pedestrian. The marshal ignored the angry man's shaking fist and epithet and replied calmly, "Oh, they're around right enough, but you won't see them advertised as such. Damned if Arizona didn't pass a prohibition law last year," Truesdale said in disgust. "Them psalm-singin' bastards finally got the votes to do such a damn-fool thing, and anyone wearin' a badge in this state has been regrettin' it ever since, even though nothing's really changed. You can still get a drink and get laid same as ever in any of the private clubs. The problem is a peace officer has less control now over what goes on inside compared to when the saloons were public. Before last year, the laws involvin' what you could and couldn't do in a saloon were strict and easy to enforce. It ain't so now. The whores are now workin' alongside where the booze is sold, which wasn't the case when they had to stay in the cribs behind the saloons. And because of that, Saturday nights is worse than ever what with drunk miners fightin' over the same whore." Truesdale shook his head and added somberly, "Morgan, I'm gettin' too damned old to put up with this crap much longer."

Truesdale pulled up in front of a two-story brick building with an empty lot on either side of it. The bars on the windows flanking the heavy door and on the double-row of smaller windows positioned along the sides of the building easily identified its purpose. The imposing building across the street with the traditional columned façade resembled nearly every court house Morgan had ever seen.

"I figured you might want to see Frank right away, so I brought you here first instead of taking you over to the hotel or one of the boarding houses. After you visit for a spell, I'll give you a suggestion or two about where you might want to bunk in. It all depends on how long you're gonna be around."

Morgan understood the marshal's last comment was a thinly-veiled attempt to learn how long he planned to stay in Adobe Wells. In reality, he hadn't made up his mind. He left Albuquerque with the expectation of being gone only long enough to see Frank and arrange for the lawyer he correctly assumed his brother had not yet hired. With a trial date scheduled little more than a week away, there was little point in leaving now until it was over, one way or the other.

Morgan followed Truesdale through the front door, and the familiar and unmistakable jail odor immediately filled his nostrils. The combination of gun oil, antiseptic, and the faint odor of urine was ubiquitous to every jail he had ever been in to include the one he had presided over in Las Cruces more than ten years ago. To the left and right of the entrance was a waiting area containing worn benches and an assortment of mismatched wooden chairs. The floor around the spittoons was tobacco-stained. The reception area and office section was separated by a wooden rail. Mounted on a wall behind the rail was a rack with rifles and shotguns chained together. In front of the rack was a desk at which sat a stern-faced, bespectacled man in his early thirties with bulging arms that strained the fabric of his shirt. The spectacles the burly man was wearing might have softened the features of most men; with him, it seemed to have the opposite effect. He had a badge similar to the one Truesdale wore pinned above the left pocket of his white shirt with the word 'deputy' above the encircled star. The deputy's attention was fixed on a woman awkwardly balancing an infant on one hip and clutching the hand of a small boy with the other. She was pretty enough in a coarse way, and the thin, faded dress she was wearing did little to conceal a shapely figure.

"Kincy, this here is Morgan Westphal, Frank Shaw's brother," Truesdale interrupted, paying no attention to the woman. "Kincy Blaylock is one of my deputies. He ain't the friendliest man around, but he does a good enough job, that is when he ain't workin' hard to get himself elected marshal," Truesdale added with a humorless laugh, that left Morgan thinking relations between the two men were strained.

Expressionless, Blaylock acknowledged the introduction with only a curt nod. Morgan wondered if the deputy was naturally unfriendly or if there was something else behind his demeanor. Blaylock's attention shifted back to the woman who was looking at Morgan with a quizzical expression. Briefly their eyes met before she looked away and directed her attention to the deputy.

Truesdale led the way toward a door at the back of the room. Behind him, Morgan heard the woman say, "But, Deputy Blaylock, how am I gonna feed my babes if my husband ain't found? It ain't like Willard to go off and leave us like this."

He heard Blaylock's unsympathetic, brusque reply. "Mrs. Merrick, we'll take a look around. He's probably sleeping it off up in one of the gulches. In the meantime, there's the miner's welfare store the next street over...." The rest of the conversation was lost when the door closed behind them.

Morgan followed Truesdale down a short hallway at the far end toward a stout metal-slatted door. Halfway down the hallway, Truesdale stopped at the entrance of a small office and motioned him inside.

"You can set your bag here while I have Myron take you up to see Frank; Myron's the jailer."

Truesdale paused and looked inquisitively at Morgan before asking, "You packin'?"

"It's in the suitcase," referring to the .44 caliber Army Colt at the bottom of his suitcase. After leaving Las Cruces, where as marshal the pistol was necessary, there had seldom been an occasion to use it. Occasionally, he wondered why he still bothered to bring it with him. It was too large to carry comfortably in the shoulder holster for any length of time, and it was an all-too grim reminder of why he had left Las Cruces. He reasoned it was a habit he hadn't found a reason to break.

Truesdale nodded and said over his shoulder, "Leave the bag in my office" and walked across the hall to a smaller office. A moment later, Truesdale emerged with a stocky man walking behind him and carrying a ring of keys. The jailer's broad shoulders, thick upper arms, and protruding belly resembled the build of a professional wrestler. In stark contrast to the deputy in the other office, the jailer stepped forward with a friendly smile and outstretched hand. Without waiting for Truesdale to introduce him, he said, "I'm Myron Hickman. It's a pleasure to know you, Mr. Westphal. Your brother's been looking forward to your arrival. Follow me, and I'll take you right up."

Truesdale remained behind while Morgan followed the jailer through the slatted metal door and toward an iron circular staircase.

After climbing to the next floor, the two men approached still another solid metal door. The jailer selected a key from the dozen or so attached to the ring and unlocked the padlock securing the thick sliding bolt to the door frame. Morgan followed the jailer into a cell block where the walls, ceiling, and cells were painted a featureless gray that even the shafts of sunlight streaming through the narrow windows failed to brighten. There were six small cells clustered in two back-to-back rows located in the center of the room. The roofs of the cells were sheet metal and separated from the building's high ceiling. The two center cells were enclosed by solid metal walls on all sides except the side facing the outside corridor which consisted of thick iron slats instead of the cylindrical bars typical in most jails. The four end cells had the luxury of being open-sided on the corner walls. The room was hot and stifling. Morgan immediately removed his suit jacket and loosened his celluloid collar.

"The marshal put Frank up here on account of how serious the charge is against him," the jailer said. "Hardesty was popular, and there's some in the town got some hard feelings toward your brother. Marshal Truesdale thought it would be safer to keep him up here. He's the onliest one here, but it ain't a bad place to be this time of year on account it's a lot cooler up here than in the cells below." The jailer then called out. "Hey, Frank, you got a visitor come to see you."

Morgan heard a shout from the far end of the room, "Is that you, Morg?"

Hearing the eagerness in his brother's voice, he felt a sudden rush of guilt for his near decision not to come to Adobe Wells. Ruefully, Morgan thought some things would never change; his brother would always require his help, and he would always feel guilty if he didn't give it. One of these days, he was going to say no to Frank, and it might surprise both of them. The thought caused him to consider whether there would ever be a next time should Frank be found guilty.

"Yeah, it's me, Frank."

The jailer led him to the opposite corner of the room where a sweat-soaked Frank stood dressed only in his underwear, each hand grasping a metal slat. His brother's face was wreathed in a broad, welcoming smile. Morgan noticed a nasty gash on Frank's forehead. He thought Frank's features resembled their stepfather who had been unusually handsome. It was also an unfortunate attribute that was often the cause of Frank's troubles. Frank liked women, and they reciprocated whether they were married or not. In contrast to Frank, he knew he was physically unremarkable. Women told him he was "interesting" and distinguished-looking rather than handsome.

Morgan conceded that it wasn't Frank's good looks alone that made him so appealing to women. He envied Frank's charm that made every woman he met feel she was the center of his attention, which at the time was exactly what Frank both intended and firmly believed. Frank's sincerity always was always convincing because it was genuine. Morgan learned long ago his brother had the capacity to tell you something and make you believe it even when later it proved not to be exactly the way things were. Frank didn't actually lie and would have been deeply offended if accused of it. Rather, he simply stretched the truth or omitted details to create an impression or ensure a conclusion Frank wanted you to have.

"Morg, I knew you wouldn't let me down," stretching both hands through the slats and grasping Morgan's hand firmly. The comment made him wince, and another wave of guilt swept over him.

Morgan turned to the jailer. "What's the chance of letting Frank out?"

The jailer shook his head and apologized. "Sorry Mr. Westphal, the marshal says I can't let Frank out. I can let you in if you want, but I'll have to lock the door."

"It's all right," Morgan replied and stepped aside while the jailer unlocked the cell door.

The small cell contained a metal bunk with a striped mattress on top of which was a folded blanket, pillow, and Frank's shirt and trousers. Under the bunk next to Frank's shoes was an enamel jug with a tin cup upended on top Morgan assumed contained water. A waist-high funnel with a hinged top was connected to a tube welded to the interior wall served as a urinal. The cell was no worse and some better than others Morgan had seen.

Morgan waited until after he heard the door to the cell block clang shut. "Now, Frank, tell me what happened."

Chapter Two

"Morgan, I swear on our mother's grave, I never killed Hardesty!"

"All right, for the time being, I'll accept that as the truth." In order to remain objective, Morgan tried to resist the automatic skepticism he had for nearly anything his brother had ever said.

"What do you mean for the time being? I'm telling you, I didn't do it."

"If I'm going to help you, I need to know the truth and with as much detail concerning what happened as you can remember."

"Hell, Morg, you know I wouldn't tell you different," he responded, giving Morgan an injured look.

"There are too many times in the past where you managed to leave out a few things, things that somehow or other ended up costing me both time and money. This time not telling me the whole truth might cost your life."

His feelings hurt, Frank sat down on the bunk, his hands on either side of his face, he stared morosely at the floor. "Shit, Morg, if you feel that way, why'd you bother comin' here?"

Morgan remained silent, resisting the urge to tell him he almost didn't. He waited for his brother's mood to rapidly shift as he knew it would. Without fail, Frank's sullen face quickly brightened.

"Never mind me, Morg. I'm just a little touchy what with being cooped up in this tin hell-hole. I'm real glad you came."

Morgan leaned back against the slatted bars opposite the bunk. "All right Frank, let's begin with what happened, what you know, and where you were when this man Hardesty was killed."

"Well, it was five days ago. I was drilling the last two holes on a face in one of the drifts down on the third and bottom level of the Emily."

"Were you alone?"

"Yeah."

"I thought drilling was always done by two-man teams."

"Not since the new percussion drills came along about four years back. The Leyner drills took care of that. Not so good for the drillers but cheaper for the mine owners since fewer drillers are needed. Anyway, I had to stop and change a bit. I was running a little behind, and it was getting close to the end of my shift, somewhere around eleven at night, I'd guess. The shift I was on starts at noon and goes to midnight, depending on if everything goes the way it's supposed to with no misfires or other problems."

"What do you mean, 'other problems'?"

"There's a lot of things can go wrong, time it takes to find a charge that didn't go off, a ceiling collapsin', hard rock that takes longer to drill, busted drills, and time wasted to get replacements. If you don't finish drillin' on time, you don't get paid for any time spent past your shift."

Listening to Frank's explanation, Morgan was reminded why he had no desire to follow his father's footsteps. Even the thought of going down hundreds of feet underground was enough to make Morgan shudder. In his younger days he tried it in one of the mines near Prescott, but after two weeks, he'd had enough and was more than glad to volunteer for Roosevelt's newly-formed Rough Riders and fight in Cuba. At the time, he had no idea what the fuss with Spain was all about and didn't really care. It was a chance for a better alternative to hardrock mining.

"I was just about finished replacing a drill bit when I realized I didn't hear sounds of any drilling over in the drift Hardesty was working. At first I thought maybe he was either taking a piss or changing a bit like me. Then I heard voices coming through the crosscut." Seeing the frown on Morgan's face, he elaborated. "Drifts are usually connected by a crosscut. That's a small passageway running at a right angle to the vein to connect two seams and provide more ventilation. The crosscut was maybe fifteen to twenty feet behind me and the face I was drilling. I wasn't sure I'd heard anything what with my ears ringing so bad. I took the cotton out of my ears and listened again thinking maybe Cardwell was making another round, but I didn't hear anything."

"Who's Cardwell?"

"Tate Cardwell's the shift boss. Well, I was thinkin' if it wasn't Cardwell, then Hardesty must've been talkin' to himself 'cause like me, Hardesty was workin' by himself. I thought it was kinda strange at the time Cardwell would be there since he had already been around less than an hour before."

"How often does Cardwell make his rounds?"

"He usually comes around three, maybe four times a shift. He's pretty regular."

"When does he normally make his last check?"

"After the charges have gone off, and the all clear is given, we still can't leave the drift until Cardwell says we can. Once he's satisfied with the haul, then we log out to go topside. By the time I finished changing the bit, I heard Hardesty drillin' again. About thirty minutes later, I finished the last hole and took the drill off the jackleg and carried it back up the drift out of range of the blast. When I went back to get the jackleg, I stopped at the crosscut and yelled to Hardesty to see if he was gettin' ready to set his charges. He yelled back his charges were already set. I checked my watch and saw it was five minutes past eleven. I knew I was behind and if I didn't hurry up, I'd be working for nothin' after the shift ended."

"Was it necessary to coordinate the time when you and Hardesty would light the fuses?"

"We're supposed to, and if the drifts had been closer together, we would've done that. Before you light the fuses, you're supposed to yell down the tunnel to warn anyone close by you're about to light the charges. It took me about thirty minutes to finish packing the dynamite in the holes and cuttin' the fuses. I just finished sliding the last of the charges into the drill hole and was starting to gather the fuses in the splitter when I heard Hardesty yellin' his fuses were lit. I finished cuttin' my last fuse a few minutes later. I lit the fuses and walked back to the main tunnel to wait and count the explosions as the charges went off. I expected to see Hardesty already there, but he wasn't. Well, my charges started goin' off, and I started counting keeping my fingers crossed I'd count fifteen explosions. I counted only fourteen, and right away I knew I was gonna be in for a longer shift. I'd been rushin' too fast and got careless. What surprised me was a minute later Hardesty's charges started goin' off."

"Why was that surprising?"

"Because he had already lit his fuses before I finished cutting mine. Hell Morg, he was at least five minutes ahead of me, and then his charges went off way after mine. He must've set some mighty long fuses is all I can figure."

"After you realized one of your charges didn't go off, did you wait the thirty minutes you were supposed to?"

"Hell, yes." Frank answered a little too earnestly. Morgan knew he was lying and repeated the question impatiently, "Frank, did you wait the full thirty minutes?"

"Well, maybe it wasn't quite that long, maybe closer to half," Frank admitted. "I was late, and the only way to make up for it was to cut back on the waiting time. What's the difference anyway?"

"Probably none, but it might be important. Stick to the facts, and it will help both of us. What did you do next?"

"I went back to the face to see if any of the charges didn't go off and hopin' if by chance one didn't, I'd find the charge still in the hole then all I'd have to do is set another fuse. The worst is when you can't find a charge."

"What do you do then?"

"You have to look through the ore until you find it. It's dangerous on account it could still go off. Anyway, I got as far as the crosscut and where some of the ore had blown and saw Hardesty layin' on his back with some of the ore partly covering his feet. I figured he must've been killed real quick 'cause his face was pretty much smashed up."

"Were you sure at the time it was Hardesty?"

"I didn't have no reason to believe then or now it wasn't."

"What did you think happened?"

"I dunno, Morg. I don't remember thinkin' much at all except that somehow it was my fault. I thought maybe Hardesty wanted to count the explosions from inside the crosscut instead of goin' all the way back to the main tunnel. It didn't make sense then or now why he'd risk coming into my drift before my charges went off."

"So at the time, you thought it was your blasting that killed Hardesty?"

"I did for a fact 'cause I had no goddamn reason to think different."

"What did you do then?"

"I ran back to the main tunnel and started yelling for help. Some of the muckers were already starting to show up, and Cardwell was just coming toward me a little way down the tunnel."

"What happened next?"

"I ran back to Hardesty with a couple of the muckers. Cardwell showed up about a minute later. After checkin' to make sure Hardesty was dead, Cardwell told me and the muckers to carry the body up to the top and wait with it until he got there. I told him I couldn't leave because I had a misfire. Cardwell really cussed me out good. He was more upset about the misfire than he was about Hardesty. He accused me of being careless and threatened to fire me along with being responsible for what happened to Hardesty. It weren't fair what Cardwell said. I got a reputation for being one of the best drillers in the Emily with the least number of misfires over the past six months."

Morgan thought so far there was little difference between the summary version Truesdale related and the more detailed account Frank had given. If Frank was telling the truth, whoever was talking to Hardesty when Frank was changing the drill bit might either be the man responsible for killing Hardesty, or conceivably an unknowing witness to what had happened. He needed to find out who Hardesty had been talking to. He wondered if it was Cardwell.

"How well did you get along with Cardwell before the incident?"

"Well enough, at least about as good as it ever is between a shift boss and the men workin' for him. Cardwell treated everyone all right. Sometimes he'd be on the prod about something or other. A shift boss is gonna be a prick now and then even if things are goin' okay just to remind everybody he's the boss. I figured he was upset over what happened. Shit, I was too."

"When did you find out Hardesty had been murdered?"

"The next day when Deputy Blaylock woke me up with a pistol in my face and told me I was being arrested for murder. At first, I thought it was some kind of joke until he hit me on the head with the pistol barrel. When I told him I wasn't goin' anywhere until he told me who it was I was supposed to have murdered, he wouldn't say, only hit me again. Blaylock brought me here, and Marshal Truesdale told me Hardesty was stabbed in the back. He said I was accused of doin' it. Sure, maybe in some way I might be responsible for Hardesty gettin' himself killed, but it was an accident. We had our differences, but they weren't enough reason to kill him. Anyways, I figured the cards were stacked against me, and that's when I asked Marshal Truesdale to send you a telegram."

"Tell me about Hardesty."

"What's to tell? He was just another driller. We weren't friends if that's what you mean, but I wouldn't say we were exactly enemies either."

Morgan saw his brother's eyes shift and knew there was more. "Marshal Truesdale told me you and Hardesty had a fight or two. Tell me about it."

"It was nothin' really, just a couple of guys with too much to drink and not much else to do. Shit, there's always fightin' on Saturday nights in Adobe Wells; that's just the way it is."

"C'mon, Frank, what did you and Hardesty fight about?"

"He was lettin' it be known I was signed up with the union, and it wasn't true. Me and most of the Emily workers were free workers and didn't want no truck with anybody tryin' to recruit for the Western Federation of Miners. I accused Hardesty of workin' for the WFM, and that was what got us both three days in here for disturbin' the peace."

"Was that the only confrontation you had with Hardesty?"

"Well, there might've been a couple more over the past several months, but we settled things mainly in private."

"Was it common knowledge you and Hardesty didn't get along?"

"I suppose so, but there was nothing serious enough between us that would've caused either one of us to want to kill the other. Sure, we had our differences, but it never went farther than a few punches. We also didn't take any of our disagreements down in the mine."

"Did Cardwell know you and Hardesty didn't get along?"

"Maybe he did. I never thought about it."

"Would Cardwell have kept the two of you on the same shift if he had known you didn't get along?"

"I don't think it would have mattered to Cardwell. He expects the men to leave their personal grievances on top, and we did. Things are dangerous enough a thousand feet down without addin' to it. You'll have to ask Cardwell."

Morgan resolved to do just that.

"What're you thinkin', Morg?" Frank asked after a few minutes of silence while Morgan considered what his brother had so far told him.

Morgan stared at Frank and pondered how best to answer the question. Frank's situation was worse than he had feared and, assuming he was telling the truth, there was no point in glossing things over.

"Frank, I won't try to make it look better than it is. Unfortunately, the circumstances are not good. Absent any other facts or someone else to back up your story, getting a jury to believe you is another matter."

"Christ almighty, I've told you all I know."

Morgan hated to see the desperation in his brother's face. Truesdale was wrong. Frank knew the possibility was very real he might be found guilty and executed for Hardesty's murder. Morgan thought Frank's understanding of how serious his situation was might be the best guarantee his brother, for a change, was telling the truth. There was also the possibility Frank knew or saw more but didn't realize it.

"First of all, I'm going to get you a lawyer. When he comes to see you, tell him what you told me all over again and anything else you may have forgotten to pass on to me. While you deal with the lawyer, I'll dig around and see what else or who else may come out of the shadows to shed some light on what happened in Tunnel 3."

"I knew I could count on you Morg!" Frank exclaimed. "Now you're here it's gonna be all right."

Morgan thought he was the one who should be trying to reassure Frank and not the other way around. He chose to leave it like that before saying anything Frank would know was nothing more than holding out false hope. He heard the rattle of the bolt and padlock followed by Myron's footsteps coming down the corridor.

Morgan took in his brother's somber expression and said, "I've got things to do, but before I go, is there anything I can get you?"

"Well, there's one thing. The marshal allows meals to be sent in instead of what they cook up in the jail kitchen downstairs. I'm sick and tired of beans and burned potatoes. If you'd fix it so I can get at least one good meal a day, I'd be obliged."

"I'll take care of it." It was no surprise when Frank didn't offer to pay for it.

Morgan walked into Truesdale's office and said, "I guess I'll be around awhile. Got any recommendations for a place to stay?"

"There's a widow by the name of Rachel Johansen. She lives over on Madison Street and takes in boarders by the week or more. It's quiet, clean, and the rate's a lot cheaper than the hotel. The food's good, too. I make a point of takin' my evening meals there whenever I get the chance."

"Sounds fine. I'd be obliged if you'd arrange a room for a week, on second thought, it could be longer. I'm going to look up the lawyer you mentioned and talk to the coroner who examined Hardesty. I'd also like directions for the TJ&M offices."

"Looks like you ain't gonna leave things up to the lawyer neither."

"I'll depend on the lawyer to take care of Frank in the court, but it's been my experience what gets said and done in the courtroom depends on what you find outside it."

"If there's anything I can do, officially that is, let me know."

"I appreciate the offer. There are a couple of other things you can do to help. I'd appreciate if you could arrange for Frank to get a decent supper each evening. I'll pay for it, and you'll be able to save the cost of having to feed him the one meal."

"No problem. A dollar a day should cover it. Ten bucks should do fine for now. We'll see after that if Frank will be here longer."

Morgan handed the marshal a ten-dollar bill, wondering if Truesdale's last comment was predicated on being able to prove Frank's innocence or if it was a pessimistic prediction of his brother's chances.

"What else?" Truesdale said.

"I'd like you to keep Deputy Blaylock on a short leash around Frank, and that may go the same for me. I don't think I like him."

Truesdale nodded. "Sometimes you just have to hire the help that's available rather than what you'd like to have." Recalling his own days as a sheriff, Morgan knew he had been exceptionally fortunate to have had William Cosgrove as a deputy instead of a man like Kincy Blaylock.

"Want me to take you over to the boarding house first?"

"Thanks, but I want to talk to the coroner, and I need to get Frank a lawyer. If you don't mind, I'd appreciate it if you'd take my bag over there, and tell Mrs. Johansen I'll be in time for supper."

Chapter Three

In his experience, Morgan had visited enough morgues to know it was never pleasant and rarely helpful. He didn't expect his time with Dr. Ian Chambliss would be any different. In his opinion most of those who carved and probed a corpse cared more about the fee they were paid than the information concerning the circumstances of death. His brief association with the Pinkerton National Detective Agency in Cripple Creek, Colorado years ago had been unfortunate, but it did serve to expose him to the embryonic field of police forensics which the Pinkertons had helped to advance. He hoped the coroner would at least allow him access to the autopsy report if not to Hardesty's body.

A receptionist at the hospital front desk told him the doctor was performing an autopsy and directed him to the basement.

He descended two flights of wide marble stairs to the basement floor. The faint pungent odor of formaldehyde became stronger as he walked down a long corridor painted an incongruous bright yellow. Morgan wondered if the cheerful color was an attempt to make less grim the place where grim things took place. He passed several closed doors and proceeded as instructed toward the far end of the hallway where a door with a small glass panel allowed him to see inside the morgue. The floor was a non-descript gray tile as were the walls halfway to the ceiling. Three men dressed in neck-to-ankle length smocks leaned over the partially dissected body of a man. An elderly distinguished looking individual with snow-white hair, a neatly trimmed moustache, and short-pointed beard fit the description of Dr. Chambliss.

Morgan opened the door and walked in causing the three men to turn toward him in startled surprise. He had hardly taken a step when the elderly man who looked to be well into his seventies spoke sharply in a surprisingly deep voice. "Here now, you can't just walk in here."

"The receptionist upstairs said I'd find Dr. Chambliss here."

"I'm Doctor Chambliss, and if you want to see me, make an appointment. I'm busy."

"Excuse me, Doctor. I know you're a busy man, but then so am I. Marshal Truesdale assured me you would be more than willing to help me out. He also said you were a rude, old son of a bitch and stubborn as a mule." The faces of the two other men went from shocked surprise to relief when Chambliss tilted his head back and laughed with infectious humor.

"Well, you tell that…never mind, I'll tell him myself. Now just who in the hell are you, and what do you want?"

"My name is Morgan Westphal. I'm assisting Marshal Truesdale with the investigation into the death of Philip Hardesty."

"You mean murder, don't you?" was the blunt response. "It's plain enough for any imbecile to see and for at least a few of the doctors I've known to see he was murdered. Very well, wait outside, and I'll give you a few minutes," he said and turned his back in dismissal.

"Pardon me, Dr. Chambliss, but I'd also like to see the autopsy report and the body if possible."

The doctor froze, and one of the assistants gasped. Slowly Dr. Chambliss turned to face Morgan with a baleful stare. "Mr. Westphal, I'm beginning to lose my patience and my inclination to give you any time at all. Give me one good reason why I should talk to you let alone give you access to the autopsy report much less the body."

"Doctor, the man accused of killing Hardesty happens to be my brother, and I believe he's innocent. His trial starts in eight days in a town I'm led to believe is already convinced he's guilty. Frank Shaw has a lot less time to waste than you do. Is that reason enough?"

Morgan saw the doctor hesitate and hoped he had made the telling point.

"All right, Westphal, I'll listen to what you have to say, and then I'll decide whether or not to grant your request. Now, before I give in to my better judgment to wish you no more than good day, I suggest you leave and allow me to finish what I'm doing here."

Satisfied, Morgan quickly withdrew to the corridor. To his surprise, it was only a quarter hour later when he was summoned back into the laboratory by one of the young assistants. Dr. Chambliss was standing next to the gurney when Morgan entered the room. This time the corpse was covered by a stained sheet that may have once been white but had since become a dingy gray.

"Who are you, Westphal? You're not one of the marshal's deputies, because I know all of them. By the way, why isn't your name Shaw?"

"Frank Shaw and I had the same mother, different fathers. I'm a senior partner in a private company that conducts investigations. Before that, I was the sheriff in Las Cruces, New Mexico; consequently, over the years I've gained some experience in investigating homicides including determining the cause and time of death of a victim. Marshal Truesdale has known me for almost twenty years and can vouch for my credentials."

Morgan thought he saw interest and a sympathetic glint in the doctor's eyes. Without saying a word, he glanced at one of the assistants who threw back the sheet shrouding the corpse.

"Westphal, this is Phillip Hardesty. He's merely the latest, and literally, near faceless victim of the human species unlimited capacity to take the life of his fellow man. I am not authorized to show you the autopsy report; however, I will provide you with an oral summary of my findings. Now, please pay close attention and don't interrupt." Briskly and clinically, Chambliss began the examination as if he were conducting a lecture to a room full of medical students.

"The victim is a Caucasian male five feet, ten inches tall, approximately 30-35 years old, and weighs 190 pounds. Apart from some softening of the tissue in the region of the lower torso, his body muscles were highly developed, and his hands were calloused indicating he was employed in some form of manual labor." Chambliss regarded Morgan and added with a hint of dry humor, "Since the body was found in a mine, it can be reasonably conjectured he was a miner by profession. An examination of the liver showed early signs of cirrhosis, and the additional fatty tissue around the belly suggested he was a heavy drinker, a not too uncommon, and I might add, a perfectly understandable trait for someone engaged in the mining profession. He has numerous small scars on his lower forearms, and there is evidence of a previous fracture of the left tibia. He is missing the tip of his left forefinger although it is difficult to tell from the general condition of the hand whether the loss was a pre-existing condition or resulted from the explosion. He must have recently shaved his moustache as the skin on the upper lip and along the side of the mouth is much lighter than the rest of his face. As you can easily see from the condition of the face, the victim received a severe blow to the right side of the face fracturing the cheekbone, nose, and severely abrading the skin from the forehead down to the chin. The one undamaged eye–the other was crushed–was brown. In addition to the blow to the face, he received abrading wounds to the upper torso and on both arms and legs. Although severe, the visible wounds you see were not immediately life-threatening. Serious as it was, the facial wound need not have been fatal if he had received treatment quickly to clear the nasal passage, without which the swelling and bleeding would have caused eventual suffocation. Had he lived, the victim would have suffered permanent disfigurement. From the uneven serrations, the facial wound was caused by a large rough object. The other wounds to the arms and torso are also consistent with impact wounds also caused by uneven objects. The presence of minute pieces of rock imbedded in all the wounds seems to confirm he was struck by the debris from an explosion as was reported when he was brought here."

Morgan bent over to take a closer look at Hardesty's mangled face and the wounds to the dead man's upper body. He had seen enough blunt impact wounds of various kinds to see something the doctor may have missed.

"Do you think it curious the skin and flesh of the facial wound appear to stretch downward from the margins of the wound, while the tissue in the lower wounds at the top and bottom of each wound seem to have torn upward toward the head?"

"I fail to see your point, Mr. Westphal."

"First, the depths of the wounds below the neck are significantly less than the wound to the face. One of the objects that struck the victim on the left side of the torso was nearly as large as the one that hit the victim's face, and yet the wound is not as deep. It also seems to me it may have been caused by a glancing blow since the tissue has folded upward. The latter might indicate the victim was lying down when the debris struck him. The facial wound looks as if the object came straight down in comparison to the glancing trajectory of the objects striking the lower body."

"Is that really relevant to the cause of death?" the doctor queried with a hint of impatience.

"Perhaps not to the cause of death, but it may be quite significant to where he received the fatal wound in the event whoever struck the fatal blow wanted to make the death appear accidental and caused by the explosion."

"Now I understand what you mean. I compliment you on your observation," Chambliss acknowledged with genuine admiration. "Until you pointed it out, I must admit I failed to note any significance to the angle of the objects that struck him." He paused and continued, "It's also possible the facial wound resulted when a large rock struck the tunnel ceiling first before descending downward toward the victim."

Morgan nodded, "I agree that is certainly a possibility including falling rock from the tunnel ceiling dislodged by the blasting."

Chambliss shrugged, "I concur and will amend my report to document either possibility. Now let us examine the other side of the body." Doctor Chambliss signaled to the two assistants to turn the corpse over and resumed lecturing.

"Observe there are no obvious injuries to the back, buttocks, and legs. There is, however, a cranial abrasion low on the left side of the occipital bone and bridging upward from right to left across the lambdoid suture. The scalp is torn; however, there's no sign of any indentation of the occipital bone. During the initial examination before I had the wound cleaned there was considerable blood in the hair, on his neck, and left shoulder consistent with severe bleeding of the scalp. The bleeding also indicates he remained alive for some period of time after he received the blow to the head. Although I did not examine the brain, the blow would have doubtless caused a severe concussion and some internal hemorrhaging; however, in my opinion, the wound probably wasn't severe enough to cause any permanent impairment."

"Is there any chance the blow could have been caused by a fall?"

"It's not very likely. Had that been the case, the wound boundaries would be uneven, and the wound itself would not have been as deep. Further, the location of the wound in relation to the occipital region is not consistent with someone falling backward where the head would more likely be tilted back. With the head bending backward, the injury would be higher on the parietal region and over a wider area than is the case here. No, the victim was struck forcefully with a heavy rounded object such as a metal pipe. And whoever struck Mr. Hardesty was most probably left-handed considering the position and angle of the wound."

Morgan winced at the last comment. Frank was left-handed.

"Now let us move to the actual cause of the victim's death. Notice the small puncture wound just to the right of the spine. The small size and triangular shape of the wound is very curious, and possibly made by a small dagger or stiletto. Now if this was somewhere in Northern Virginia in 1864, I would swear this was made by a bayonet. I was a young surgeon during the war, for which side is irrelevant. Unfortunately, I had the opportunity to see enough such wounds. But I digress. The fatal instrument entered between the fourth and fifth ribs. Whoever it was must have thought stabbing the victim in the back would inflict an immediate and fatal wound. Had the weapon not been impeded when it struck the cartilaginous joint between the two ribs, it is very possible it would have. As it was, the blade did not reach the heart but did puncture one of the main arteries."

"Would he have survived the wound?"

"Any competent surgeon would have been able to save him had he been given immediate professional care. Under the circumstances and deep underground that was not possible. Given where the fatal wound was inflicted, he had at best but a short time left to live. The person who struck him on the head may have wanted to make certain Mr. Hardesty did not leave that mine alive. It is also quite possible there was more than one assailant."

"What do you mean two assailants?"

"This may be more your department than mine, but the reason I think there may have been two assailants is the position and angle of the wounds. It is my presumption the fatal wound was delivered second. The victim did not die instantly from the head wound as was expected; therefore, he was stabbed. I would further posit that Mr. Hardesty was bending down at the time he was struck, again based on the angle and location of the wound so low on the back of the head. The angle and position of the puncture wound in the back indicates an upward thrusting motion by a right-handed person who was…" Frowning Chambliss stopped then said, "I do find the position of the puncture wound quite curious."

"In what way?"

"It's obvious the individual who stabbed the victim knew nothing of anatomy. The location of the wound would not have caused immediate death. Indeed, most stabbing wounds to the back, particularly knife wounds, are not immediately fatal as this one was not, too many ribs in the way. It would take someone skilled with a knife and familiar with the most vulnerable areas of the human anatomy to deliver a lethal blow effective enough to cause immediate death. The depth of the wound was also shallow."

"Doctor, you said the penetration was impeded by striking the rib cartilage which might explain why the wound was so shallow."

"Correct, and does pose the question why the assailant didn't try and stab the victim again."

"What if the assailant didn't intend to kill him?"

"Mr. Westphal, my point is the assailant was an amateur, not that he was unsuccessful. I fail to see where you're going with this."

"And my point is what if the wound was accidental?" Dr. Chambliss stared at Morgan in irritation. "Assume the possibility the victim fell backward on a sharp object. You said yourself the shape of the wound was strange, suggesting perhaps it was not a knife at all. I think we can both safely rule out a bayonet." Morgan pursed his lips and grew silent, his forehead furrowed in thought. "Consider if the victim was struck on the head first when he was he was standing up, would he have pitched forward or backward?"

"In most cases, someone struck a sharp blow from behind such as this was and hard enough to induce sudden unconsciousness would fall forward not backward."

"If the victim was not immediately unconscious, is it possible out of reflex he arched his back before falling backward?"

"An interesting possibility," Chambliss replied, "What made you think of it?"

"In Cuba, I saw a Spanish soldier shot in the back while he was running up hill and leaning forward. Before he fell, he threw up his hands, and instead of falling facedown, he went backward. He was still alive when I passed him by."

"I see your point although in this case I cannot endorse your theory."

"But is it a possibility you cannot rule out?"

"I think it's improbable although I'll concede your point. Understand, Westphal, my conclusions are based on conjecture and practical knowledge gained from years of professional experience including too many battlefields. What actually happened may be far different from my observations. Only Mr. Hardesty and the person or persons in the mine tunnel at the time can tell us what really occurred; regrettably, Mr. Hardesty is unable to speak of it."

"On the contrary, Dr. Chambliss, I believe thanks to you, Mr. Hardesty has said a great deal."

"I wonder if I've really helped your brother. What I've told you will inevitably be repeated in court at your brother's trial, and perhaps it will do more to contribute to his guilt than his innocence."

Without providing the reason he felt differently, Morgan responded, "Doctor Chambliss, if the jury hears what you have explained to me, it will do more to help than harm my brother. Frank said he heard voices. Since you've posed the possibility of two assailants it may help to corroborate my brother's claim."

"There is little doubt in my mind as to that question."

"Are the victim's clothes and personal effects here?"

"His things, or what's left of them, are in the storage room. In the course of removing his clothes, some items had to be cut off. I seem to recall there were very few personal effects. You're welcome to inspect them if you wish. Jordan, bring the box containing the victim's effects."

One of the young assistants disappeared briefly into a small storage room and returned carrying a small carton which he placed on an empty gurney. Morgan opened the box and found on top an inventory list of the items inside. Scanning the list, he saw the doctor was right; there was little there and included just about what he would have expected a miner might have working underground. The first item he examined was a dark, shapeless felt hat stiffened with resin to provide some protection from falling rock. There was no blood on the hat. The next item was a tattered blood-stained jacket and underneath that a blood-stained and badly torn, collarless linsey-woolsey shirt with large buttons down the right side. Wide cloth suspenders were buttoned to heavy work trousers that had been patched in the seat and knees. The trousers were also torn and bloody. Long underwear that may have once been red but was now a faded pink was also stained with blood. There was a pair of thick, wool socks and a pair of ankle-high work shoes showing considerable wear and tear. The clothing and boots were still quite damp to the touch giving some indication of the wet conditions in the Emily. A small envelope was the final item at the bottom of the box. Morgan opened the envelope and spilled the contents on the gurney. There was very little in the way of personal effects. He was surprised to find the stub of a white stearic candle, the same type of smokeless candle he had used during his one and very brief stint as a miner. He had assumed electric lights and carbide head lamps had made candles a thing of the past. He opened a small tin container and found a half-dozen sulfur matches. There was a small change purse containing less than a dollar in coins, a small pocket knife, an inexpensive pocket watch, a key much smaller than for a normal door lock with the number 149 stamped on it, and a printed chit entitling the bearer to a free drink at the Arabian Club. The name 'Adele' was scribbled on the back of the slip of paper and underneath was "Thurs night." Morgan placed the effects back in the box without comment. There was nothing exceptional about any of the items he had just examined, and yet he had the nagging feeling he had missed something. His gaze wandered back to the corpse, and he took in the mangled face. He turned to Dr. Chambliss and asked with a thoughtful expression.

"Are you certain the dead man is Phillip Hardesty?"

Momentarily startled, Doctor Chambliss replied, "Well, if he isn't Hardesty then someone else will have the name Phillip Hardesty on his grave when this man is buried in a few days. But that's an interesting question, Mr. Westphal. What prompted you to ask it?"

"No reason Doctor, at this moment no reason at all. As you say, it's an interesting question. Perhaps some effort needs to be made to confirm his identity."

"Strange you should say that," The doctor responded, his brow furrowed reflectively.

"What do you mean?"

"Nothing really, it's that what you said was similar to what Mr. LaTrobe told me when he asked for an autopsy of the victim."

"Mr. Latrobe requested the autopsy?" Morgan asked in surprise. "It's curious Mr. Latrobe asked for one. Wouldn't the procedure be performed as a matter of routine?"

"Not necessarily if there was no reason to believe there was foul play."

"But then you had no suspicion the victim had been murdered until you examined the body and discovered the puncture wound. Therefore, until then there was no reason to suspect Hardesty had died under suspicious circumstances."

"What you say is true enough," the doctor conceded with a perplexed expression.

"Did you ask why Mr. LaTrobe wanted the autopsy?"

"No. I assumed it might have had something to do with determining if personal negligence or company procedures were at fault in the event of a lawsuit."

Morgan thought the doctor's conjecture was reasonable enough, but he still intended to ask Latrobe about it.

"Dr. Chambliss, I won't take up any more of your time. You've been most helpful."

Chapter Four

Six blocks from the hospital at the far end of an unpaved side-street and sandwiched between a cinema and a barber shop, Morgan found the office of Mr. Samuel Spencer, Attorney-At-Law. Morgan hesitated before entering. The location and peeling paint on the clapboard façade and window badly in need of washing did little to inspire confidence the lawyer's practice was thriving. He recalled Truesdale's endorsement of Spencer along with his warning to be quick if he wanted a lawyer from out of town. The reality was Frank had no time. He walked in.

If the exterior of the office was not impressive, the inside of the narrow office was even less so. Just inside the door was a small reception area made smaller by two overstuffed leather chairs with a round wooden table between them. A faded settee that would have looked more appropriate in a parlor was positioned opposite the chairs.

A young, plain-featured woman sat behind a desk beyond the waiting area, her fingers tapping efficiently on a typewriter. Apart from the clatter of the typewriter, the funereal silence was broken only by the faint sound of a piano from the cinema next door. A telephone sat on a small table next to the desk. The woman's brightly colored dress and the sparkling brooch fastened above her left breast were the only hint of color in a room dominated by hues of brown and gray that did little to dispel the gloom. A man Morgan assumed was Samuel Spencer was hunched over a desk at the far end of the room.

The slender woman stood up and greeted him with a warm smile, "May I help you, sir?"

"Yes, you may. If possible I would like to see Mr. Spencer."

"And who may I say is calling?"

"My name is Morgan Westphal, and I'm here to engage Mr. Spencer's services."

"If you will please wait, I'll see if Mr. Spencer has time for you now, or you can make an appointment to see him at a later date."

"I'm afraid it's a matter of some urgency. I must see him now. I might even say a man's life is depending on it."

She paused and her brows knitted in concern. "Very well, I'll see what I can do." The heels of her shoes drummed hollow on the wooden floor as she walked back to the rear of the room. She returned a moment later and said, "Mr. Westphal, Mr. Spencer will see you now." She stepped aside and gestured toward the seated lawyer.

Morgan passed several book cases filled with thick books uniformly bound in green and brown. He assumed the books represented the approved laws of the United States and the new state of Arizona. He hoped somewhere in those bound volumes, there would be a page or two that might benefit Frank.

Even in the dim light, it was easy for Morgan to see the man waiting for him was gravely ill. He was much older than Morgan expected. Either that or the ravages of the disease now consuming him had prematurely aged him. He saw why Truesdale had added the caveat about him lasting long enough to finish the trial, for it was clear Samuel Spencer was in the final stages of consumption. His face was the color of old parchment. The lawyer's sunken cheeks were even more pronounced by high cheekbones and a thin, hawk-like nose. Except for sparse tufts above his ears, he was nearly bald. Morgan thought the lawyer might at one time have been handsome. The piercing black eyes regarding Morgan with intelligence and interest were as vibrant and full of life as his body was not.

The lawyer did not offer to shake hands. Gesturing to a chair to one side of the desk, the spectral figure said, "Mr.

Westphal, you interest me. Please sit down and tell me how I can be of service."

"Mr. Spencer, I'm the half-brother of Franklin Shaw who is currently in jail and accused of murdering a man by the name of Phillip Hardesty. I arrived here in Adobe Wells a few hours ago from Albuquerque to seek counsel for his defense. Marshal Truesdale suggested you might help. Do you have experience in such cases?"

"Yes, Mr. Westphal, I do." Spencer carefully placed his pen into its holder and leaned back in his chair. "Allow me to briefly acquaint you with my bona fides. I have extensive experience in the litigation of criminal charges including those similar to what your brother is now facing. I confess most of my experience has been with the courts in the state of Virginia. I might also add the murder cases I've handled are not as recent as I might wish since coming to the Territory of Arizona four years ago for reasons of health. My specialty in Virginia was criminal law where I defended quite a number of individuals accused of capital offenses."

"May I assume you were always successful?"

"You may, but it would be disingenuous on my part to allow you to think so. The truth is the most artfully constructed and eloquently argued defense will not save a truly guilty person if the facts of the case are irrefutable and compelling. Some of my clients went to the gallows in spite of my best efforts. Still, I am gratified to say my record was quite admirable. Judge Breen is familiar with my background should you care to make enquiries of him."

Morgan thought the candid answer did more to reassure than to cast doubt on Mr. Spencer's qualifications.

"I am also familiar with the broad circumstances of your brother's case. Judge Breen has already approached me with the possibility of assuming your brother's defense. I've been somewhat reluctant to accept the judge's request. I dislike admitting this for my hesitation is based purely on pecuniary reasons. The fees authorized by the state are limited and exceedingly slow in reaching a court-appointed advocate. Having said that, I was prepared to tell the judge tomorrow I would accept the appointment. In short, my friend, I think it only fair to advise you to leave my office now, and in so doing, it will be to your certain financial benefit although not to mine. I might also add to my further detriment, I will do my best to defend your brother regardless of whether you or the state of Arizona provides payment for my services. "

Morgan liked the man's forthright manner. "What then are your fees?"

"I require 20 dollars for each day out of court I spend in preparation for trial. If for some reason your brother does not go to trial because of a plea arrangement I have devised, I will expect a fee of one-hundred dollars to close the case assuming it is resolved in the interest of the client. If the case goes to trial, my fee is 25 dollars for each day spent in court. Post-trial services will be negotiated as necessary. I will bill separately for any investigative services that may be required. If you find my fees too high, we can, of course, reach an accommodation if only because your brother's case offers the possibility of welcome relief from the tedium of drawing up wills, defending drunks, and matters involving probate."

Morgan nodded and replied, "Then you may inform Judge Breen I will pay for your services instead of the state of Arizona; however, it will be quite unnecessary to engage anyone to perform any investigative services. I am well-qualified to assist you in that regard. In fact, I will insist on it." Morgan briefly outlined his background.

"Excellent, Mr. Westphal, I'll accept your brother as a client as well as your assistance. I'll draw up a document summarizing our legal arrangement that will be ready for your signature in the morning. Miss Ottmier will have the document available in the event I'm not here. It is customary to provide a modest retainer fee in any amount of your choosing which I will credit to your account."

Morgan reached for his wallet and took out a five-dollar bill and placed it on the desk. He was struck by the near skeletal hand that retrieved the bill and dropped it in one of the desk drawers.

"Now, Mr. Westphal we will, as they say, get down to the nub of things. The trial date has been set, and regrettably time is not on our side. We have no time to waste. I'll naturally file a motion for extension, but since Judge Breen is seldom inclined to grant such motions, it would be a mistake to delay doing all we can to present a defense on the date now scheduled."

"What is the chance of moving the trial to another town?"

"Why would you wish to do so, Mr. Westphal?"

"My impression is my brother is facing a potentially hostile environment generally prejudicial to a fair trial."

"I see. And why do you think that is the case?"

"My brother is being confined in isolation for his own safety, and the victim apparently was popular in a way that Frank evidently is not. I also have the impression the superintendent of the TJ&M may be trying to make an example of Frank to satisfy his own purpose. Since the superintendent is both prominent and influential in Adobe Wells, I believe any local jury selected may be unfairly biased."

"That would, of course, be Victor LaTrobe. Yes, you have a point. Adobe Wells tends to move in the direction Victor LaTrobe points. Again, I do not entertain high hopes the judge will approve it, but I'll file a motion for a change of venue just the same. I assume then you have talked to your brother?"

"I have at length. He claims he's innocent. For once I tend to believe him. Regrettably, that has not always been the case. After talking to Dr. Chambliss who performed the autopsy, I am more convinced than ever Frank did not murder Phillip Hardesty or whoever the unfortunate victim is they carried out of the Emily Mine."

The lawyer's surprise was clearly evident. "I must say, you've been busy in the short time you've been here. I'm most anxious to hear what you have to say, but I believe before we get into the particulars of the case, I want you to tell me about your brother first. I am intrigued by your comment—I believe your exact words were, 'for once I tend to believe him'. "

While Spencer listened attentively, Morgan proceeded to give a cryptic and objective description of his brother and ended by saying, "Frank has many faults: he's impulsive; he has a hot temper; and his judgment is questionable. To make matters worse, he has also shown on several occasions he can be violent when provoked. One such instance put him in Yuma prison for a year. Having said all that, I don't think my brother is capable of premeditated murder. What I've learned so far suggests Hardesty's murder may have been premeditated and carried out by more than one individual. Even the location of the murder may be significant to the act as well."

"I must say that is a most interesting and provocative hypothesis. It would seem appropriate at this point to tell me what you have so far learned since thus far my knowledge has been confined to the basic facts as related to me by Judge Breen and arrest document." Morgan summarized what Frank had told him and what he learned at the morgue and conversation with Doctor Chambliss. When he finished, the lawyer said, "Now I would be interested in your thoughts why you think your brother is ...."

The comment was interrupted when the lawyer quickly pressed a handkerchief to his mouth to stifle a sudden and violent coughing spell. Morgan saw the handkerchief was flecked with red as the lawyer returned the cloth to his coat pocket. Before continuing to speak, Spencer reached into one of the desk drawers and retrieved a small bottle, unscrewed the cap, and took a drink of the dark liquid inside. Morgan easily recognized the size and shape of the bottle. Toward the end of his mother's life, the only relief from her body-wracking coughs came from the laudanum she drank in the year before she died.

"My apologies Mr. Westphal. As you can see, I'm unwell; however, I assure you I am in no danger of expiring before I finish defending your brother. I was about to ask why you think your brother is innocent?"

"If Frank had committed the crime, it is absurd to think he would contrive to make it look like an accident in the drift he was working. It would seem more logical to have left the body in the drift Hardesty was working in and make it appear it was caused by an accidental, premature explosion."

Spencer countered by asking, "True, but what if leaving the body where it was found would be so obvious as to eliminate your brother from suspicion for the very reason you cite?"

"Perhaps, but that doesn't explain the wound to the back which is unlikely to have been caused by accident."

"Also true, but that is an *a priori* hypothesis based solely on the expectation no autopsy would be performed; therefore, the actual cause of death would not have been discovered at all." Seeing the troubled frown on Morgan's face, the lawyer added, "Forgive me for sounding negative. It is not my intent to dismiss your theory lightly, particularly when it is both logical and compelling if not necessarily persuasive. You must realize my comments are precisely what the prosecution would be apt to point out during a trial. From time to time, a well-argued hypothesis is sufficient to create doubt in the minds of a jury. A better and preferred approach is to rely on facts and corroborated testimony than unsubstantiated theory. We must do our best to find both. If Dr. Chambliss is right concerning more than one assailant, it means there are at least two people alive who know what happened; we only need the testimony of one of them to either free your brother or—"

"Or to convict him in the event Frank really was an accomplice."

"Mr. Westphal, the question of your brother's guilt or innocence is neither a deterrent nor an attribute in preparing his defense. We have an arcane but extremely important tenet underpinning our entire judicial system, a person is presumed innocent until proven guilty. The prosecution has the burden to prove Frank's guilt. We don't have to prove your brother is innocent; we only need to cast doubt on the prosecution's efforts to prove him guilty."

Morgan stood up to leave. "I'll keep you informed on the progress of my inquiries."

"If I may ask, how and where do you intend to proceed?"

"I'll concentrate on finding who else was in the drift with Hardesty. I intend to talk to Mr. Cardwell, the shift foreman and with other men on the shift with Hardesty. I'll also attempt to find out more about Phillip Hardesty and to learn who else may have had a motive to kill him. I think it may also prove useful to talk with Mr. LaTrobe."

"Victor LaTrobe?" the lawyer asked in surprise.

"Yes, I want to know why he wanted the body autopsied. I find it peculiar a man in his position would be concerned to the extent he seems to be. And there is the fact he personally contacted Dr. Chambliss to press for an autopsy."

"You have good instincts, Mr. Westphal. I'll be most interested in learning what you find out. If it is more convenient, you may call me on the telephone. Simply give the operator my name or ask for party number 19."

Back on the street, Morgan noted the deepening shadows and realized it was growing too late to accomplish anything else except to find Mrs. Johansen's boarding house.

Chapter Five

With Marshal Truesdale's roadster parked in front, Morgan had no difficulty identifying which home on the quiet side street was Mrs. Johansen's boarding house. He climbed the porch steps and knocked on the door. An attractive middle-aged woman wearing an apron and a friendly smile opened the door.

"You must be Mr. Westphal from Albuquerque?"

"I am, and I hope I'm not too late for supper."

"Not at all, I'll be serving dinner in a few minutes, and there's a place for you. You'll have a chance to meet the other guests then. I've had your bag taken to your room."

Morgan followed Mrs. Johansen to the stairs opposite the front entrance and past a dining room on the left. A soft glow emanating from rose-colored kerosene lamps on either side of a black horsehair settee identified the parlor on the right where two people were occupied in a lively discussion. A stocky man with close-cropped gray hair was talking to a young, attractive woman. The woman glanced curiously at Morgan and gave him a slight nod. Morgan thought if she was one of the guests, the boarding house had more than decent food to commend it.

He followed Mrs. Johansen up the stairs to a small but comfortable room overlooking the backyard. After pointing out the lavatory farther down the hall, she left him to unpack. The first thing he took from the suitcase was the Colt revolver, which he placed in the bottom drawer of the bureau where he expected it to remain during his stay in Adobe Wells. By the time he finished unpacking and made an attempt to comb his thick, unruly hair, it was time to meet the other guests.

"Mr. Westphal is from Albuquerque. He'll be staying with us for a week or more," Mrs. Johansen announced to the three men and two women filing into the dining room where Truesdale stood waiting. "Mr. Westphal, if you'll take a seat next to Mrs. Pomeroy," pointing to a severe-looking matron whose pinched expression and dark attire suggested a humorless and sour disposition; it would not take Morgan long to confirm his initial impression. The younger woman whom he had seen in the parlor was introduced as Miss Flynn, an attractive, slender woman. From the jut of her chin and her direct way of looking at him, he had the impression she was used to speaking her mind.

The man he had seen in the parlor talking to Miss Flynn was Mr. Elias Stockwell. His burly frame strained the fabric of a badly rumpled broadcloth suit. Mr. Stockwell did not hesitate to mention the fact he was a representative of the miner's union. A badly stained, loosely tied cravat suggested Stockwell's indifference to personal appearance. His gruff manner and solid build suggested he was a man who had been used to hard work and was not ashamed of it.

With his attention fixated on Miss Flynn, Mr. Henry Dahlgliesh, a haberdashery salesman, barely acknowledged the introduction before moving quickly to the table in order to seat the young woman. Morgan noticed Miss Flynn did not appear particularly pleased at the attention.

The third man was introduced as Mr. Hanson Markham who spoke with a noticeable English accent. He was an engineer who had recently come from England to work for the Sandusky Mining Company. He had not been long in America and proved later to be an entertaining raconteur easily filling in the conversation voids with lively and humorous comments on his impressions of America and the American southwest.

During the casual dinner conversation, Morgan preferred to remain silent, responding only when someone directed a comment or question to him. After a long, all-night train ride and a busy day, he was willing to remain in the background. Morgan noticed Elias Stockwell kept looking at him with an intensity bordering on rude.

"Mr. Stockwell, I don't wish to be impolite, but is there something about me you find objectionable?"

Mr. Stockwell flushed. "I'm sorry, but you look familiar to me. I seldom forget a face, and I'm certain we've met somewhere before."

"It's entirely possible. I travel a lot, but if we've met, I regret I'm unable to recall when or where it was."

"Where do you travel?" Miss Flynn asked.

"Texas, California, Colorado, on occasion Arizona."

"And why have you come to Adobe Wells?" Miss Flynn continued.

Morgan shot a look at Truesdale and replied, "I've some personal business to attend to," and in attempt to forestall any additional questions he had no wish to answer, he added, "I once lived here in Adobe Wells as a young boy, and frankly, I was curious to return."

Frowning, Mr. Stockwell asked, "Westphal, you say you've traveled to Colorado. By any chance, were you there in 1903?"

"I was there briefly about that time. That was more than ten years ago, Mr. Stockwell, and I've been to Colorado, Denver in particular, on a number of occasions since."

"By any chance were you in Colorado City in 1903?"

"As a matter of fact, I was. Why do you ask?"

His eyes narrow slits, Stockwell leaned forward and said in a low voice, "I told you I never forget a face, and I saw you there. You were with those damned Pinkertons, and don't deny it."

"Mr. Stockwell, mind your language!" Mrs. Johansen said. "I'll not have that kind of talk in my house." By now the other guests had stopped eating and were looking in astonishment at Stockwell.

If Stockwell heard the admonishment, he ignored it. "Westphal, you helped the Pinkertons bust the union. On account of you and the rest of them bastards, over thirty miners were killed for trying to get a fair wage and a decent workday."

"Mr. Stockwell, perhaps this might be a discussion more appropriate for another occasion," Morgan said, doing his best to control his rising temper. "I'm quite certain my brief stay during that unfortunate time had little bearing on the actions of either the mine owners or the union. To be perfectly honest, I..." his words were interrupted by Stockwell's angry accusation.

"For what you and the rest of them sons of bitches did, I hope you rot in hell!"

Morgan quietly placed his napkin on the table and pushed his chair back. In alarm, Truesdale leaped up to intervene in a situation he was certain was about to get out of hand.

Morgan put up a reassuring hand and said, "It's all right, Dan. Mrs. Johansen, my apologies to you and the other guests for being an unwitting cause for this disturbance. It would perhaps be best if I leave now to avoid inciting Mr. Stockwell any further. To ensure there is no possibility of further unpleasantness, I'd better find lodging at the hotel."

"No, Mr. Westphal, please be seated. It is Mr. Stockwell I wish to leave the table. Tomorrow, you will need to find other accommodations. You are no longer welcome here."

From Stockwell's startled expression, it was apparent he had been oblivious of the other guests focused as he was on the disastrous outcome of the 1903 Colorado labor war. Morgan almost felt sorry for Stockwell as the red-faced man stood up.

"With the exception of Mr. Westphal, I apologize to all of you. Mr. Westphal, you are scum, and I advise you to avoid crossing my path during your visit to Adobe Wells. Mrs. Johansen, I'll pack my things and leave tonight." Without another word, Stockwell stalked out of the room.

Morgan sat down and calmly attended to dinner although his appetite was somewhat diminished. Even though conversation resumed, it was muted. Morgan looked up from his plate and caught Hanson Markham covertly studying him, his brow knitted in deep thought. When their eyes met, Markham put his fork down and asked, "What is it you do, Mr. Westphal? do you work for the Pinkerton Detective Agency?"

Morgan hesitated, reluctant to reveal his occupation and true purpose for being in Adobe Wells. He saw no point in avoiding the truth. "Actually, I am a senior partner in Westphal & Cosgrove Investigations based in Albuquerque."

"What is your real reason for being here, Mr. Westphal? I warrant it has to do with something more than revisiting boyhood memories."

"Unfortunately, you're correct. I happen to be related to Frank Shaw, the miner now in jail who's accused of murdering another miner a few days ago. I believe my brother has been falsely accused. My purpose for coming to Adobe Wells is to assist in his defense by helping the marshal find who committed the murder."

"Marshal Truesdale, do you think Mr. Westphal's brother is innocent?" Markham asked.

"I have my doubts; therefore, I'm happy to have Mr. Westphal's assistance. I don't think it's in the best interests of Adobe Wells and the state of Arizona for an innocent man to hang."

Markham stood up to leave and said, "According to what I've read in the newspaper, you have a difficult task. I hope you and the marshal find the guilty party and prove your brother innocent."

"Well, I must say the evening has been somewhat more lively than usual," Mrs. Johansen declared to no one in particular.

One by one the other lodgers including Mrs. Johansen excused themselves and left the room leaving only the marshal, Miss Flynn, and Morgan to linger over coffee.

"Morgan, what was Stockwell talking about?" Truesdale asked.

"There was big trouble between the miners and mine owners in Colorado in 1903. He thinks I was part of what happened to the miners in Cripple Creek. I was in Colorado all right, and Stockwell probably did see me in the short time I was there. Too bad he didn't let me finish, or maybe he wouldn't have gotten so riled."

"What were you doing in Colorado?"

"One of the first big jobs my partner and I agreed to do was in support of a contract the Pinkerton Detective Agency had with the mine owners in and around Cripple Creek and Colorado City. Stockwell was right about the mine owners wanting to prevent the union from shutting down the mines. Pinkerton was short-handed and hired a number of other companies similar to mine that had investigative or security-related experience. My partner Will Cosgrove and I had just formed Westphal and Cosgrove Investigations the year before. At the time, we didn't have much business coming our way, so we weren't too choosy. As it turned out we should've been. It took only a few weeks to realize signing that contract was a huge mistake."

"Why was it a mistake?" Miss Flynn asked.

"What Stockwell accused the Pinkerton Agency of was essentially true; the agency stopped at nothing to break the strike. Most of what the miners and mill workers were doing to disrupt the mining companies were instigated and done by contract detectives posing as union workers. I went to Colorado believing our job was to help out local marshals by identifying the troublemakers. I didn't have any particular sympathy for the union, but I sure didn't want to be a part of making a bad situation worse. When my partner and I discovered most of the trouble was being caused by

Miss Flynn smiled. "That's right, but I'm only the receptionist. The only time I ever see Mr. LaTrobe is when he passes by my desk. I doubt he'd even recognize me if he walked in here, and that goes for Mrs. LaTrobe as well. Marshal, what you said about her is certainly true. She's beautiful, but we call her the ice princess. If she ever smiled I think her face would shatter." Morgan detected only detached objectivity in her remark without a trace of envy or malice.

Truesdale stifled a yawn. "It's been a long day. I believe I'll turn in early." Morgan noticed when he left the dining room, the marshal did not head for the front door but turned left toward the back of the house increasing his suspicion it wasn't for the food alone Dan Truesdale chose to come to Rachel Johansen's boarding house.

Morgan considered following the marshal's lead but was reluctant to leave Miss Flynn's company, especially since she appeared to be in no hurry to leave either. He glanced at her and saw she was looking at him with open curiosity.

"Did you really live in Adobe Wells?" she said.

"I did, about thirty years or so ago, give or take."

"It must've been a lot different then."

"That's probably an understatement."

Chin propped on her hand, she said, "What was it like back then?"

"I hardly recognized the town or Mesquite Flats when I got here. What I remember of Adobe Wells was a raw mining town with more tents than houses. It was primitive, and I loved it. I was eight years old when my father brought me and my mother here from Prescott. Back then, Adobe Wells was nothing but a collection of rude shacks. Mesquite Flats was a metropolis in comparison. By the time we left two years later, both towns were already beginning to look different."

"Tell me about your life here." She caught herself and apologized, "I'm sorry, but it's so completely different from the world I grew up in."

"You make me feel ancient, someone out of a history book."

"Not at all, I'm only curious about a time and place that's so removed from what I was used to where I grew up. I'd like to know what an eight-year-old boy thought about Adobe Wells."

"He smiled, warmed by her interest.

"It was an exciting place to live, but then I was young and saw only what a young boy saw. I liked hearing the steam whistle signaling another blast followed soon after by the faint shaking of the ground under my feet. I used to stand in front of the mercantile store after a shift change hoping the miners passing by might be feeling generous and throw me a penny for a piece of candy. Most of all, I remember watching the mule skinners riding the rear mule of the twelve-mule teams, handling the jerk lines that helped keep the heavy wagons loaded with copper ingots heading down the hill to the rail siding at Mesquite Flats. I can still hear the sharp crack of their blacksnake whips, and I was convinced when I was older, I was going to be a mule skinner, swaggering around with a whip curled over my shoulder and a sheath knife on my belt. I wanted to learn how to swear like them; nobody can out-swear a mule skinner. I had several goats and sold the milk to help out a little."

"Why did you leave Adobe Wells?"

"After my father was killed in one of the mines, mother and I went back to Prescott. He's still underground along with a dozen other men who died when the tunnel they were in collapsed. Mother and two of the other wives who also lost their husbands pleaded with anyone who would listen to recover the bodies, but it came to nothing. The excuse was it was too risky to excavate that section. The real reason was it wasn't profitable to waste time and money digging up dead bodies; it was more economical to start another tunnel." He paused and stared off into space. "Funny, I didn't cry because my father was gone, at least not right away. I cried when I had to leave my goats behind. Doesn't make a lot of sense I suppose, crying over some animals when you just lost your father."

"How did you happen to become a private investigator?" she asked when Morgan remained silent.

He considered beginning with his arrival in Albuquerque without mentioning the circumstances that took him there. For some strange reason, he felt like telling her what happened before he went there.

"I was on my way back to Prescott after the war ended in Cuba, and I passed through Las Cruces, New Mexico. I liked what I saw, stayed, and got hired as a deputy marshal. I met someone; her name was Lydia Forrest. We were married a year later after I was elected town marshal. The two years in Las Cruces were the best years of my life."

"What happened to change it?"

"Lydia and I were on our way to church one Sunday morning, not that we were regular church goers. It was also the morning she told me she was with child. She felt we ought to get in the habit of going to church every Sunday now that we were about to become a real family. It was a big mistake getting religion on that particular morning. A cowhand I arrested for disorderly conduct the night before stepped out of an alley and tried to shoot me in the back. He was drunk and hit Lydia instead. She died in my arms."

"I am so sorry."

"It was a long time ago. For years, I felt guilty I was the one who walked away and not Lydia."

"What happened to the man who shot her?"

"I killed him. Will Cosgrove, my deputy, found him holed up in a brothel in Mesilla, a Mexican town just outside of Las Cruces. I went there to arrest him—at least, I told myself that's what I was going to do, and Will thought so too. The

65

cowhand was still drunk and went for his gun just exactly as I knew he might and hoped he would. I suppose if he hadn't made a move, I might not have had any choice but to arrest him and let him stand trial. The truth is, I wasn't going to take a chance he was going to get off with a few years in prison. I resigned the same day I buried Lydia. I ended up in Albuquerque, and Will joined me not long after that. We pooled everything we had and hung up a sign, Westphal & Cosgrove Investigations, on the front of a small building near the railroad depot."

Aware he had talked enough about himself, Morgan asked, "How long do you expect to be in Adobe Wells, Miss Flynn?"

"Please, Mr. Westphal, now that we know one another, it's Cady."

"Then call me Morgan."

"As for how long I'll be here, who knows? I'll probably stay put long enough to earn enough money to go someplace else. I've thought a lot about going to California, maybe San Francisco, and I seem to be getting closer each time I move."

"What are you looking for Cady?"

She shrugged and shook her head, "I'm not sure. I always move to a new place thinking I'll find a reason to stay, but I never do." She smiled. "For the time being, Adobe Wells is home, at least until I can save up enough to go farther west and closer to California. Perhaps I'll actually get there one day. There's always the possibility."

"I hope one day you will." After she left, he realized he had said more about himself than she did. He resolved to change that the next time there was a chance. He hoped there would be. On the way upstairs he suddenly felt guilty. During the time with Cady Flynn, he had forgotten about Frank locked up in the town jail.

Chapter Six

After breakfast, Morgan called and made an appointment to see Victor Latrobe at 11 o'clock. With ample time before the appointment, he went to see Frank, in part to see how he was doing, but also to ask a few more questions prompted by the time spent with Dr. Chambliss.

Deputy Kincy Blaylock wasn't there when Morgan arrived at the jail. Another and friendlier deputy obligingly summoned the jailer who once again led him up to the second-floor cell block. Myron informed him Frank had already received a visit from Samuel Spencer. It was encouraging the lawyer had wasted no time in seeing his client. Morgan surmised Frank's glum mood was the result of the lawyer's visit had further emphasized the reality of his situation. He thought the lawyer's cadaverous appearance probably hadn't helped to inspire confidence.

The jailer started to open the cell door. "That won't be necessary."

"Then I'll leave the cell-block door unlocked. You can leave when you want."

Morgan waited until he heard the cellblock door close before saying anything. His attempt to get more than a monosyllabic response caused him to lose patience.

"Frank, this is getting us nowhere. You're going to have to do better than one-word answers. Now let's start over. Tell me about Hardesty; what did he look like, what kind of man was he, who did he spend time with, what was the reason, or reasons, you didn't get along with him?"

With an effort, Frank sat up and looked apologetic. "Sorry, Morg, I know you're doing all you can, but it's hard sitting in here knowing I don't deserve to be and thinking maybe the deck is stacked against me. I ain't no angel, and you of all people know that, but gettin' a noose around my neck for something I ain't done is hard to take."

Mollified, Morgan replied, "I understand, Frank, and I'm not going to waste words and time telling you not to worry. I need to know as much about Hardesty as I can. There are at least two people, maybe more, who wanted Hardesty dead, and the only way to find out why and who they are is to learn everything about the man. So talk to me about him."

"Well, some would say we looked more like brothers than you and I do. We were about the same size; he was a little heavier. Nice lookin' fella, I guess. He had an easy way with women, even better'n me." The last was said objectively and absent of any false modesty.

"What color were his eyes?"

"Jesus Christ, who gives a shit what color his eyes were?"

"Calm down Frank, and answer the question. I've got my reasons,"

"I dunno, brown, I think. Hell, I can't remember."

"Was there anything about his facial features that was striking or unusual?"

"Not really. Like I said, he was nice-looking. Before we got crosswise, we used to have a lot of fun together. Why are you asking questions about what he looked like? The man is dead. It doesn't matter anymore what the hell he looked like."

"You may be more wrong than you think if the man you're accused of killing isn't Phillip Hardesty."

"What are you talking about? Of course, it was him. I knew the man for better'n a year. Who else could it be?"

"How can you be sure it was really Hardesty? I saw his body. His face was practically gone."

"You're not making any sense at all. There wasn't anybody else down there in that end of the tunnel except me and Hardesty."

"You said you heard voices so there was someone else besides Hardesty. The coroner told me it's possible there were two people involved in the murder."

"I'll be damned!" Suddenly animated, Frank stood up and began pacing the cell. "That will prove I've been telling the truth about hearing voices."

"Hold on a minute. It doesn't prove anything. All it means is that someone else besides you might have been involved. The coroner said one of the men was probably left-handed; Frank, you're left-handed."

"Shit! It all still comes back to me," Frank said in disgust, sitting back down on the bunk.

Morgan did not respond to give Frank time to regain his composure. A few minutes later, Frank asked in a quiet voice, "What else do you want to know?"

"You said earlier you and Hardesty got 'crosswise.' Tell me about it."

Frank shifted uneasily and seemed reluctant to answer the question. "It was back in Colorado."

"Colorado? I didn't know you two knew each other in Colorado."

"What does it matter when I met him?"

Morgan concealed his exasperation. "Just tell me about Colorado."

"Well, we were teamed together and double-jackin' in a gold mine near Telluride last year. It was his turn to hold the drill bit. He got careless. We had a pretty good time the night before and were pretty hung over. Anyway, his forefinger got on top of the drill. I came down with the hammer and took off the end of his finger. He said it was my fault, and I knew it wasn't. I was sorry it happened, but didn't figure I had any reason to apologize. I guess that kinda got things started between us. He wouldn't let it go, and we split up after that."

"Which finger was it?"

"The left forefinger. Why?"

"Just curious, that's all."

"Soon after that, the foreman started coming down on me pretty hard and making a point of searching me when I came out of the mine. He accused me of high-grading."

"What's that?"

Frank shrugged, "Some would call it getting paid what you're due. The mine owners call it stealin'. Now and then depending on the mine, a sharp eye can spot a piece of ore that's showing real good and maybe worth a couple of bucks on the side. When no one's looking, you slip it in your pocket. I knew a fella once who carried a pouch down inside the crotch of his pants."

"Were you high-grading?"

"Damn right, but then so was everyone else, except I was the only one getting searched regular like. I knew Hardesty had put the foreman on me even if he wouldn't admit it."

"So how did you manage to wind up together in Adobe Wells?"

Frank hesitated and appeared reluctant to answer the question. "TJ&M was hiring in Adobe Wells, and the ore was playing out in Telluride. It wasn't like we planned to come down here together. You go where the wages are, and the wages were down here in Arizona."

Morgan thought there was more to it and probed deeper. "Why didn't you go to Bisbee? It's bigger than Adobe Wells."

"Well, we didn't," Frank replied. "In hindsight, I damn sure wish I had!"

"Was the Emily the only mine hiring when you got here?"

"I don't know. There might've been other mines hiring. I don't recall."

"So even though you two didn't get along, you both came down to Adobe Wells and coincidentally happened to sign on at the Emily."

"I didn't know he had. He got here a week or two before I did."

"Did you know he was coming to Adobe Wells when he left Telluride?"

"I suppose I did. I figured the place was big enough we could stay out of each other's way."

"Did Hardesty have any enemies that you know of?"

"If he did, I don't know who they are. It wasn't like we were around each other much."

"What were you and Hardesty fighting about that got you locked up?"

"Like I told you before, it wasn't anything important. We had too much to drink, and things just got of hand."

"Did Hardesty get jailed, too?"

"No."

"Why not?"

"Because he was in the hospital," Frank replied sounding like he didn't want to answer.

"For God's sake, what did you do to him?"

"I threw him down the stairs."

"Frank!"

"All right, it was after I busted a chair over his head. He spent the night in the hospital."

"You must have been really angry."

"I had a right to be. He pulled a knife on me. I guess I lost my head."

Morgan looked at his brother with sudden interest. "What kind of knife was it?"

"I dunno, just an ordinary knife. There wasn't anything special about it. All the drillers carry knives for cuttin' fuses includin' me."

"Look, Frank, this could be important," Morgan said trying to ignore Frank's apparent indifference to such a critical detail. "Was it a wide blade, narrow, short, long? Try to remember."

"It was pretty much like the jack knife I carried." The answer was disappointing.

71

"Did you ever carry any other kind of knife down in the mine?"

"What are you getting at?"

"I mean like a dagger or thin bladed knife?"

"What would I be doing with a useless piece of shit like that in a mine, picking my teeth?" The sarcastic reply left no room to doubt Frank was telling the truth. Morgan changed the subject.

"How did you and Hardesty end up working so close together on that particular day?"

"That was where Cardwell put us."

"Does he change the assignments for each shift, or do you go back to the same drift you were in during the previous shift?"

"Mostly we keep on working the same face from one shift to the next until the vein peters out. If a drift is showin' real good, the top drillers will get assigned there. I ain't braggin' none, but Hardesty and me were the best there was."

"Were the drifts you and Hardesty working considered richer than the others?"

"Yeah, I reckin' they were, but then the copper all through the bottom level was prime compared to the upper levels. A few times I saw rock where the copper veins were as thick as your little finger. I figured it was just a matter of time before TJ&M was gonna take the risk and go deeper."

"What do you mean 'take the risk'?"

"Besides the normal hazards in any mine, the Emily has mine gas. That shit will take a man out before he knows he's a goner. It settles down in the lowest levels. The ventilation shafts and air pumps control it well enough on the upper levels, but you can't always depend on clean air at the lower levels. That's why we use candles down there. A candle flame will go out several minutes before a carbide headlamp. As they say, when the candle flame starts flickerin', you best be gettin' out real fast. Otherwise someone will carry your ass outta there."

Morgan recalled the candle stub in Hardesty's pocket and now realized its significance.

"Where was Hardesty working before he was assigned to the drift next to you?"

"I'm pretty sure he'd been working in Tunnel 2."

"Were you surprised when he was assigned to the drift next to you?"

"Yeah, I was. Like I said, the drift wasn't showin' all that good. And there was another problem with that particular face."

"What do you mean another problem?"

"The vein was anglin' the wrong way. It was starting to move in the direction of the Imperial Mine located next to the Emily. Everybody knows there's hard feelin's between Sandusky and LaTrobe on account the SMC is suing the TJ&M for encroaching on the Imperial claim. There's speculation the drift Hardesty was in might've already been in the Imperial, and if it wasn't, sooner or later it would've been the way the way the vein was shifting. Anyway, I heard, there wasn't supposed to be anyone workin' that close to the Imperial until the lawsuit is settled. Didn't matter none to me. I wasn't being paid to worry about things that weren't my business."

"Gold and silver are valuable byproducts in copper mining. Did Hardesty's drift have ore in it besides copper?"

"Not a chance. Sure there's gold and silver in that drift just like all the others, but it ain't like a regular gold or silver mine where you can see the stuff. It's all mixed in with the copper. You can't really recognize the gold or silver just by looking at the ore-bearing rock. And when you can, it ain't more'n a fleck and not worth bothering with. It's only after the ore gets smelted when the gold or silver is recovered. I know what you're thinking. You're wonderin' were we high grading. Well you can forget it. It ain't likely in a copper mine." Morgan realized he would have to keep on looking for another reason Hardesty had been killed.

"Where did Hardesty live?"

"He was living in a boarding house somewhere over on 3rd and Jefferson."

"Who's Adele?"

Frank looked perplexed. "I don't recollect the name. Where did you come up with it?"

"It was written on the back of a card in Hardesty's pocket. The card offered a free drink at the Arabian Club. Is the Arabian Club a whorehouse?"

"I suppose. Just like the other private clubs, it's got whores in cribs out back. Maybe this 'Adele' was one of them. I might recognize her if I saw her, but the name don't mean a thing. Jesus, who the hell cares what a whore's name is? When a man's got a few drinks in him, he ain't thinking about much of anything else except getting his dollar's worth, and he sure ain't gonna spend his fifteen minutes having a conversation. For all I know, I might've been with her a half dozen times over the past few months."

Morgan tried a different tact. "You said yesterday Hardesty was letting it about you were a union man, and you denied it. Why did he accuse you?"

Frank shrugged and his response was non-committal, "Search me." Morgan knew Frank was holding back and wondered why.

"Come on, Frank, it's not like you're admitting to a crime if you're a union man. You want to try another answer?"

"Morg, admitting you're union in the wrong part of town or in the wrong company is enough to get a man's hands busted, or worse."

"We're alone here, Frank, and I'm your brother trying to help you. I get the feeling you're not playing square with me. Chances are I'm going to find out one way or the other if you are for the union. It will save time now if you don't hold back on me, and it will be a whole lot better for you in the long run."

Frank hesitated and then said in a lower voice, "Not exactly."

"What's that supposed to mean? You either are or you're not. Which is it?"

"I've been talking to one of the union reps on the quiet like. He was gonna pay me a lot of money for signing up with the WFM and a bonus for every man I got to sign on as well. But I didn't agree to it. I told him I'd think about it."

"Was the man you talked with named Stockwell?"

Astonished, Frank asked, "How did you know?"

"It's not important. Who else suspected you were leaning toward the union?"

"Nobody I know. I don't know how Hardesty even knew, unless someone saw me talking to Stockwell and told him."

"Did you go to Stockwell, or did he find you?"

"I didn't know who he was until he bought me a couple of drinks and asked if I would meet him outside. He gave me five dollars just to hear what he had to say. That's almost a day's wage. He said it would be worth my while if I did. I know what you're thinking.. You've got to understand he was offering decent money, and I admit I was tempted, and maybe I might've done it. Anyway, I don't see what this has to do with anything or why Hardesty was killed."

On the surface, Morgan had to agree. The conflict between union and nonunion workers Truesdale described the night before might have been enough justification for a fight between his brother and Hardesty, although Frank's flirtation with the union hardly seemed serious enough to provoke murder. Morgan took out his pocket watch and saw the time for his appointment with LaTrobe was not far off.

"Frank, I've got to go now. Can I bring you anything?"

"I could use another shirt and a pair of trousers and some underwear. The one's I'm wearing are gettin' a bit ripe."

"Where are your things?"

"I'm bunked in with a man by the name of Otis Crandall in a little adobe shack at the end of 6th Street right off Tanner

Gulch on the west end of town. You can't miss it; it's the last house on the left."

Chapter Seven

Miss Ottmier flashed a bright smile that helped to dispel Morgan's gloomy frame of mind. The visit to Frank had been informative, yet he still had a nagging feeling Frank was holding back.

"Mr. Spencer is in court this morning. He said you would be dropping by to sign the contract," she volunteered and handed him two typewritten pages. Morgan scanned the pages and was satisfied they described the verbal agreement the day before. He accepted the pen Miss Ottmier offered and signed the document below the lawyer's signature.

"He also said to give you this," handing him a slip of paper with a name and address typed on it. "It's the name and address of Mr. Hardesty's landlord. He called Mr. Landen this morning and got him to agree to allow you to look over Mr. Hardesty's personal effects. He's expecting you. The room Mr. Hardesty was staying in has already been rented, but his bags are still in Mr. Landen's possession. He plans on selling what's in them to pay the rent to pay the rent the victim still owed."

Morgan was impressed. The lawyer had anticipated him, saving him the time and trouble of tracking down where Hardesty had lived. He doubted he would find anything of significance, but it was simply a possibility that had to be checked if only to verify the clothing and shoe sizes matched those in the morgue. After telling the secretary he would try and stop by at the end of the day, he left for the meeting with Victor Latrobe.

Morgan was about to enter the large building occupied solely by the TJ&M when he saw her come out of the front entrance. She was doubtless one of the most beautiful women he had ever seen. Tall and willowy, she was dressed entirely in black that highlighted her delicate, porcelain features. In defiance of the trend for short hair, her long ash-blonde hair was upswept in a fashion reminiscent of an earlier decade. Briefly their eyes met, and he caught a faint scent of her perfume as she swept past him. He touched the brim of his hat, and she acknowledged his greeting with a polite but disinterested nod. He paused to watch her walk to a parked touring car where a liveried chauffeur waited with the door open. Had he noticed, Morgan would have seen several other men equally transfixed. When the automobile pulled away from the curb, she never glanced right or left but stared straight ahead either uncaring or oblivious to the attention she had inspired. He heard a chuckle behind him and turned to see Dan Truesdale smiling at him.

"Yep, she does have that effect on men, and the other women hate her for it."

"Who is she?"

"Why, that's Olivia LaTrobe, Victor LaTrobe's wife. I told you she was a looker."

"I confess your comment didn't exactly prepare me for the reality. What are you doing here?"

"Actually, I came to help you. Sam Spencer said you were going to see Victor LaTrobe today. I called to find out when your appointment was. I thought it might help if I came over first and let him know I'd appreciate any assistance he can give you. I thought a comment from me might make him a mite more cooperative."

"You didn't by any chance tell him Frank is my brother?"

"Nah, I thought you'd be better off if he didn't know. I sorta made it look like you was helpin' me out some."

"It might help since I want to talk to the men on shift with Hardesty that night. I was hoping to save time running all over Adobe Wells to find them by interviewing them while they're all together on shift. It would also give me an opportunity to get a better idea of where the murder took place, although I suspect by now it looks a lot different."

"Maybe not, but on the other hand, you may not be able to get down there either."

"Why not?"

"I understand the Emily's bottom level is shut down on account of the floodin' that started the day after Hardesty was killed. They've been pumpin' ever since. About the time the doc determined Hardesty was murdered, it was too late to go down there and have a look."

"I didn't know there was a water problem in the Emily. Frank never mentioned it."

"Most of the mines around here have water problems, and some are even worse off than the Emily. One or two mines have been shut down for good because of water they can't pump out fast enough to bring out the ore."

Morgan recalled the Hardesty's damp boots. If what Truesdale said was true, seepage was a common enough occurrence that Frank might not have considered it worth mentioning.

"Is the Imperial flooding?"

"Nope, not that I heard, and that must be gravelin' LaTrobe somethin' terrible knowin' Sandusky is still diggin' away," Truesdale said with a smile. "The thought of LaTrobe havin' a bad day is enough to brighten mine. You'll find out soon enough what I mean when you meet LaTrobe."

The first thing Morgan noticed when he entered the foyer was Miss Cady Flynn sitting behind a desk. She looked quite professional in a modest but attractive long-sleeved blouse and a plain gold necklace. A small watch was pinned on her blouse above the swell of her left breast. She looked up and gave him a smile of recognition.

"Morgan Westphal, you look different in the light of day, and, I might add, not quite so serious."

"At the risk you might take offense, I can say the same, Cady."

He liked the way her face lit up when she laughed.

An imperious voice stopped further conversation, "Miss Flynn!" Morgan saw a cadaverous, bespectacled man with a receding hairline wearing a gray striped business suit standing in an open doorway behind her. He had a sour expression Morgan suspected was permanently etched on his face. "If that is Mr. Westphal, please have him come into the inner office. Mr. LaTrobe is waiting."

"That's Mr. Warren, Mr. LaTrobe's personal secretary," she whispered. "We call him 'The Warden'," she added, making a face.

Mr. Warren acknowledged Morgan with a condescending nod and without a word entered the office, evidently assuming Morgan would follow. The 'Warden' marched rather than walked to a closed door at the other end of the room. After wrapping lightly on the door, the personal secretary opened it and announced pompously, "Mr. Westphal is here to see you, sir," and stepped aside to allow Morgan to enter.

"Mr. Warren, if you would be good enough to hold this until I leave," Morgan said and gave his hat to the secretary who took it automatically, mouth open in shocked surprise. Morgan heard a snicker from one of the secretaries before the door closed behind him.

In contradiction to Truesdale's opinion, Victor LaTrobe in his late forties proved to be personable and engaging. He was shorter than Morgan expected. His smile was slightly unbalanced apparently due to what appeared to be a slight paralysis on the left side of his face. His long black hair was neatly combed straight back from a broad forehead.

Limping slightly and favoring his left leg, the local superintendent of TJ&M Enterprises with outstretched hand met Morgan halfway across the spacious wood paneled office. His grip was strong and firm. He noticed LaTrobe's

left hand was clenched. Morgan wondered if LaTrobe had suffered a mild stroke.

"Won't you please be seated?" LaTrobe gestured to an expensive ensemble of comfortable-looking leather chairs in a corner of the office. Morgan sat down in the chair indicated by Victor LaTrobe while the mine superintendent took a seat in a straight-backed chair opposite. Morgan realized he was sitting slightly lower than LaTrobe and knew it had been intentional.

"Marshal Truesdale prepared me for your visit. I confess until his arrival, I was at a complete loss to know why you wished to see me. I'm still not altogether clear how I can be of any assistance."

"There are a few loose ends concerning the miner's death in the Emily Mine that need to be tied up before trial."

"Such as?" There was no longer the trace of a smile on his face.

"We'll need formal statements from the shift foreman and the men who were working on Hardesty's shift."

"I thought they had already given statements." LaTrobe's brow lifted in surprise.

"That was before the coroner ruled it was a murder and not an accident," Morgan adlibbed.

"Yes, I see, but you hardly need my permission to talk to them."

"True, however, it would expedite matters if I can talk to them while they're on shift. And since I will need to see the location where the crime was committed in order to sketch it for the benefit of the jury, it would be helpful to accomplish both at one time." Morgan hoped it sounded smooth and convincing.

LaTrobe eyed Morgan sharply. "Mr. Westphal, you are working for the prosecution, I presume?"

"It's my job to provide the prosecution with all the facts to be certain the perpetrator of the crime gets his just due," Morgan said without emotion. "Marshal Truesdale and I have known each other for many years, and he's quite familiar with my investigative background. Since I happened to be in Adobe Wells, I was happy to extend a professional favor."

"You just happened to be in Adobe Wells?" LaTrobe asked sounding suspicious.

"Yes. In fact, I once lived here as a boy when my father worked in the mines. The changes since I was last here are quite extraordinary."

Reassured, LaTrobe commented with some irritation, "I'm really not persuaded further investigation is necessary, Mr. Westphal. The man now in jail is clearly guilty and will hang for it. It seems a lot of unnecessary time and trouble for a matter so clear cut."

"Unfortunately, Mr. LaTrobe, the case is not as solid as you may think. It would be true if the accused confessed to the crime. He has not; therefore, those of us involved in preparing the case for trial must go to greater lengths to see the killer hangs for the crime. Without a witness present, the evidence is purely circumstantial."

"Are you saying there's a chance this man Shaw will not be found guilty?"

"It's possible, but I think with a little more probing we'll have the necessary evidence for a conviction."

"What do you consider convincing evidence?"

"An eyewitness would be best. A more convincing motive would also be helpful."

"I've been led to believe the victim and Shaw did not get along."

"I'm aware of that. It's also true there are some ready to say they were the best of friends. Now you see the obstacles the prosecution has in obtaining a conviction. Not that it can't be done, it's that in the little time left before the trial date, it will be necessary to expedite the investigation to ensure a conviction. It's unfortunate Judge Breen saw fit to schedule such an early trial." Morgan had the satisfaction of seeing LaTrobe shift uneasily in his chair.

"It's possible I can have a talk with the judge and see if the trial can be delayed in the event you and Truesdale need more time. I'm afraid I might have had something to do with urging a quick resolution by suggesting it to Judge Breen."

"As superintendent of TJ&M, why do you care one way or the other? It seems a low-level matter for someone as busy and as far removed from the victim and perpetrator to be concerned at all."

"That's where you're wrong, Mr. Westphal. I am directly responsible for the smooth operation of our business interests here in Adobe Wells. Whatever affects the mines, no matter how incidental it may be, has a direct impact on TJ&M stockholders, and it doesn't stop there. Adobe Wells is also affected since we are the largest employer here. Needless to say, the TJ&M Board of Directors will view my performance unfavorably if there is adverse publicity in addition to the risk of a slow-down in production. So you see, that's why this matter must be taken care of as quickly as possible before the union exploits the incident for their own purpose."

Morgan noted LaTrobe's increasing agitation. Gone was the calm, affable demeanor of a few minutes ago. The man seated before him now was tense with an undercurrent of restrained anger. Morgan had noticed earlier LaTrobe had the unconscious habit of occasionally reaching over with his right hand to gently massage the left hand. LaTrobe was now gripping the paralyzed hand tightly. He thought the remark about the union was strange as thus far there was no apparent involvement or interest by the union. The remark was curious enough to explore further.

"I fail to see how the union would profit from this particular affair."

"It's easy to see you don't have the same experience with the union that I've had. The socialists will stop at nothing until they control every industry in the country with their godless philosophy. I've reason to believe Hardesty was either secretly working for the union or was a union sympathizer. I've made a point to keep my eye on any of my workers who might be sympathetic to the WFM."

Morgan was mystified not only about LaTrobe's assertion Hardesty was somehow affiliated with the mine workers' union, but also why he would be so concerned about the death of someone who may have belonged to an organization he so thoroughly detested. He though it was worth pursuing.

"If Hardesty was a union man, why are you so concerned with ensuring Shaw is held accountable? From your earlier comments, I would think you would be satisfied with Hardesty's death and unconcerned who may have killed him."

LaTrobe looked momentarily surprised or startled at the question. Morgan was unable to tell which. "The reason Shaw must hang is very simple. If he doesn't, the union will make Hardesty a martyr to their cause. I, TJ&M Enterprises, cannot afford to allow this to happen."

"What if Hardesty wasn't a union man?"

"It doesn't matter, Mr. Westphal. The union people will say he was, and then the trouble will start. Have you ever seen what happens during a strike?" Morgan shook his head. "It's an ugly thing to see. Innocent people are injured or killed, production stops, and business suffers. The union thinks perversely they've won when the mines are forced to shut down."

Oddly, Morgan was beginning to understand the superintendent's biased view of the murder. LaTrobe didn't care whether Frank was innocent or guilty. He needed to prevent a fire from being started. Apart from a fundamental hatred of the WFM, LaTrobe viewed Frank's predicament purely in terms of business. The fine point of guilt or innocence was incidental to LaTrobe whose sole interest was preventing an unwelcome business outcome. If an innocent man was hanged in the process, well that was merely an unfortunate consequence.

"Dr. Chambliss said you called him and insisted an autopsy be conducted even though at first Hardesty's death was believed to be accidental. Why did you make that call?"

"I wanted to be sure the death really was accidental and not the work of someone trying to set up a liability claim against the TJ&M. I must be constantly vigilant; the TJ&M cannot afford anymore litigation."

"When you learned Hardesty had been murdered, you must have been relieved it was not the result of an accident for which the company might be held accountable."

"I hadn't really thought of it in that manner." There was a tap on the door, and Mr. Warren entered the room and approached LaTrobe. He leaned over and whispered in the superintendent's ear. LaTrobe's taut face relaxed.

"You're in luck, Mr. Westphal. I was about to tell you I would be unable to approve your request to go down into the Emily because of the flooding we've been having on the lower level. It seems everything is now under control, David, contact Mr. Cardwell and inform him Mr. Westphal is to be permitted access to the Emily during the second shift. I want Mr. Westphal to be treated as my personal guest and given complete cooperation in the investigation of Mr. Hardesty's death."

"I appreciate your assistance and your time, Mr. Latrobe," Morgan said after the private secretary departed.

"Not at all, it's the least I can do," LaTrobe responded, once again relaxed. "The second shift starts in thirty minutes and will end at midnight. When you're ready to go down into the Emily, ask the lift operator for Mr. Cardwell, he's the shift foreman. For your own safety, I would ask you to pay close attention to anything Cardwell says. You may find him a trifle overbearing, although I've never known a successful mine supervisor to be anything but."

"I'll keep that in mind."

"I advise you to dress warmly. You'll find it both cold and very damp where you're going. It's also dangerous so you will have to sign a release absolving TJ&M of any responsibility should you meet with an unfortunate accident. Please see Mr. Warren, and he'll provide you with the form."

Morgan stood up to leave, "My thanks for your courtesy," and headed for the door, taking one last look at the ornately decorated room. With his hand on the doorknob, he heard LaTrobe call his name.

"One more thing, Mr. Westphal, I would consider it a personal favor if you would keep me informed on the progress of your investigation."

"I'm sorry, Mr. Latrobe. Ethically I really cannot oblige you. The results of my investigation will be turned over to Marshal Truesdale."

"Oh, I don't mean to interfere, and I'm not asking for details. I'm merely curious as to the general progress you make. After all, TJ&M is not exactly a disinterested party."

Morgan wondered what to make of the superintendent's request and was about to repeat his refusal when he thought better of it. He thought there might be some benefit in such an arrangement.

"I suppose a general appreciation of the case would not jeopardize any confidence," Morgan replied with a suitably reluctant expression.

"Splendid, Mr. Westphal, splendid. I'm grateful for your understanding. In the future, if you wish to see me, it may prove more convenient for us both to come to my house and avoid the distractions and protocol of an office visit. I shall instruct my house staff accordingly. Goodbye, Mr. Westphal, and thank you for coming."

Chapter Eight

Morgan realized if he was going down into the Emily, he needed clothes and footwear more suitable than anything he had with him. He remembered Frank's earlier request for clothing and regretted he and Frank were not remotely of similar size. There was no other choice but to purchase what he needed. Before exiting the TJ&M building, he stopped and asked Cady Flynn where he might obtain the items he required. She directed him to the Mercantile Emporium several blocks away.

The Emporium clerk took one look at Morgan's suit and raised a skeptical eyebrow when he was asked to show garments more suitable for going into an underground mine.

"I work for a newspaper," Morgan explained, "and I'm here in Adobe Wells to write a feature about the hazards of working underground. As you can see, what I'm wearing is hardly practical for the job."

"You ain't working for one of them union rags, are you?" the unfriendly clerk asked. Since the Mercantile Emporium was owned by TJ&M, the clerk's prejudice was not surprising.

"Not a chance, you couldn't pay me enough to work for a socialist newspaper," borrowing LaTrobe's descriptor. "Nah, I'm strictly a free enterprise man myself."

The admission seemed to have the desired effect, and the clerk's attitude quickly transitioned from truculent to helpful. This time it was the clerk who looked around and lowered his voice. "Since you ain't really gonna be working down there, it don't make sense in buying new stuff, if you know what I mean. We got some used things in a back shed we sell at discount. Sometimes a man comes up short before payday and sells some of his gear to make up for it. You're welcome to look if you've a mind."

Morgan thought it was an excellent suggestion. That the clerk was competing in the backroom with TJ&M did not offend his sensibilities in the least. For next to nothing, he purchased a hat, denim trousers with a set of frayed braces attached, a heavy shirt, wool socks, a pair of work boots only slightly larger than his own size, and a carbide lamp that still looked serviceable. He drew the line on the long underwear and purchased those new.

He was on his way out of the store after arranging to pick up the bulky package before closing time when he saw by chance a glass case full of knives. The knives were of varying types and sizes most of which were folding pocket knives similar to what Frank described. It was clear from the size and shape of the blades such knives would not have caused the wound in Hardesty's back.

Morgan left the emporium and followed the directions to Hardesty's lodgings. He had ample time to get the clothes his brother wanted and drop them off at the jail before going to the boarding house to change clothes. He didn't want to go into the Emily until late in the shift to watch one of the drillers setting the charges. He needed to gain a better insight of the sequence of the actions, time required to set the charges, and examine the blast results.

The dilapidated Hotel Territorial, a two-story frame building where Phillip Hardesty had lived, was nothing more than an isolated and lingering survivor of a neighborhood that had been displaced by the spread of active claims in the relentless pursuit of commercial grade ore. During the time Morgan had lived nearby, the house had been grand and centered in the main commercial center of Adobe Wells; however, the intervening years had not been kind to it, and the building now bore little resemblance to the one he remembered. The few houses and fewer businesses still left in that part of town were equally rundown. The once verdant hillside overlooking the forlorn enclave where he had once played was now a featureless spill of gray tailings. Morgan thought the industrial yard with its stacks of square-cut timbers and machinery farther down the gravel road was about where he had lived in a small four-room shack with another family whose names he no longer remembered.

Contrary to what Miss Ottmier had led him to believe, Mr. Landen was not happy to see him when Morgan introduced himself. Apparently the aging and unkempt manager with tobacco stains at the sides of his mouth and on the front of his unbuttoned shirt had second thoughts about permitting an examination of Hardesty's luggage. Morgan assured him he was not there to appropriate the bags or any items toward reimbursing the town for Hardesty's burial expenses. The hotel manager remained unconvinced and uncooperative. Finally out of patience with the persistent refusal, Morgan asked to use the telephone. When asked who he wanted to call, Morgan said he was going to have Marshal Truesdale obtain a court order to remove the luggage to the jail. Mr. Landen quickly changed his mind and led Morgan to a small storage room at the back of the house. The hotel manager pointed to a large leather suitcase and a carpet bag he identified as Hardesty's; both bags were battered and worn.

Under the baleful and watchful gaze of the landlord, Morgan picked up the bags and carried them out to the back porch.

"Probably ain't nothin' in them bags gonna cover the rent he owed me," Landen remarked.

Since it was clear the irritating man was not about to let him examine the contents of the bags by himself, Morgan thought he may as well see if Landen had anything useful to say about Hardesty's habits.

"Did Mr. Hardesty have any visitors?" Morgan asked as he unbuckled the first of the two leather straps that held the leather suitcase together.

"Not many."

"Did you know any of them or recall any names?"

"The fella down in the jail they say killed Hardesty used to come now and then." Morgan assumed Frank's visits were before the two men had a falling out. On second thought, he considered that might be an unwarranted assumption.

"When was the last time you saw Frank Shaw come here?"

"I recollect t'were late last week...mebbe early Thursday morning I reckin'." Morgan cursed under his breath. What the hell was Frank seeing Hardesty about, and why didn't he tell him about the visit? He left Frank with the impression the two had not spoken or seen each other outside the Emily for some time.

"The reason I remember was Shaw was bangin' so hard on Hardesty's door it woke up some of the other men, and one of them came and got me. It was plain Shaw had been drinking. He didn't pay no attention when I told him to leave. Finally, Hardesty opened the door and invited him into the room. Things settled down for a time then their voices got so loud some of the men started complaining again, and I had to go back there and take care of things. The second time I took my shotgun. Both of them fellas was big men, and I ain't so young no more. I pointed the shotgun at Shaw and told him to leave and be quick about it. Yes, siree, you better be sure he left then."

"What were they arguing about?"

"I wouldn't know about that 'though it didn't seem like they was arguin' so much as talking loud." Morgan thought the comment was surprising, given the supposed animosity between them.

Morgan opened up the suitcase and was struck by how carefully the clothing had been packed. Glancing at the hotel manager, he asked, "Did you pack these bags?"

"No, they was already packed when I went in to get the room fixed up right after I heard he was dead."

"Was there anything left in the closet or bureau?"

"Nope, all I found was them two bags. The rent was due on Saturday, and I got a notion Mr. Hardesty was about to skip."

Morgan wondered why a man about to go to work would pack all his things. If he was planning to go somewhere after his shift ended. Logic would suggest he would pack when he returned and after he had a chance to clean up. Since his shift didn't end until after midnight, where would he be going so early in the morning, particularly after working a hard, dirty twelve-hour shift? He wondered if Frank knew Hardesty was leaving and where he might be going.

"Who else do you recall coming here?"

"Nobody I can remember." Landen scratched his bulging stomach thoughtfully. "He used to get phone calls, usually on Friday mornings just before he left to go on shift. Since the phone is on the wall outside my door, most of the time I was the one answered it."

"Was it the same person each time, and did he give a name?"

"Yep, and no, she never said who she was."

"She?"

"I guess I know a woman's voice when I hear one."

"Is there anything else you can tell me about Hardesty?"

"Nothin' else comes to mind 'cept maybe one other thing. Damn he was one good lookin' fella. He coulda been one of them actors in the flickers they make out in California. If I'd ever looked like him, I reckin' I wouldn't be wastin' my time with a flophouse like this."

"Thanks for your time, Mr. Landen. I won't keep you any longer from whatever you were doing. I'll be sure and repack everything as I found them." The attempt to discourage Landen from looking over his shoulder finally succeeded. The landlord took the hint and left Morgan to sift through the contents of the bags.

The shirts and trousers looked to be the same size as those he had examined in the morgue. The clothes were neither stylish nor expensive and generally representative of what a working-class man would wear during his time off. The only clothing approaching formal wear consisted of a modest brown-striped suit with matching vest. An Arabian Club card in the left vest pocket was identical to the one included in Hardesty's personal effects at the morgue. Nothing was written on the back. There were two collarless white shirts and an assortment of celluloid shirt collars stored in a cookie tin. A small box held a set of inexpensive mother-of-pearl cuff links and shirt studs. A leather case contained a hairbrush, a pair of combs, and a straight razor with a tortoise-shell handle. Toiletries in a side pocket consisted of a toothbrush, small tin of toothpaste powder, a leather strop, shaving brush, and a ceramic shaving mug. A moustache cup similar to the one he owned was packed at the bottom next to a pair of ankle-length, button-top shoes. The shoes were worn but neatly polished. In a cardboard box, were several tins of vulcanized sheaths.

The carpet bag proved equally disappointing, containing nothing but a Newsboy flat cap, underwear, socks, and soiled clothing in a separate laundry bag. The contents of both bags said little about the man who owned them except that he had been neat, frugal, and careful with his possessions. The rubber sheaths indicated he was just as careful sexually. The thought reminded him of the Arabian Club and whether or not it would be worthwhile to go there and find "Adele". Perhaps she was the reason for the quantity of sheaths.

The one conspicuous thing missing was a wallet and any personal papers that it may have contained. There was no wallet among Hardesty's personal effects at the morgue leaving him to suspect someone at the morgue had pilfered it, or Landen was lying about not opening the bags. In either case, the chance of recovering it was doubtful at best.

Morgan began folding and replacing the items in the bags as neatly as possible. He soon accepted the reality he was not going to succeed in packing them as well as they had been before. He recalled from their brief honeymoon, Lydia had been a meticulous packer as was his mother. There were some things women did naturally better than men, and packing had to be counted among them. Hardesty's bags looked as if they had been packed by a woman.

Morgan was winded by the time he climbed the steep, winding gulch and found the tin-roofed adobe shack at the end of 6th Street where Frank lived. He knocked on the door and heard a sleepy voice ask, "Who is it?"

"Morgan Westphal. I'm here to pick up a few things for Frank."

"Just a minute," the voice replied. A moment later, Morgan heard a bolt slide and a tall, lanky young man with tousled hair and dressed only in his underwear asked, What do want?"

"Are you Otis Crandall?"

"That's right," he said, trying unsuccessfully to stifle a yawn.

"I'm Frank's brother. He asked me to get some of his clothes."

"He never told me he had a brother," Crandall said skeptically. "If you're his brother, how come you ain't got the same name and you're so much older?"

"We're half-brothers. We had the same mother, different fathers."

"How do I know you're Frank's brother? You got any proof? Maybe you just want to help yourself to Frank's stuff."

"Look, if I were here to rob Frank, I doubt I would be dressed like this and knocking on the door in broad daylight. The sooner I can get some clothes for Frank, the sooner you can get back to bed. Or if you like, I'll give you the list of things he wants, and you can take them down to the jail, it's your choice. Now what's it going to be?"

The effort to process the request was visible on the young man's face. To his relief, Crandall finally grasped the logic of the argument, flashed a smile, and waved him inside.

"I guess you must be Frank's brother at that, but you sure don't look like him."

"I never said we were twins. Mr. Crandall…"

"Call me Otis. Me and Frank been bunking together since Hardesty moved out and went on over ta live in the old Territorial. I was sure sorry to hear what Frank done. He ain't a bad fella, and it sure surprised me to learn he killed Hardesty."

"Did you know Hardesty?"

"Nah, I just knowed who he was, that's all. Saw him back in Telluride a bunch of times and a few times over in one of the sportin' houses drinkin' with Frank, back when they was still friends."

"What did Hardesty look like?"

"He was a helluva good lookin' sunnuva bitch, I'll say, or my name ain't Otis Crandall. Say, why're you interested in Hardesty?"

"I'm trying to help Frank by finding who killed Hardesty."

"If it weren't Frank that did it, who do you think did?"

"Well, Otis, that's what I'm working on."

Otis knitted his brow and said, "Mister, I sure hope you find the man 'cause I don't want to see Frank hang for somethin' he ain't done."

"That makes two of us—make that three of us counting Frank. Do you recall any visitors Frank had?"

"There was a big fella, kinda mean-faced, with short gray hair come lookin' for Frank here not too long ago." The description fit Elias Stockwell. Frank warn't here, and the man left. He looked like one of them union fellas. I told Frank that night if'n he was to join the union, he'd be livin' by hisself pretty damn quick."

"You don't much care for the union, do you, Otis?"

"Well, if I did, I sure wouldn't admit it none, leastways where anyone workin' for TJ&M might hear. It ain't just a question of keepin' your job. A man could get hisself hurt real bad. You know, an accident that warn't no real accident a 'tall, if you know what I mean."

"Have there been any such 'accidents' in the Emily?"

The young man's face took on a guarded expression. "Mister, maybe I don't wanna say no more, and maybe I already said more'n I should've."

"I understand, Otis, but have you ever thought Hardesty may have had one of those 'accidents'?"

"Goddamn, I never thought of that. If it's true, then Frank got no chance a 'tall, 'cause LaTrobe will make certain he don't the same as he done up in Telluride."

"What happened in Telluride?"

"Word got out a fella by the name of McPherson was signed on with the WFM. Mac was on the same shift I was and a mucker like me. It warn't too long 'fore Cardwell—"

"The same Cardwell who's working as a shift boss in the Emily?"

"That's him. Anyway, Mac got pulled off the drift he was muckin' out and told to go help out on one of the ore chutes takin' the ore from an upper level stope down to the ore cars on a lower level. Well, they said he done fell in the chute, but if you ever seen one of them chutes, it'd be pretty hard to fall in, and Mac went down that thing headfirst. Shit, everybody knowed 'tweren't no accident, but that's the way Mr. Cardwell reported it. It ain't healthy to talk union around a TJ&M mine, and if you're dumb enough to be lettin' on you're a union man, you gonna be a dead union man for too long."

"Have there been any other accidents in any of the TJ&M mines here in Adobe Wells?"

"I heard a driller over in the Pearl lost a hand. Coulda been a real accident. They been havin' some problems with the dynamite and blasting' caps. Some are blamin' the union. They say the union is fussin' with 'em and sayin' it ain't safe to get the drillers to strike. Mister, it may be just talk, maybe it ain't. Best be careful with your questions and where you ask them is all I gotta say. Now if you don't mind, I need to get some shut-eye. Them things over there on that side belong to Frank. Help yourself, and I'd be obliged if you'd let yourself out."

Otis Crandall was snoring loudly before Morgan finished stuffing a laundry bag with the clothing Frank wanted.

Chapter Nine

Truesdale drove him up the short winding road to the Emily just as the sun dropped below the mountains. The mine's head frame was silhouetted against a cloudless sky rapidly changing from rose and turquoise to deepening shades of azure.

The headlamps revealed a stream of water splashing noisily down the tailings into the canyon below. The pulsing throb of the water and ventilation pumps reminded him of a rhythmic heartbeat. The volume of water pouring down made him wonder how much water was still left in Tunnel 3.

"I'm still not sure what you're lookin' for and what you expect to find," Truesdale said.

"To be honest, I'm not either. I'm hoping I'll know after I've had a look around down there. Dan, there's something that's right out in front of me, but I can't make out what it is. If I scratch around long enough, maybe I'll find something that might start making some sense. By the time I get back up on the surface I may have nothing to show for it but wet feet, a cold ass, and sincere regret for having made the effort."

The marshal maneuvered the roadster around a stack of square timbers, past a hissing steam engine and across a set of narrow tracks leading to the cage platform located directly underneath the head frame. The loud grinding of the hoist wheel and whine of the cage cables were reminders in a few minutes he would be lowered into the darkness below; the thought was enough to consider changing his mind. Too late, Truesdale pulled to a stop, and Morgan climbed out of the roadster donning the light jacket he had delayed slipping on until now. He knew in the cold, damp mine below he would miss the hot, dry breeze now blowing through the canyon.

With one hand on the gear lever and an eye on a dial showing the rate and progress of the descending cage, the operator was also paying attention to a half-dozen sweating Mexicans loading a stack of heavy timbers into the other and considerably larger equipment cage. Evidently the loading was not going fast enough to suit him.

"You goddamned worthless greasers, get your asses moving else I'm gonna put my boot up where the sun ain't never shined." Morgan realized there had been many changes since his brief mining experience; however, the vignette before him made it obvious some things had not.

Morgan approached the cage operator who was old enough to be his grandfather and introduced himself. "The name's Westphal. I'm here to see Mr. Cardwell."

The operator glanced at Morgan, spat a stream of tobacco juice to one side. "Been expectin' you. The boss said to send you right down." He looked closely at Morgan's clothing and nodded approvingly, "Looks like you been underground before."

"A long time ago I did a little hardrock digging over in Prescott," without mentioning it was an unwelcome, short-lived experience.

"Well, least you look and sound like you know somethin' about it. Best get your headlamp on. It ain't exactly daylight down where you're goin'." After helping Morgan fasten the carbide headlamp around the brim of the resin-stiffened felt hat, the cage operator adjusted the water valve to start the drip into the calcium carbide chamber. "That should do it," then struck a match to ignite the gas. "You got a candle?"

Morgan shook his head and replied, "Didn't think I'd need one."

"Well, young fella, you best take this since you're going all the way down to Tunnel 3." He handed Morgan the stub of a stearic candle. "There ain't been any problems with gas since they put in the new blowers last week, but you never can tell. Now when the cage comes up, jump in and hold on.

Better keep everything inside the cage, and that includes your prick, hands, and feet, else you ain't gonna have 'em anymore by the time you gets to the bottom. You'll be at the bottom level in a lil' over one minute. When the cage stops, be quick about gettin' off. More'n likely, you'll find Mr. Cardwell at the control station 'bout twenty yards down the tunnel on the left."

With a clatter, the cage suddenly appeared and came to a stuttering stop. Morgan jumped on and gripped one of several leather straps suspended from the top of the cage. He was enveloped in a cold updraft coming up from the shaft that quickly replaced the hot, dry surface air with refreshing coolness. He felt the cage move ever so slightly and then his stomach heaved upward as the cage plunged downward in a rattling descent into the depths below. His ears crackled and finally popped with the change in pressure. He wanted to close his eyes to keep from seeing how the headlamp illuminated the rock sides of the shaft passing by in a blur.

Imperceptibly at first then more noticeably, the cage began to slow down until with a sudden jerk that bent his knees, it came to a halt. He wasted no time in heeding the operator's caution for a quick exit. A bell rang, and the cage lifted upward into the darkness as fast as it had come down. He found himself on a wooden platform next to a group of men apparently waiting for the other cage to come down to unload the timbers the Mexican workers had been loading. He was struck how much they resembled each other in the dimly lit tunnel with their dirt-encrusted faces obscuring or shadowing their features. They were all dressed similar to him in dark clothing and felt hats. Most wore long moustaches the same as his. Even a short distance away in the gloom, they would be virtually indistinguishable from each other. He resisted the impulse to go over and talk to them about Hardesty out of concern Cardwell might take exception. Without the supervisor's cooperation, he would gain nothing except a fast exit back up to the surface.

In the distance, he heard the faint percussive noise of the drills, the rumble of ore cars, and unidentified sounds that could have been the earth itself shifting. He recalled a veteran miner telling him after his first day underground, if you heard the mine groaning and grinding, it was only Mother Earth complaining. It was what you didn't hear that would kill you.

Lit by a string of dim overhead lights, Tunnel 3 stretched into the distance. The lights glinted off shallow pools and the polished metal tracks leading to the cage platform. The tracks ran down the center of the tunnel; every few yards, the tunnel widened a few feet to allow pedestrian traffic to get out of the way of the ore cars. As directed by the cage operator, he followed the tracks in search of the control station. He hoped Cardwell wasn't off somewhere on his rounds.

By the time he got to the station, his shoes and the bottom of his denim trousers were soaked. His feet were already cold, and he knew they would be colder still by the time he got back to the surface.

Setback about eight feet from the tunnel, the station was lit by two bare overhead lights. Rough planking provided a few inches of clearance above the floor. A telephone and a network of wires snaking to a signal box were attached to a board fastened to one wall. Next to each switch was a small light and number. Morgan assumed any call coming in would also trigger a light in case the noise in the tunnel drowned out the audible signal. Below the telephone was a chest-high wooden table set at an angle that served as a desk. A man deep in thought and smoking a cigar leaned on the table studying a diagram of the Emily Mine.

Large and brawny Tate Cardwell nearly filled the narrow alcove. In spite of the cold temperature, his jacket and hat were hanging on a nail beside the desk. His shirt sleeves were rolled up revealing heavily muscled arms. His broad, sloping shoulders, heavy brow, and prominent jaw reminded him of a troll-like creature he had once seen in a book illustration. Cardwell turned to face him, and his unfriendly expression was enough to tell him the shift boss was less than overjoyed to see him.

"You're Westphal?" It was more an accusation than a question. When Morgan nodded, he said, "I'm Cardwell." He didn't offer to shake hands. "You took your own sweet time coming. I expected you hours ago. Apart from knowing LaTrobe let you come down here, I don't have a goddamn clue what you're after."

"Sorry, I didn't realize there was any particular time I was expected." Morgan replied and briefly explained his reason for being there. He concluded by saying, "I wanted to come in on the last half of the shift to observe some of the drilling and blasting."

"What for?"

"To get a better understanding for the time it takes to drill a round, set the charges, and inspect the results."

"Well, it's your time, and as long as you don't get in my way or interfere with the men, I suppose I ain't got any objection. If you do get in the way, you'll be outta here faster than you came down. Personally, I think you're wasting your time and mine."

The telephone above the desk rang and a light on the panel next to it began blinking. With a muttered curse, Cardwell lifted the instrument off the cradle and asked, "What now, Dawson?" He was clearly annoyed at the interruption. Cardwell listened for a moment, reached under the desk for a ledger, and after thumbing through it, began writing on one of the pages as he listened occasionally asking questions. Cardwell wrote the notations with his left hand.

The conversation ended and Cardwell faced Morgan. "Since you're here, take a look at this," pointing the cigar at a map of the mine's third level. "This'll give you some idea of how the tunnel is laid out. I'm gonna let you move around on your own. You can't get lost since all the drifts and stopes connect to the main tunnel. As you can see, Tunnel 3 starts curving from about fifty yards from where we're standing at the main shaft and continues to curve until it finally turns sharply from south to northeast. The tunnel ends here about where the boundary is between the Imperial and Emily; that's also where the last drift runs almost due east."

"I understand Sandusky has filed suit against TJ&M for encroachment."

"Yeah, that's right. It's all bullshit. Sandusky is sore because the Emily is showing better ore. La Trobe is getting ready to counter-sue the SMC. In the end, the lawyers will be the only ones to win."

"Is there any encroachment?"

"Shit, all the mines encroach to some degree whether it's intentional or accidental. Who the hell really knows? In the Emily alone, we've got miles of tunnels, drifts, and crosscuts at three levels down to more than 1100 feet—that's from surface level not sea level. The drifts follow the veins. We measure from the shaft and take bearings and still you can be off 30-50 feet, especially when the tunnel slopes downward, which in the case down here, it does and toward the east. Hell, we've got winzes, ventilation shafts, going up through the Imperial, and at least one of the Imperial shafts is connected to one of ours; you can see it right here intersecting on the other side of the tunnel where Hardesty was killed. Same is true with winzes connecting the west side of the Emily with the Pearl."

"Tell me about Hardesty and what you think happened to him."

Cardwell gave him a calculating look, took a deep drag on the cigar, and exhaled. Morgan was enveloped in a cloud of acrid smoke he knew was deliberate and meant to intimidate.

"I already told the marshal what I know. It was a short conversation. Why don't you ask him?"

"Because he didn't know Hardesty, and you did. And because you were down here, and he wasn't."

Cardwell was silent for a moment as if considering whether to cooperate. Finally, he shrugged and said, "All right. There ain't much to tell. Hardesty was a good enough driller and better'n most. Had a bad temper, but I didn't hold that as being a problem for me. Shit, most of the men down here ain't exactly the kind you bring home to your wife for Sunday dinner. They know any of 'em crosses me, they get this first," holding up a ham fist. "If there's a second time, they draw their pay."

"So Hardesty never gave you any trouble in or out of the Emily?"

"Say, where're you going with this? I never had a beef with Hardesty, and as far as I know, he didn't have one with me."

"What about Frank Shaw?"

"About the same, I'd say."

"Do you think Shaw killed Hardesty?"

"If it wasn't Shaw, who else could it be? Westphal, I don't really give a shit who killed him or why. The only thing I care about is I'm short three drillers now that Merrick's skipped out, and I'm more concerned with getting them replaced than I am whether or not Shaw gets hangs for murder." The name Merrick sounded vaguely familiar, but Morgan was unable to recall where he'd heard it. "With Hardesty killed and the goddamned tunnel flooded for three days, production is down, LaTrobe's temper is up, and my bonus ain't gonna be for shit this month."

"Did you know Hardesty and Shaw didn't get along?"

"So what, most of the men down here don't like someone else on the shift. If I had to take into consideration whose a friend and whose not, Christ, I'd never get any ore out of this goddamned tunnel."

"So it was an accident they ended up in adjacent drifts?"

"You might say it was at that. I switched Hardesty over to that drift three days before he was killed when the vein in the drift he'd been drilling petered out. Shaw had been working where he was for more'n a week. I keep the drillers working the same drifts for as long as the ore holds out; the drillers get so they think a drift belongs to them, if you get what I mean. They're more likely to hustle their ass a bit more when they're working the same drift."

"Tell me about the night the murder took place. When was the last time you saw Hardesty alive?"

Cardwell cocked his head. "I'd guess maybe between 10:00 and 10:30 p.m.. Hardesty was down to the last couple of holes, and it looked to me he was gonna finish the shift on time. He was dependable, not like a few of the others who I've got to kick their ass at quitting time on Saturday when we shut down for twenty-four hours so's they remember what they're supposed to do when they come back. And then I got to kick 'em again when they come back to work to remind the sons of bitches what I said the day before. For once, Shaw looked like he was doggin' it, and I told him to get his ass moving, or he was gonna get docked. Anyway, I always make my rounds an hour or two before blasting and then right after the charges go off so's I can report to the foreman what I think the muckers are going to send up."

"How were you notified about what happened?"

"I got a call someone was hurt and got down there as quick as I could."

"When you reached Shaw's drift, what did you find?"

"Shaw and the men working the stope nearby were standing around Hardesty. It was plain enough Hardesty was dead. From his face, it looked like he caught the blast right square in front."

"What did Shaw say?"

"He was upset. Claimed it was an accident, and it was his fault."

"Did you believe him?"

"At the time, I had no reason not to. I did think it was strange where the body was, but I guess I thought maybe Shaw had carried Hardesty back from the face."

"Was anyone else near or at the end of the tunnel besides Hardesty, Shaw, and the men working in the stope?"

"No. The closest anyone else was to Hardesty and Shaw were the five men working the stope; it's, maybe fifty yards west of where Hardesty and Shaw were working. They had no reason to be anywhere except there."

"What about other men delivering dynamite down to the drillers?"

"I got a team of muckers bring the dynamite down toward the end of the shift. It's their responsibility to take the dynamite to where the drillers are working. The drillers carry their own fuses and blasting caps."

"What about replacement drill bits?"

"Each driller is expected to pick up at least two drill bits at the machine shop before they come down. Two is usually enough. If they need another, there's a call box close by they can call the parts and equipment man. It happens now and then, but not too often."

"Were there any calls for parts from either Hardesty or Shaw at any time during the shift?"

"No."

"Is there any other way to get to the drifts Hardesty and Shaw were in besides going down the main tunnel?"

"What the hell do you mean?"

"You said there were a couple of winzes providing ventilation in that part of the tunnel with at least one connecting the Emily with the Imperial. Is it possible someone came down one of the ventilation shafts to get into Hardesty's drift?"

He saw Cardwell's eyes narrow as he considered the question. "I suppose it's possible but unlikely."

"Why?"

"I think you'll know when you look at one of those shafts. They're narrow, not like the tunnel behind you. They twist and turn according to where the rock was the softest. They're also steep as hell. Christ, it'd take a monkey to get up one of those goddamned things."

"That may be true, but monkeys didn't dig those shafts, men did. That being the case, someone could enter and leave at that end of the tunnel, and no one would ever know it."

"I'm not sure where you're going with this."

"It's possible Shaw is telling the truth, and someone else killed Hardesty then used a ventilation shaft to escape."

Cardwell's skepticism was plain to see. "The ventilation shafts were dug from the surface down to the first tunnel then extended downward to the next level after that. A man would have to be out of his mind to risk climbing up over a thousand feet through one of those shafts."

"Or desperate," Morgan responded. "Maybe it wasn't necessary to go up a thousand feet, only 200-300 feet at the most and leave the mine through the tunnel above."

"Not a chance, Westphal. Shaw did it as sure as I'm standing here. You'll see after you go and take a look at those shafts."

"When the shift is over, how do you account for the men; is there a roll call taken?"

"You bet your ass there is. When they come on shift, I log them in right here. The same is true when they finish, I log each one out."

"Did you log everyone out on the night Hardesty was killed?"

Cardwell's eyes blinked rapidly, and the shift boss hesitated before answering. "Of course, I did. Why wouldn't I?"

"There was confusion that night. I'm only suggesting the possibility normal procedures may not have been followed as carefully as they would have been had there not been a death."

"I know and do my job, and I'm telling you everybody got logged out at the same time."

"What about the two men you sent up with Hardesty's body? They went up before the rest. Did you log them out, or were you still at the end of the tunnel where Shaw was still working to find the misfire?"

Morgan noted the flicker of doubt in Cardwell's eyes. "All right, I see your point," the shift boss conceded. "But I logged them out later when the rest of the men finished up. Shaw was the last one out because he had to stay and find the misfire."

"Do you remember who you sent up with Hardesty's body?"

"Yeah, it was Merrick and Davies."

"You said earlier Merrick had skipped out. When did he show up missing?"

"He never showed up for the next shift. Didn't much matter because by then the third level had flooded, and I released everybody except for a couple of men to help with the hoses and pumps. I told them to come back when we got the tunnel drained. That was today, and Merrick didn't show up."

"Did he tell anyone where he went?"

"Not that I know of, or if he did, I never heard. The bastard just up and left without so much as a by your leave. Didn't even collect his wages for the week."

"When you went up to the surface, was Merrick still with Hardesty and Davies?"

This time, Cardwell's eyes shot up in surprise. "Come to think of it, he wasn't. I had to get one of the other men to load the body on the truck. Never gave it any thought until now." From his years of experience, Morgan was certain Cardwell was lying.

"So the last time you saw Merrick was down here when you told him and Davies to take the body to the surface."

"I guess that's right." Cardwell's brow furrowed. "I'm not sure why you're so interested in Merrick."

"What if Merrick killed Hardesty and not Shaw?"

"What reason would Merrick have to kill Hardesty?"

"I don't know that he did. I'm only suggesting the possibility Shaw did not. For that matter, what reason did Shaw have to kill Hardesty? Perhaps he had less reason than Merrick did. Are you aware of any conflict between Merrick and Hardesty?"

Cardwell shook his head. "Like I said, how these men get along or don't on the surface is no concern of mine."

"What kind of man was Merrick? Was he a good driller, dependable?"

"Nah, he wasn't near as good as Shaw or Hardesty for certain, but he did his job all right. Quiet fella, kept to himself. I got nothing else to say about him."

Morgan concluded he had learned all Cardwell was going to tell him and left the station. As he made his way down the tunnel, he thought Cardwell was just as likely a suspect as Merrick, the missing driller. Merrick may be the key to getting Frank's neck out of a noose. He had gone only a short distance when a thought occurred to him, and he returned to Cardwell's station.

"Mister Cardwell did you pick Merrick and Davies to take Hardesty's body up to the surface, or did they volunteer?"

The shift boss looked startled. "They happened to be the ones standing closest to me so I told them to do it."

Morgan repeated the question. "Mr. Cardwell, are you sure neither man volunteered?"

"Now that you mention it, I believe Merrick did offer to take the body up—hell, it didn't matter to me who took him up. It wasn't important to me then anymore than it is now. Why do you want to know?"

"No particular reason, just curious, and it may not be important at all. Where would I find Davies?"

"He's working in the stope down close to where you want to go. Come on, I gotta go part way there. You may as well come along with me."

Morgan was struck by how Cardwell's manner had undergone a mercurial change. The shift boss was almost friendly as he pointed out various features of the tunnel and talked informatively and candidly about the challenges in mining the Emily with an unstable overburden.

Presently, they came upon two muckers in the process of replacing some shoring timbers. Cardwell interrupted what he was saying in mid-sentence and stopped to observe. One of the men labored unsuccessfully to maneuver a heavy vertical timber into position while the other, hands stretched above him, struggled to hold up the overhead cross-timber. Dissatisfied with the progress, Cardwell ordered the miner positioning the vertical support to help the one who seemed close to letting the cross- timber drop.

Effortlessly, the shift boss picked up the shoring timber and shoved it into place. He then picked up both of the heavy mauls the two miners had been using and with one in each hand began pounding the support from side to side and top to bottom with practiced blows until it was snug against the tunnel wall. Cardwell's demonstration of ambidextrous strength was impressive.

As soon as the task was completed, Cardwell berated the two men for their clumsy work. Morgan quietly moved on. Evidently, one of the men said something Cardwell didn't like for the next thing he heard behind him was the meaty sound of a fist hitting flesh followed by a loud grunt.

He thought Cardwell was another physical risk as bad as any other for any miner working in the Emily.

Chapter Ten

By the time Morgan estimated he was halfway to the east face, he was beginning to feel the claustrophobic effects of being in a dark tunnel with over a thousand feet of dirt and rock above his head. He missed the comparatively well-lit control station and the additional lights that gave some reassuring sense of security. The dim lights spaced fifty feet apart at the top of the tunnel created a tomb-like atmosphere made worse by the absence of any other signs of human life except for the muffled sounds of the hammer drills growing fainter the farther he went. Occasionally, he passed places where the tunnel had been shored up with square timbers and planks wedged behind the vertical and overhead horizontal supports. The extent of the shoring timbers served to emphasize the instability of the overburden.

The farther he went, the more frequent the presence of shoring and cavities in the tunnel roof where rocks had fallen down. Once he thought he heard the sound of a splash behind him; it was clear why the miners took pains to protect their heads from falling debris. The occasional ankle-deep puddles of icy water and damp walls were reminders of the recent flooding. He refused to dwell on the prospect of a wall of water racing down upon him, yet the specter continued to intrude each time he splashed through another low point where the water had pooled.

To get his mind off his surroundings, he forced himself to think over what Cardwell had told him. He was convinced if Frank went to trial and Cardwell repeated substantially what he had told him, perhaps Spencer would be able to raise enough doubt about Frank's guilt to get an acquittal, assuming an impartial jury would be picked. In spite of the lawyer's confidence, it would be far better to find the real murderer. The circumstances surrounding Hardesty's death were becoming more and more unclear. It all came down to motive. Did Frank have any reason to kill Hardesty apart from disliking him? He didn't want to believe Frank was the murderer. Had Hardesty been killed during a fight with Frank, it would not have surprised him based on Frank's volatile nature. What was the motive for Hardesty murder? Who would gain from his death, or who hated him enough to kill him?

The latter prompted him to think of another plausible angle. What if the murder wasn't premeditated and resulted from a spontaneous act completely unplanned? He hoped Davies could shed some light on where Merrick might be. On the other hand, if Merrick killed Hardesty, he already had four days to get as far away from Adobe Wells as possible. Finding Merrick in the time he had before Frank's trial was not a bright prospect.

He heard a faint ringing sound growing steadily louder behind him. He turned and saw a light coming toward him at a rapid pace. He barely had time to step aside in one of the pedestrian escapes when Cardwell swept past him pedaling a bicycle-like machine mounted on the rails. Considering how long it was taking him to reach the end of the tunnel, he had begun to wonder how Cardwell was able to make multiple inspections of the drifts and stopes under excavation. The contraption revealed how the shift boss was able to move about so quickly.

Morgan passed by a number of drifts meandering off to the left or right. Some were nothing more than dark openings indicating they were not being worked. He heard and felt the vibration of the percussion drills, loud or faint depending on how far back the working face was from the main tunnel. He paused briefly at the entrance to a new drift that was no deeper than thirty-forty feet from the tunnel and pulled out a wad of cotton to stuff in his ears to muffle the deafening noise of the drill. Morgan saw water splashing from the drill's water hose with drops flickering like diamonds in the light of the miner's carbide lamp and nearby candle pick. The spraying water was used to clear the debris from the hole and keep down the lethal rock dust. That explained the dampness of Hardesty's clothes. It was cold enough down here without getting wet to add further to the discomfort of an unpleasant and difficult job.

The tunnel suddenly widened, and Morgan was reminded of a small train yard as he saw rows of empty ore cars and handcarts waiting to be filled by the muckers. Barrels of nails, boxes, and stacks of timbers and planking occupied an alcove opposite the ore cars.

The tunnel took an abrupt sharp left turn and started to slope downward. He knew from Cardwell's description he was getting close to the end of the tunnel. He heard voices and the familiar metallic sound of multiple picks striking rock coming from the entrance to a drift up ahead. From the number of voices and sounds of digging, the drift must lead to the stope Cardwell had said was the nearest excavation to the drifts where Frank and Hardesty had been working. Unfortunately, the overhead lights ended, and from that point on the tunnel ahead was illuminated only by his carbide lamp. The water now covered the tunnel floor. He no longer heard the rhythmic and strangely reassuring throbbing sound of the pumps and hoped it was because the flooding had been contained. When he stopped to listen, the only thing he heard were the muted voices of the men working the stope behind him and the ominous sound of dripping water becoming progressively louder.

He turned into a narrow entrance and waded through ankle-deep water into the blackness. A few minutes later, he saw the crosscut on the left connecting the two drifts. He was now standing on or close to the spot where Hardesty had been found. He noticed several large boulders lying close together and looked up. Above him he saw a large cavity where loose rock had broken from the tunnel ceiling. The boulders on the tunnel floor were all sufficiently large to have caused the severe damage to Hardesty's face if the victim had been underneath when one or more had fallen.

A few yards ahead, the carbide lamp revealed the working face. The drift was either slanting downward or the water was slowly rising; he couldn't be sure as the water. Whatever the reason, the water now reached halfway to his knees.

Morgan moved closer to the working face and after a cursory examination of the arch-shaped excavation, he had a better feel for the pattern caused by the blast. There was no doubt Hardesty had been at the far range of the spoil blasted from the face.

The floor of the crosscut connecting the two drifts was higher than the parallel drifts and forced him to bend down to keep from hitting the ceiling. Men as tall as Frank and Hardesty would have had even more difficulty negotiating the narrow passage. With each step, the sound of cascading water was louder. Halfway through the crosscut, Morgan saw a drill bit half-submerged in the water and wondered why Frank or Hardesty would have left it there.

As soon as he stepped down out of the crosscut into the drift Hardesty was working, it was apparent from the sound of rushing water, the source of the flooding was not far away. With alarm, he saw the water level was still rising more than the downward slope of the tunnel floor could account for.

He followed the drift in the direction of the face. He moved slowly to keep from stumbling over anything that would send him sprawling in the cold water and plunge him into total darkness if the lamp went out. He resisted the impulse to turn back and make his way back up the tunnel toward the stope where it was brighter, the water was less deep, and the presence of other men would provide some reassurance. He was starting to doubt he was accomplishing anything and the deepening water was both a distraction and cause for alarm. Apart from getting some notion of the layout of the two drifts and the approximate distances from each working face back to the crosscut, he thought there was little to be gained by remaining any longer in such a nightmarish place. He overcame his urge to leave and reluctantly pressed on. He examined the working face and noted the faint impressions of the drill holes. The dark rock covering most of the cavity indicated the thickness of the copper vein starting near the top of the excavation and disappearing down below the waterline. Even his untrained eye could see how rich the vein was. It was obvious why TJ&M was willing to risk flooding, lives, and encroachment to work the drift.

According to what Frank had told him about the drilling pattern, the round appeared to have detonated as intended, leaving an excavation nearly twelve feet deep, eight feet wide at the bottom, and seven feet high. Something just didn't add up. If Hardesty had set the charges, and one or more went off prematurely then how did he make it back to the crosscut before the rest of the charges detonated? As Frank explained, the explosives were set to ignite the outer perimeter charges first followed by the remaining charges detonated in sequence within seconds and working toward the center. The center holes contained no charges at all, only five empty holes drilled to break up the final center section without the need of any explosives. If Hardesty had been struck by a premature explosion of the outer round, it was unlikely he would have had time to escape the effects of the remaining explosions. According to Frank, once the fuses were lit, the driller had at least a minute, possibly more, to get back far enough to eliminate any risk of being struck. If Hardesty had been close enough to the face to have been hit by a premature explosion, he would have been buried under tons of rock. If the round had detonated according to plan, Hardesty may have moved to the crosscut and was there when he received the fatal wound. Then after Frank moved back down the drift to the tunnel to wait for his charges to go off, the killer dragged Hardesty's body into Frank's drift in order to put the blame on him.

Hardesty had either been moved after having been killed, or as Dr. Chambliss suggested, he could have lived long enough to make it as far as the crosscut after the assailant, or assailants, left the drift. The wound in the back and the blow to the head would have been enough for the assailant or assailants to believe Hardesty would be crushed by the ore blasted from the drift face. The fatal wound was obscure enough to have been easily overlooked except for Dr. Chambliss' keen eye. If those responsible were making every effort to make Hardesty's death look like an accident, there was never any intent to frame Frank for the crime. Frank was nothing more than a secondary victim of the plot when Hardesty did not die immediately. Well, the theory sounded plausible enough; however, that was all it was, nothing more than a theoretical possibility. He needed more facts, but with the water level now up to his waist it was time to leave.

He hadn't gone very far when his attention was drawn to the east wall where water was bubbling from it. Rivulets of turbulent water resembled translucent snakes in the light of his headlamp. Curious, he moved toward the wall for a closer look. It took only a cursory examination to reveal the holes the water was coming from had been drilled. He wondered why there would be any reason for drilling toward the Imperial claim unless the objective was encroachment. He examined the east wall of the drift and saw no trace of ore-bearing rock.

In the few minutes it took to wade back to the crosscut, the water had risen two to three inches higher, and the noise of cascading water toward the main tunnel was becoming louder. With a sense of urgency, Morgan increased his pace, anxious to reach the tunnel and back toward the stope and safety of a higher tunnel floor. He had gone only a short distance past the crosscut when he saw something glinting in the water. He leaned down and saw a metal object below the surface. Careful not to extinguish his lamp, he reached down and picked it up. He immediately recognized the object as a 'sticking tommy', the iron candle holder for the candles the miners burned to warn of mine gas. The five-inch pointed shaft was triangular and suggestive of the bayonet wounds Chambliss described.

Morgan had no doubt the candle holder was the murder weapon.

Chapter Eleven

Morgan tucked the candle pick into his belt and quickened his pace toward the main tunnel. The water level was nearly half way up his chest and seemed to be climbing higher with every step he took. A few minutes later and with considerable relief, he saw the main tunnel ahead. He also found the principal source of the cascading water he had been hearing. It was pouring down from a narrow opening in the ceiling. When he took a closer look, Morgan recognized the opening as one of the ventilation shafts Cardwell had mentioned connecting the bottom level with the tunnel above. Within the torrent of water, he saw a thick canvas hose disappearing in the darkness above. If the hose was intended to pump water out of the mine, it was limp and not functioning. He wondered if the hose had been placed there recently when the flooding began, or if it had been there ever since the drift was started.

He grabbed the stiff hose with both hands and tugged on it but it didn't budge. Getting thoroughly soaked in the process, Morgan tested his entire weight on it and still the hose remained solid. He shined his light up into the opening and quickly saw why Cardwell was skeptical about someone using it to get down in the drift and then leave the same way. The shaft was almost vertical as it disappeared into the darkness above. With great difficulty, the hose could be used by someone nimble and strong enough to descend or ascend the narrow steep shaft. It was another point for Spencer to present to a jury.

By the time he felt the tunnel floor beginning to ramp upward, the water had reached his neck. In the distance, he saw lights and breathed a sigh of relief. Minutes later, he was reassured as the water had already receded to below his shoulders. He splashed the final few feet into the lighted tunnel just as the rhythmic and reassuring sound of the pumps resumed. He wondered if the pumps had stopped for some legitimate reason or if someone intended to put an end to his investigation.

Morgan entered the stope and saw a geometric maze of square-set timbers stretching high above his head. The foot-thick timbers forming square compartments resembled a giant jigsaw puzzle. The clang of shovels and thud of picks was interspersed with an occasional shout followed by the rumble of ore falling down a wooden chute placed at one end of the huge wooden structure. Multiple levels were being excavated at the same time, and the winking of the carbide headlamps between the timbers reminded him of flashing fireflies. Morgan spotted a miner sitting on one of the bottom timbers smoking a cigarette and looking in his direction. He walked over and introduced himself.

"The name's Westphal. I'm looking for a man by the name of Davies." Morgan sat down next to the miner and took his boots off to shake out water and wring out the heavy socks.

"I'm Hugh Davies. What do you want?" he asked in a broad accent unmistakably British.

"I'm an investigator and assisting Marshal Truesdale in his investigation of Hardesty's death. I have permission from LaTrobe to talk to anyone in the Emily who might know anything about his death."

The driller's face tightened. "Can't say I know anything except he was killed a few days ago before the tunnel flooded out."

"Did you know Hardesty?"

"Can't say I did and probably wouldna recognized him if I'd passed him on the street. Then again I could say that about most of the men down here except the ones I work with here."

"Were you here in the stope when Hardesty was killed?"

"I was here. These men can vouch for that if you think I had anything to do with it?"

"I don't. I'm just trying to find out how you happened to hear there had been an accident farther down the tunnel."

"Shift was about done, and we were getting ready to walk back down the tunnel to go topside when we heard someone yelling for help. I went out in the main tunnel to see what was happening, and saw a driller come running toward me. He was yelling about an accident and for someone to go down to the call box and get the shift boss. Gantwell was right behind me and took off down the tunnel to the call box, while I followed the driller. It wasn't but a few minutes later Cardwell, the shift boss, and some others came along."

"Didn't have to go far," said a voice from above Morgan. He looked up and saw a face peering down at him. "I met Cardwell coming down the tunnel long 'afore I ever reached the call box."

"Are you Gantwell?" Morgan yelled up, noticing the sounds of digging had stopped, and other faces were beginning to look down quizzically from various compartments above.

"That's right."

"How about you and the others take a break and come on down?" Morgan waited until one by one four other men sat or stood near Davies. Again, Morgan noticed how similar they all looked dressed much the same as Hardesty was, or for that matter, the clothes he was wearing. Davies was the only one clean-shaven; the others wore drooping moustaches like his. After Morgan identified himself and why he was there, he turned to Gantwell and said, "You said Cardwell was already close by?"

"Yeah, didn't have to go more'n a dozen yards and saved me going all the way back to the call box." The response differed from what Cardwell had told him when he claimed he'd been notified on the call box.

"Were you surprised to see Cardwell?"

"Nah, he usually shows up toward the end of the shift, either him or Dandridge."

"Who's Dandridge?" Morgan asked.

"Charles Dandridge. He's the assistant shift boss," Davies said. This was the first mention of an assistant to Cardwell. he wondered why Cardwell or Frank hadn't mentioned there was an assistant.

"What did you see when you got to the drift?"

"A man was laying on his back and a right mess he was. Nothin' anybody could do for him. It didn't take a doctor to see he was a goner."

"What about Shaw? What did he say, and how did he seem?"

Davies shrugged. "I dunno, seemed real upset, kept sayin' it was his fault. I didn't understand why 'cause it seemed to me any man gets himself blown up like that is either just plain stupid and doesn't know what the hell he's doing, or he was plain unlucky."

"What happened next?"

"Cardwell said we needed to get the body outta there. He pointed to me and another fella volunteered."

"Who was the other man?"

"Dunno, some driller working in one of the drifts down toward the callbox; I think maybe Cardwell called him Miller or something like that."

"Could it have been Merrick?"

"I suppose. I seen him around, but I didn't really know him."

"Before you took the body up to the surface, were you told to stay with the body?"

"Yeah."

"I understand you stayed with the body, but Merrick didn't."

"That's right. He claimed the shift was over, and he wasn't going to spend his time watching over a stiff. Then he just up and left."

"Did anyone ever see Merrick again?" He assumed the silence meant no.

"What did Merrick look like?"

Davies screwed up his face and shook his head. "There wasn't anything particular about him I remember. Anyway, I didn't take much notice of him, and it ain't exactly broad daylight down here."

"Was he clean shaven, or did he have a moustache?"

'Damned if I know." Then looking around at the other men who all but one had moustaches in various lengths, he said, "I reckon he had a moustache."

"But you're not sure?"

"Jesus, mister, like I said, I don't remember. What difference does it make whether he had moustache or not? A man was dead, and I didn't give a shit what he looked like then anymore than I do now."

"It makes a difference. There's a possibility the dead man was someone other than Hardesty."

"It was Hardesty, make no mistake," a cold voice said from behind Morgan. Morgan turned and saw Cardwell emerge from the shadows. He wondered how long the shift boss had been standing there. "I guess I know who my drillers are just as I know who these men are. I also know if you bastards don't get your sorry-asses back up there and get back to work, I'll dock your wages." There was a scramble as the miners leaped up and moved quickly up the ladders and disappeared into the labyrinth of square-sets. Moments later, the sound of energetic digging filled the stope.

"Westphal, I think it's about time you left the Emily."

"I don't think so, Cardwell. I'm not finished looking around," Morgan replied .

"That's where you're wrong, Westphal. You leave when I say it's time to leave, and that time is now. Down here what I say goes so move it, or I'll have to use more persuasive means. Believe me when I say you don't really want that to happen."

"I suggest you check with Mr. LaTrobe before you make a big mistake."

"What are you talking about?"

"Mr. LaTrobe asked me to keep him informed. Somehow, I don't believe he's going to be too happy when I tell him his shift boss for Tunnel 3 was uncooperative."

"I think you're full of shit. Why would LaTrobe care one way or the other about what happens down here as long as production stays up?"

"You'll have to ask him, and I suggest you do it now before I waste time by having to come back later." Morgan saw the shift boss hesitate uncertain whether to believe him. He wasn't confident LaTrobe would overrule the shift boss and counted on Cardwell's reluctance to call LaTrobe at this late hour.

"All right, Westphal, but if you're bullshitin' me, I'll see you regret it. Adobe Wells isn't big enough I can't find you."

"Relax, Cardwell, I'm telling you straight. We both have a job to do, so I suggest we get on with it. However, before you go, I've got a couple of more questions for you."

"What do you want to know?"

"Why are you so sure the man killed was Hardesty? The body was unrecognizable."

Cardwell's expression was perplexed. "Like I been sayin' who else could it have been?" The answer was reasonable.

"That's what I'm trying to find out. Everyone's convinced it was Hardesty who was killed and maybe it was. On the other hand, there's no way to tell for certain because of the condition of the body. You're assuming it was Hardesty only because it was his drift the body was in and not because there was anything else to confirm it was him."

Cardwell scratched the side of his jaw thoughtfully. "Maybe, except I can't see how or why it would be anyone but Hardesty. Everybody else was accounted for the night it happened."

It was time for Morgan to concede the point if Cardwell was certain everyone on the shift was accounted for and where they were supposed to be, unless the shift boss was lying. Even the discrepancies between what Cardwell said previously and what the miners in the stope had told him were not significant.

"For the time being, I'll accept the body was Hardesty, which leads to the important question, who killed him. While everyone seems to believe Shaw was the murderer, I for one am not so sure, and that's why I'd like to find Merrick. Don't you think it's strange he disappeared so quickly and never showed up the next day to collect his wages?"

"Yeah, now you mention it, I reckon so."

"How far from here is the drift Merrick was working?"

"Maybe thirty yards back down the tunnel."

"Considering the curving of the tunnel and the distance from here down to where Merrick was working, would Merrick have been likely to hear Shaw yelling for help if he was drilling?"

"Not a chance."

"And yet you found him down at Shaw's drift when you got there?"

"I guess until now I never gave it any thought."

"Tell me, did Merrick have a moustache?"

"I don't recall for sure, but I don't think he did."

"What about Hardesty?"

"I think so, but again I can't be sure. More men down here do than don't." The response explained why Hardesty's luggage contained a moustache cup.

"If the deputy shift boss is around, I'd like to talk to him."

"Dandridge? I fired that worthless son of bitch four days ago. The drunken bastard was more trouble than he was worth."

"Was he on duty the night Hardesty was killed?"

"Yeah, and it was mainly his fault the tunnel flooded. He didn't check on the seepage at this end the way he was supposed to. He also forgot to make sure the pumps were working before the shift changed. If he had, he would have seen what was happening."

"I thought the water source was down here at this level."

"The problem is, but the source ain't. It only collects here. More'n likely the water ain't even coming out of the Emily claim. It's over in the Imperial. I've been telling LaTrobe I think Sandusky is somehow channeling the water into the Emily."

"When did you start having serious flooding problems?"

"We've always had some seepage—shit, every mine around Adobe wells has, but nothing like what happened a few days ago."

"Why would Hardesty be drilling toward the Imperial mine and not parallel?"

"What do you mean?"

"I found drill holes on the east side of the tunnel not far from the working face; there's water coming out of them."

"Bullshit! The vein in that drift is going 90 degrees the other way. You must be seein' things."

"Go see for yourself. I did some double-jacking years back, and I know drill holes when I see them. I suggest before you do, wait until the water level goes down a bit."

His hands clenched, Cardwell let out a string of oaths. When he calmed down, he said, "If you're right, Westphal, then I've got more problems than water. Hardesty may have sold out to Sandusky. By God, if I'd found him drilling where you said he was, I'd have killed the bastard myself. Shaw ought to get a bonus for doing it."

It wasn't until he was back in the tunnel and Cardwell had gone to look at Hardesty's drift that Morgan finally remembered where he had heard the name Merrick. The day he got to Adobe Wells and Truesdale had taken him to see Frank, Blaylock had called the woman with the two kids standing in front of him Mrs. Merrick. The woman had been looking for her husband who had been missing for several days.

The driller tugged the last fuse into the wooden splitter where the other fourteen were gathered, pulled out his pocket knife, trimmed and cut it to the same length as the rest. Then to Morgan's consternation, Jacob Turner struck a match and lighted the stub of a cigar he had been chewing on while standing perilously close to the web of gathered fuses.

"That should do 'er, I reckon," he said in satisfaction as he flashed a smile at Morgan. The smile was a change from the cold reception he received when he entered the drift and told the miner why he was there and not a company spy checking up on the miners. During the few occasions Turner stopped drilling to check the depth of the hole he was drilling or to shift the drill to start another hole, Morgan asked the driller questions concerning the equipment, the reliability of the dynamite and fuses, and general safety procedures established for the Emily. Most of the time, Morgan stood back and quietly observed the time-consuming and laborious process of extending the face another twelve feet. He was content to stand back to avoid being liberally spattered by the wet debris blowing back from the face from the combined effect of both the compressed air and water pumping through the drill.

Apart from a renewed admiration for what his brother and the other miners did for a living, he wasn't sure he'd learned anything he wouldn't have gained by talking more with Frank. Based on what Frank told him, Hardesty must have been killed close to the end of the shift and after Cardwell made his rounds. On average, it had taken Turner from twenty to thirty minutes to drill each of the last three of the twelve-foot deep holes. Taking into account short breaks, the time it took to reposition the drill after finishing a hole, change drill bits, and the nearly one hour it took to place the charges and set the fuses, Hardesty had probably completed at least twelve or thirteen holes of his round when he was stabbed. That meant at least one of the killers, if not both, must have been present in the drift for as long as ninety minutes, possibly longer to complete drilling the round and set the charges.

That was a long time to remain undiscovered unless Frank was wrong about hearing voices when he was changing bits with two holes left to drill. It was doubtful Hardesty had finished his round by then and set his charges so quickly if the hardness of the face was comparable to the one Frank was working. Whoever had hit and stabbed Hardesty spent a lot of time and effort to cover up the murder while risking being discovered during Cardwell's routine inspection. Why was it so important to make the murder look like an accident? He needed to ask Frank again about the voices to make sure he really had heard them, and if so, when did he hear them. Cardwell claimed if he had seen Hardesty drilling on the east side, he would have killed him. Was Cardwell's comment only bluster, or did the shift boss know more than he was letting on?

"Mister, you best move on back," Turner said interrupting his thoughts. Morgan noticed the fuses were already lit and quickly got to his feet. In return for his cooperation, Morgan carried the drill mount back to the tunnel. Turner lifted the heavy Leyner drill to his shoulder and belatedly yelled, "Fire in the hole!" before following Morgan. The two men barely reached the tunnel and stood to one side of the drift entrance when the first explosion occurred followed then in rapid succession by fourteen more. A dusty cloud of smoke and dust erupted from the drift, and Morgan smelled the acrid stench of dynamite. He heard voices and saw four muckers with hand carts and shovels coming from the direction of the equipment tunnel.

"What now, Jacob?" Morgan asked as he sat down close to the driller who was already sitting with his back to the tunnel wall.

"We wait for the dust to settle and for Cardwell to come and look things over. If he says mighty fine, I get to go up and get some shut-eye. If it don't look good to him, then I'll be down here some longer than I care to be."

Thinking to pass the time until Cardwell showed up, Morgan probed beyond the technical questions he had been asking.

"Jacob, what have you heard about Hardesty's death?"

At first when the miner didn't reply, Morgan thought he was back where he started an hour ago. The driller removed the cigar from the corner of his mouth and spat. "Well, I knew from the start there was somethin' strange. Hardesty was experienced and no fool. Ain't no way was he going to get hisself killed that way."

"Do you believe Shaw did it?"

"Don't rightly know. Maybe he did, maybe he didn't. I wouldn't care to say one way or t'other."

Morgan tried a different tack. "Did you hear anything about Hardesty being a union member?"

Again, the miner hesitated, now clearly uncomfortable. "In this here mine, even the word union can get a man in real trouble. I'll say this much, when a man works in a TJ&M mine, if he's union, he better keep it to hisself. Now that ain't necessarily true over in the Sandusky mines where you got men over there ain't afraid of sympathizin' with the union as long as they do it quiet like. Sandusky is smart that way. They won't support the union, but they give their miners mostly what the union is lookin' to get."

"Did you know if Hardesty had signed on with the union?"

"I heard some talk about it—didn't give it much thought. Like I said, it ain't smart to talk union around here."

"Do you know if Cardwell or any of the other supervisors suspected Hardesty was union?"

"If they had known it, Hardesty would've been fired lickety-split."

"Did Hardesty have any trouble with Cardwell?"

"No more'n anyone else. You do your job, and Cardwell will leave you alone. If you don't, he ain't likely to ask you kindly to please move your ass. He's buckin' to be foreman for TJ&M, and I reckon by and by Mister LaTrobe gonna give him the job."

"Do you know if Cardwell or anyone else had a grudge against Hardesty?"

Turner gave him a cold look. "Mister, I don't know you well enough to answer, and that don't mean I know anything a'tall. I got no more interest in this conversation. I got me a wife and two young'uns says I got nothin' more to say about anything that happened down here the night Hardesty came up short." To further emphasize the conversation was over, Turner got up and moved to the other side of the tunnel.

Morgan saw a bobbing headlamp coming toward him. A moment later, Cardwell coasted to a stop a few feet away and climbed off the bicycle cart. Ignoring Morgan, the shift boss directed his attention to the driller. "You count fifteen?"

"Sure did," Turner answered standing up.

"Let's go see if you can count," he replied and strode into the drift seemingly unaffected by the smoke and dust still swirling about and reducing the brightness of the headlamps to a yellowish glow.

Curious to see the effects of the blast, Morgan trailed behind. He watched as Cardwell stopped to pick up and examine random samples of the rocky spoil as he made his way to the face now twelve feet deeper than it was before the shift began. Cardwell seemed satisfied after insuring there were no charges remaining. After grunting his approval, he said, "All right, Turner, your round's clean. You can go." Turner breathed an audible sigh of relief and wasted no time in leaving. Still conspicuously ignoring Morgan, Cardwell turned to follow the driller.

"Mr. Cardwell, tell me again when you made your last inspection of the drift Hardesty was working."

"Not now, Westphal. As you can see, I'm busy, and I've got three more drifts to check."

"We can talk on the way."

"You want to ask more questions, see me on the surface."

"Then I'll wait for you by the lift."

Cardwell gave him a humorless smile. "Do what you like," he retorted and continued on without looking back.

Later after waiting an hour on the surface, it became clear to Morgan the shift boss had no intention of talking any more that night.

Chapter Twelve

Morgan opened his eyes, rolled over, and checked his pocket watch to see what time it was. He lay back grateful it was still early enough to remain where he was and enjoy the blessed warmth of the rising sun through the curtained window. Already the cool night-time temperature was rapidly giving way to the promise of another scorching day, and after last night in the Emily, he welcomed it.

He thought the time spent in the Emily had been worthwhile after all. He was confident he had discovered the object used to kill Hardesty and gained a better perspective of where the murder occurred. The existence of drill holes where they should not have been was curious, although he still wasn't sure there was any connection with the attempt to sabotage the Emily and Hardesty's murder. Unfortunately and in spite of his fervent wish to believe Frank, he still couldn't dispel a lingering doubt he was not as innocent as he claimed. The lawyer told him it was only necessary to ensure the prosecutor was unable to prove guilt beyond a reasonable doubt. He needed to stay objective without dwelling on the possibility Frank might be guilty.

He began to prioritize what he had to do and who he needed to talk to. He was eager to show Dr. Chambliss the candle pick to confirm the plausibility such a tool, if not the one he found, could have been the murder weapon. Spencer would benefit from what he had learned in the Emily to continue building a strong defense. He had to find Merrick. By now he might be back with his wife, or she might at least know where he was. His disappearance and absence was suspicious. He was either somehow involved in Hardesty's death or he knew something about it. He also had the feeling locating Merrick would not be easy or the possibility he may have also become a victim because of what he did or knew. If Blaylock didn't know where Merrick was, the deputy might know where his wife lived.

He needed to talk to LaTrobe again. Not for the purpose LaTrobe wanted but for his own reasons. LaTrobe's interest in the murder and the progress of the investigation was way out of proportion to his position as TJ&M's superintendent. There had to be a reason well beyond the explanation LaTrobe had given, which, while superficially reasonable, did not overcome the nagging feeling the superintendent had another reason for requesting an autopsy. He wanted to maintain the superintendent's confidence to gain access to people or find leads that might otherwise be unavailable. The drill holes he discovered in Hardesty's drift might help to establish his credibility.

Finally, he needed to locate the woman named "Adele" whose name Hardesty had scribbled on the back of the card found in his pocket. The Arabian Club seemed an obvious place to find her.

After leaving the lawyer, Morgan's spirits remained upbeat even after being informed Judge Breen denied the motions requesting both a trial delay and a change of venue. If not overconfident, Spencer was pleased with the progress of the investigation so far. Morgan gave the lawyer a sketch of the two drifts Hardesty and Frank were working showing the location of the crosscut and ventilation shaft. He also gave him a list of those he had interviewed the previous day and night. While Miss Ottmeier recorded, he summarized the pertinent information each potential witness would be expected to provide in court if asked to testify. In all probability, some of the same men would also be witnesses for the prosecution. When Morgan finished, Spencer claimed if he had to go to trial tomorrow, Frank's chances for an acquittal were by no means assured, they were at least considerably improved.

Back on the street, Morgan headed toward the jail. In the distance, he thought he heard shouting and wondered what the disturbance was about. He noticed there seemed to be fewer pedestrians than usual, and most shops were closed.

Deputy Blaylock was inspecting a shotgun when Morgan entered the jail. The deputy looked up, removed his rimless spectacles, and continued cleaning them without saying a word.

"Is the Marshal in?" Morgan said.

"No," was the curt answer.

"Do you know when he will be?"

"He didn't say."

"Do you know where I might find him?"

"Can't say that I do."

"Perhaps you can help then." Blaylock made no reply and continued to polish the spectacles, his face expressionless.

"When I arrived here with Marshal Truesdale, you were speaking to a woman you addressed as Mrs. Merrick. She had a couple of kids with her and was looking for her husband. Do you know if she ever located him?"

"No."

Morgan made an effort to conceal his irritation. "No, as in you don't know, or she didn't find her husband?"

Blaylock shrugged, "I don't know or care if she did or didn't."

"Do you happen to know where she lives?"

"I don't believe I do."

"You have no record of her visit and where she lives?"

"I didn't think it was important."

"A man is missing for a couple of days, his wife is asking for help, and you don't think it's important? I'm beginning to wonder what you do around here. You don't seem to know very much including where your boss is."

The deputy flushed and his jaw tightened. "Westphal, I don't like your brother, and I think I like you even less,. You shouldn't have told the marshal what you did about me. You want to be careful what you say about other folks; they might take offense. Your brother might be sorry you did."

He now understood the reason for the deputy's hostile, uncooperative behavior. "Blaylock, if you've got a problem with me, it would be better for you to keep my brother out of it, or I may take exception."

"You're a little old and maybe just a little long in the tooth to be talking that way."

"It's all right because when I get pushed too far I make up for it by fighting as dirty as you can get. I'd like to see my brother."

"Sorry, it ain't visiting hours."

"When are the visiting hours?"

"When I'm in charge, it's when I say they are, and it ain't now."

Morgan concluded there was no point in prolonging the conversation. The deputy had the upper hand, and they both knew it.

"Tell the marshal I was here."

"I'll try and remember, but I got this problem lately about remembering things that don't seem important."

"Blaylock, I'm trying real hard to find something about you I like. I believe I'll give up."

Morgan walked to the door only to stop when he heard Blaylock say, "Be careful, Westphal, I can fight dirty, too." Morgan turned and saw the deputy pointing the shotgun at him. "Bang, bang," he said with a smile.

Morgan walked past a row of clubs bearing names such as the Orient, Emerald Palace, and Egyptian Paradise until he came to the Arabian Club. In different ways the sandwich boards in front offered whatever a miner happened to want–any time, day or night. In fresh paint and smaller letters close to the bottom of the signs, were the words 'Private Club – Members Only.'

Morgan walked through the open double-door of the Arabian Club where a bored, sleepy-eyed young man sitting just inside at a small table pointed wordlessly to a sign also freshly painted, 'Membership 25 cents.' Morgan fished out the necessary coins and handed them over, receiving in return a printed card identical to the ones in Hardesty's pocket and luggage. The card entitled him to one free drink.

A long polished bar along one wall ran the length of the narrow room. Rows of liquor bottles were arranged on shelves below a dusty mirror. Beside the mirror hung a large, badly-painted picture of a naked woman lounging on a couch holding a strategically-placed fan. The provocative pose was obviously intended to inspire the painting's admirers to visit the cribs out back. Business was slow. Two men, elbows propped on the bar, each with a foot resting on the brass floor rail, were drinking beer. On the other side of the room were felt-topped poker tables and a roulette table. Morgan heard the tapping of a roulette ball before it dropped into one of the pockets accompanied by more shouts of dismay than joy. At the far end of the room, two men were playing pool, the click of the colored balls audible above the noise of the men clustered around the roulette table.

Morgan walked over to the bar and presented the card to the bartender polishing a row of shot glasses. The bartender paused briefly and asked, "What'll it be?"

"Only some information," Morgan responded.

The bartender's eyes narrowed. "Are you the law?" When Morgan shook his head, he said, "Then it all depends on what you're asking."

"I'm looking for Adele."

The bartender relaxed and replied with a leer, "Well, that information is free enough even if Adele ain't." The bartender chuckled at his reply and pointed at the far end of the room. "You see that big man over there wearing the derby? His name is Nat Hoskins; he's the one you want to see. Nat takes care of the Adele's time." Morgan nodded and headed toward the back of the room. "Hey, mister, don't you want your drink first, or are you coming back for it later?" Morgan didn't bother to turn around and kept on walking. He heard the bartender say, "Suit yourself," and then in a lower voice mutter, "I bet your prick ain't as stiff as your neck."

Broad-shouldered and pasty-faced, Nat Hoskins was big enough to discourage any unruly behavior, and if his large size was not enough, the blackjack tucked in his belt was apt to be. Morgan noticed he had a reptilian way of constantly licking his lips as he looked up from his game of solitaire and said with a smile that never reached his eyes, "The name's Nat. Can I help you friend?"

"Where can I find Adele?"

"She's got a place out back."

"Can you be more specific?"

"I can, but I won't unless you care to tell me what it is you're looking for and how much you're offering. She's particular about what she'll do with a customer. Now, I've got a couple gals outback will do anything you ask, but Adele...well, like I said, she's downright particular."

"I only want a few minutes of her time, not to buy any services."

"Oh, well, that's a new one. Friend, if you're worried about catching a dose of the clap then don't 'cause all my whores are clean. They're checked regular-like. I think we can arrange something, but it'll cost you just the same whether she takes off her clothes or not."

Irritated at the man's assumption, Morgan said, "Look, I'm not here for anything like that. I need to talk to her about something else, and it has nothing to do with professional services of any kind...and she can keep her clothes on."

"What do you want to talk to her about?"

"That's my business."

"Look, friend, Adele is 'my business,' and unless you tell me what you're after, you ain't gonna be doing any business with Adele. Understand, friend?"

135

Morgan took out his wallet from the inside pocket of his jacket, silently extracted a five dollar bill, and laid it on the table. The amount was nearly twice the going rate.

"Well, my friend, I guess that's all I need to know," the man said, deftly pocketing the bill. "This will get you a half-hour with Adele. Of course, this only covers my expenses. You're going to have to make your own arrangements with Adele. If I was you, I'd go ahead and get my money's worth and do more than just talk," he added with a knowing smirk.

Hoskins beckoned to a thin, pimply-faced youth wearing a flat bill cap pulled down low on his forehead. "Edgar, go wake up Adele and tell her she's got a gentleman caller then come back here and show the man where she is." As the boy departed through a back door, Hoskins turned to Morgan and suggested, "Now, friend, why don't you sit down and have a drink while Adele's making herself presentable."

Morgan merely shook his head and remained standing. Hoskins shrugged indifferently and resumed his card game.

A few minutes later the boy reappeared wide-eyed and breathless. "Mr. Hoskins, come quick!" he said, a note of urgency in his voice. "There's somethin' wrong with Adele. I think she's dead."

Morgan followed Hoskins and the boy out the back door and across a narrow, dusty street where a long row of small unpainted, cheaply constructed houses stood side by side backing onto the side of the canyon. Ten feet or so above street level, the cribs were similar in appearance. Wooden steps led to small covered porches where even at this early hour scantily clad prostitutes sat or lounged in various stages of undress. They were doing their best to look desirable and interested as they competed for the attention of a half-dozen men strolling by. When the women saw the two men and boy racing up the narrow street, the prostitutes stood up and watched their progress with growing interest.

Moving quickly for such a large man, Hoskins hurried ahead of Morgan and bounded up the steps. The house was small but twice the size of the others. Morgan paused at the steps long enough to restrain the boy from going any farther. "Go back to the Arabian and tell the bartender to call the jail and get someone down here from the marshal's office right away. Now go!"

He took the steps two at a time and entered a parlor. The furnishings were not what he would have expected on that street, but then Hoskins had said she was high-priced. The décor and stuffed furniture would have compared favorably to a suite in a decent hotel. Hoskins stood in a short hallway mutely staring into a bedroom. Morgan pushed past him into a room furnished just as comfortably.

The woman at the jail Blaylock addressed as Mrs. Merrick was lying on the bed with her eyes closed. With her lips slightly parted, she might have been asleep. She wasn't especially beautiful, but her features were regular enough to be pleasing. He noticed her cheeks were streaked as if she might have been crying. The position of her body was relaxed with the left arm extended along the left leg, the right arm draped limply across her stomach. She was nude except for linen knee-length drawers sheer enough to reveal the shadowy triangle of her pubic hair. One white stocking was on her leg, the other wrapped around her neck. Her shapely hips emphasized by the thin and tightly stretched fabric of the undergarment, narrow waist, and full breasts made the painting in the bar look even less appealing. It was easy to see why Adele encouraged a clientele willing to pay extra for a few minutes of her time. Even with her features slightly distorted in death, he recognized her.

"Jesus Christ!" Hoskins said. "She was one of the best whores I ever had."

Morgan touched the woman's arm to test for body warmth. The skin was cold. He estimated she had been dead for hours. "If you can contain your grief long enough," Morgan said, "who was her last customer?"

"I don't know. On Thursday nights she has only one customer. It was a private arrangement for all night."

"Who made the arrangement?"

"She did. From the time she got here, she said she would be engaged on a private basis every Thursday night with a 'Mr. Smith'. Under no circumstances would she be available that night of the week for any other business. She told me if I didn't like it, she'd go over to one of the other clubs. It didn't matter to me none since she paid me more than she would have made in one night. I could be wrong, but I got the impression she knew the man from wherever she'd been before."

"And you have no idea who this Mr. Smith is or what he looks like? Or is it because you won't say?"

"If I knew, I'd say so after what happened to her. He always came late at night and sometimes not at all. Even when he didn't come, he still paid for her time. Who the hell are you, and what did you want with Adele?"

"I'm helping Marshal Truesdale investigate a murder. I thought she might know something useful. How long has she been working in Adobe Wells?"

Hoskins shrugged. "Maybe six months or so."

"What was her last name?"

"Belden, or at least that's what she called herself."

"What can you tell me about her? Was she married? Did she have any kids?"

"Nah. Only whore I know that's married and has any kids is Josephine Dylan, and she ain't one of the regulars. She's married to Ed the bartender and works part time when one of the gals is sick or has the monthlies. Sometimes she works extra when her old man loses too much playing faro."

"How many kids does this Josephine Dylan have?"

"A couple of youngsters…one's a baby, the other one is a little older. They ain't Ed's brats."

Morgan was willing to bet another five it was the same two children he'd seen with Adele. He wished he could ask her why she was pretending to be Merrick's wife. Was it to set up some kind of explanation for Merrick's disappearance, or was it to underscore the fact he was missing? In either case, it brought into question once again who it was in the morgue–Merrick or Hardesty?

"Did she have any other regular customers besides this 'Mr. Smith' or someone who may have seen her more times than the other customers?"

The man shook his head. "I can't say anyone else comes to mind. She was no ordinary whore like the rest of them. She had class and was choosy about who she spent time with. The other whores might have 15-20 or more customers, on a slow night, but she worked strictly by appointment, and sometimes not at all if she didn't feel like it."

"What about somebody who wasn't a customer she may have been seeing on the side?"

"Not a chance. If she was seeing someone on her own time, I would of knowed it."

"How can you be sure? You didn't know who she was seeing on Thursday nights."

"Well, it ain't exactly all that private back here. The whores got no place to go except over in the club to have a drink now and then with a customer if that's what the man wants."

Morgan took note of the position of the body. The bedcovers were not rucked up indicating there was no struggle, and her hands were relaxed with no sign of any scratches or broken nails. If she had had intercourse during the night, it wasn't evident. Possibly she was killed before the business of the evening got underway. He bent down and lifted one of her eyelids to examine the pupils; they were unusually small. He leaned closer to her face and confirmed the faint odor of laudanum. The woman had been heavily sedated when she was strangled. He carefully undid the tightly wound stocking from her neck. He noticed the skin was slightly discolored, and there was evidence of bruising and abrasions consistent with strangulation. The laudanum had made the task of killing her easy. It was possible she may have been already dead before she was strangled.

"Did she take laudanum a lot?"

Hoskins lifted a shoulder. "I suppose. Most of them do. It helps them forget who and what they are."

"Did she use it more than most?"

"Yeah, she was pretty hard on the stuff."

"Mr. Hoskins, why don't you go outside and wait for the marshal while I have a look around?"

Morgan heard him muttering under his breath as he left, still bemoaning the financial loss her death had caused.

The sound of an automobile pulled up outside, and a moment later, he heard booted feet coming up the wooden steps. Morgan was relieved it was Truesdale and not Blaylock that walked into the bedroom.

"I'll be damned. What're you doin' here?" Truesdale asked when he saw Morgan on his knees pulling a small trunk out from underneath the bed.

Morgan put the trunk on a table and replied, "I was following a lead. Her name was written on the back of a card found in Hardesty's pocket; it turned out to be her," he added pointing to the dead woman. "She was also posing as Mrs. Merrick when you introduced me to Blaylock the day I arrived in Adobe Wells. Willard Merrick was a driller in the Emily the night Hardesty was murdered. He helped carry Hardesty's body to the surface and then disappeared right after that."

Truesdale whistled softly, "And you ended up with a dead lead."

"That's about the size of it. I'm still not positive the dead man is Hardesty."

"You think it could be Merrick?"

"It's possible. If what happened to the dead man's face wasn't accidental, then somebody went to a lot of trouble to make sure the body in the Emily wouldn't be recognized.

I'm not sure right now whether I'm looking for Hardesty or Merrick. And since Chambliss thinks there may have been a second assailant, Merrick might be the dead man, and Hardesty's the one I'm really looking for."

"What about her? What do you know so far?"

"Her name's Adele Belden according to the man who was managing her time. I suspect she had enough laudanum in her to drop a horse. If she took it herself or someone gave it to her, it made it real easy to strangle her. As you can see there's no sign of a struggle."

"Don't see how a whore would be mixed up in this."

"If she knew something about Hardesty or Merrick, and I think there's a strong possibility she did, she may have been killed for what she knew and might say. If I can find out who killed Hardesty, then maybe we'll know why this happened and who did it."

Truesdale headed for the door. "I'll stop by the coroner's office and get the body moved over to the morgue. Anything else I can do for you?"

"I could use one of your deputies to give me a hand...that is anybody but Blaylock."

Truesdale shook his head. "Sorry, but I can't oblige. That's probably the one thing I can't do. In fact, I need to ask a favor. Will you help me out on this," gesturing to the dead woman. "Right now I got more problems runnin' after my ass than I got deputies to take care of 'em. Most of the mines except those owned by TJ&M are on strike. LaTrobe has armed men around the entrance of his mines and is escortin' his men to and from the mines. I got me a powder keg just about ready to blow. Sorry Morgan ain't much I can do to help you out."

Morgan pursed his lips and gave Truesdale a speculative look. After a thoughtful silence, he said, "Maybe there is one thing you can do. Have you got the authority to deputize?"

"Well, yes, I do. In fact, I just got the mayor's permission to bring on some extra men an hour ago. But I can't see where bein' a deputy is gonna do you any good, if that's what's on your mind."

"A badge might give me a little more leverage, open up some doors and get answers a faster."

Without another word, Truesdale fished in his pocket, pulled out a badge, and in the presence of a dead whore, swore in another deputy for Adobe Wells and promptly left.

Morgan opened the trunk. The first thing he noticed was how neatly the contents were arranged and folded. He carefully removed a variety of shirtwaists, dresses, stockings, a corset, and various undergarments, some designed to be seen, others for practical wear. A box contained hair ribbons, buttons, and several pieces of cheap jewelry. Another box turned out to be a small sewing kit with an assortment of pins, needles, and spools of thread. Farther down were several pairs of shoes wrapped in paper, heavier winter-weight dresses, more underwear, and a black ankle-length coat with an imitation fur collar. At the very bottom of the trunk was a thick envelope containing over five hundred dollars in various denominations. Morgan put the envelope in his pocket resolving the money would be better used for her funeral expenses than providing a windfall for Hoskins. The last item was a picture frame with three photographs. The center photograph was badly faded and showed an older man and woman. From the faint resemblance of the dead woman, Morgan assumed they were her parents. The picture on the left was a younger picture of Adele taken perhaps five years before. She was dressed primly in a high-necked dress with a lace collar. She wasn't smiling although her features were softer than when he had seen her at the jail. The third picture was a man dressed in a pin-striped suit. Clean-shaven and staring directly at the camera was a handsome man who looked to be in his mid-thirties. Morgan wondered if he was, or had been, a husband or simply a close admirer to have been included in the triptych. He removed the photograph of the young man and saw the date, September 16, 1914, written in pencil on the back. He removed the photograph and put it in his coat pocket.

After placing everything back in the trunk, he resumed his search of the room. There was little left aside from a few garments hanging in a closet. The bureau was full of filmy and lacy things one would have expected to find belonging to a woman in her trade. A suitcase also under the bed proved to be empty except for two hats. Several pairs of shoes were placed side by side against the wall.

Morgan left the bedroom and went down the hallway to a small kitchen with a wooden table and four matching chairs, a small black stove with a kettle and a skillet on top, and a pantry with a double-set of glass doors. The pantry was stocked with cans and bags of various sizes that proved to contain coffee, sugar, and other vegetables. A smaller cabinet adjacent to the stove contained cups, saucers, plates, and an assortment of cutlery.

Morgan surveyed the backyard and noticed a pile of refuse near the opening of a partly collapsed mine shaft a few steps beyond the privy. He walked over to the refuse pile and saw several empty bottles labeled 'Laudanum' lying on top. He noticed a kerosene lantern sitting on a tree stump near the entrance to the mine shaft. He stepped closer to the shaft and realized the entrance was now little more than a narrow slit. He felt a faint cool draft on his face along with the smell of damp earth and mold. Beyond a few feet there was nothing but uninviting blackness.

Morgan returned to the house and took one last look around before leaving. Hoskins was in the street surrounded by a small crowd of prostitutes and curious patrons from the clubs across the street. One of the women whom he assumed was a prostitute was standing off to one side holding a baby with a small boy sucking his thumb clinging to her skirt. She was the only woman dabbing her eyes. Morgan walked over to Hoskins and showed him the badge. "Lock up the house and open it only for the coroner's office." Hoskins gave him a surprised look, nodded, and resumed his lurid description of what happened to Adele.

Morgan went over to the weeping woman and asked, "Excuse me, but by any chance, are you Mrs. Dylan?" The woman nodded and gave him a guarded look. "How well did you know Adele?"

The woman lifted her shoulders. "Well enough," was the non-committal response.

"Would you mind telling me what you know about her? It might help to find who killed her."

"Not much to tell. She was just another whore. Ain't no one gonna care who killed her."

"I care, and I'd like to find who did it."

Her face softened. "Adele came here about six, seven months ago from somewhere in Colorado. Before that, who knows? She'd been whorin' maybe five or six years. Said she'd been a nurse before she got in the trade. Told me she got into some trouble and ended up like a lot of women to make ends meet."

"Did she have any steady customers she used to talk about?"

"She never said."

"Hoskins said she had a regular customer every Thursday night. Do you know anything about him?"

"Yeah, I forgot about him. She never talked about him. Except once she said it was the easiest money she'd ever made. He never wanted to do anything but talk, play cards, and watch her take her clothes off. Occasionally he would sleep with her for an hour or so. She thought it was funny he never wanted to do anything but sleep." She looked faintly embarrassed. "Well, you know, there's some men are just lonely and all they want is a woman to talk to. Whore's are just as good at listenin' as they are spreadin' their legs, and it's a lot easier."

"Did she ever say anything else about the man or describe him in such way that might help to identify him?" She shook her head. "Do you know if she saw anyone else, a man or woman friend, who wasn't a customer or regular client?"

"If she did, she never mentioned it, and I never noticed. I don't think so. She wasn't like the other women workin' here. She thought she was better'n them, and in a way she was. It wasn't like she put on airs or anything. It was more like she didn't fit in. The other women were jealous, bein's she didn't have to work the way they did. I was the only one who'd even talk to her. She was always nice to me. Once she give me some money when my husband lost a lot playin' cards. I didn't ask for it, she just done it on her own."

"Does the name Willard Merrick or Phillip Hardesty mean anything to you?"

"Nah, I don't recollect hearing those names."

"Did she ever refer to herself as Mrs. Merrick?" She shook her head. "Do you have any idea why she gave a very convincing performance at the jail three days ago when she identified herself as Mrs. Merrick and said her husband was missing?"

The woman shook her head. "Mister, if there's one thing a whore does best, it's giving a convincing performance, else they ain't gonna be in business long. I got no idea why Adele would say that, 'cause she wasn't married, I'm certain of it."

"Why did she have your children with her when she reported him missing?"

Josephine Dylan's eyes flew open in surprise. "What're you talkin' about? She offered to take them down to the Mercantile and give me a chance to get some rest. As far as I know during the hour she was gone, that's what she done."

Morgan saw no point in questioning her further. Her answers, uninformative as they may have been, had the ring of honesty. Someone had a reason to make sure Adele Belden died, and he was certain it was somehow connected to Hardesty's murder.

145

Chapter 13

Morgan walked back toward the center of town and caught a taxi out to the hospital. When he arrived, he told the driver to wait for him and then went in search of Dr. Chambliss. He found him eventually on the third floor where the doctor had just completed morning rounds. This time the physician was friendlier than their first meeting, greeting him with a grimace that may have passed for a smile.

"Good morning, Mr. Westphal, and how goes your investigation?"

"Not well, I'm afraid. In fact, soon you will have another body to examine, a woman this time." Morgan briefly summarized the circumstances of Adele Belden's death and his conviction there was a link to Hardesty's murder.

"I believe she was heavily sedated with laudanum before she was strangled. The position of the body and absence of any struggle suggests she was unconscious when she was strangled, or possibly already dead."

"I see. I'll keep your observations in mind during my examination, unofficially, of course."

"Actually, you can consider them officially. I am now a town deputy duly sworn in by Marshal Truesdale."

The physician's eyes widened in surprise as he said, "You don't say. I imagine the trouble that started this morning is keeping the marshal busy. He isn't the only one. I've already treated three broken heads–one quite nasty–and a broken arm. What this town, including this understaffed hospital, doesn't need is another labor strike."

"I just heard about it from the marshal. I gather this isn't the first time."

Chambliss yawned, "No, and it likely won't be the last until either the union or the companies win. Frankly, as unpopular as the idea might be with most of the people I know, I'd like to see the union win then maybe the trouble will stop."

"What's the union after?"

"The same as they've been after over the years–higher wages, a shorter day, and safer conditions. Can't say as I blame them for wanting to get paid for whatever they're ordered to do. They don't even get paid for jobs like shoring up the tunnels or hauling timbers."

"How did the strike get settled before?"

"The mine owners brought in enough of their own men, mostly from Colorado, the locals finally gave up and the strike ended." Morgan thought that was about the time or soon after Frank and Hardesty had come to Adobe Wells. He wondered if Merrick had also come then. Well, the strike was a distraction although its outcome hardly mattered to him unless it got in the way of the investigation. LaTrobe was probably going to be less accessible, and that would be a problem, if he determined there was a reason to go back in the Emily. Fortunately, at this point he saw no reason to go back and hoped circumstances would not make it necessary.

"I suppose La Trobe is the main reason the owners' won't give into union demands."

"He is. I wonder how well he'll be able to deal with it this time," Chambliss said speculatively, a thoughtful frown furrowing his brow.

"What do you mean by that?"

As if roused from some inner thought, the doctor looked momentarily discomfited and replied, "Oh, nothing at all, just an old man getting lost in his thoughts." He smiled and brushed it off by saying, "Westphal, you'll find when you get to be my age, your mind is easily distracted and begins to wander." Morgan thought Doctor Chambliss may be long in years, but he was still as sharp as he had ever been.

He remembered the cab waiting outside and the main reason he wanted to see the doctor.

"Dr. Chambliss, I went down in the Emily last night to take a look at where the murder took place. I found what I think was the murder weapon." Morgan held out the candle pick. "Do you know what this is?"

"Yes, of course. I should have thought of that before. The size and shape of the wound would seem to fit very well, I should think. It also explains the similarity to the bayonet wounds I saw during the war."

A sudden thought struck Morgan, and he reached for the photograph of the young man he'd found in the woman's trunk. "Do you think this could be the man you examined?"

Dr. Chambliss took the photograph and moved closer to a window for more light. After studying the portrait closely, he handed it back and said, "It's possible; however, there's no way I can be certain. The cheek has the same general shape, but then again the same can be said about you or half the men in the ward behind me. I'm sorry, but his face is too badly mutilated for me to tell. Is it a picture of Hardesty?"

"I think it might be. I'll know soon enough when I show it to someone who knew him."

Morgan took his leave and returned to the waiting taxi. The hospital was higher up than the nearest buildings, and as he stood on the steps, he saw the head frames of some of the nearby mines. The hoists were silent, and there was no rumble of ore cars or the rattle of rock falling down the wooden chutes to the collection bins below. He saw crowds of men milling about and heard faint shouting.

He climbed into the car and told the worried driver to take him to the jail. The taxi driver warned he would have to take a longer way around to get to his destination to avoid the possibility of running into any of the strikers. The driver claimed this was his last fare and was going straight home after he reached the jail.

Morgan paid the driver and stepped out of the car. Blaylock was just coming out the door as he approached the entrance. With a sneer, the deputy said, "The marshal still ain't here, and it still ain't visiting hours."

"It is now." Morgan pulled out the badge and had the satisfaction of seeing Blaylock's jaw drop. "I saw Marshal Truesdale earlier this morning. I now have the authority to visit anytime I want. Now Blaylock, why don't you just go along about your business, if you have any, and I'll get on with mine." He left the stunned deputy standing speechless on the sidewalk.

Morgan entered the jail and found Myron sitting at Blaylock's desk. He showed the jailer the badge and said, "I need to spend a few minutes with Frank." After Myron identified the keys to use, Morgan bounded up the stairs. He surprised his brother when he unlocked the cell door and walked in. Morgan didn't waste any time. He pulled out the photograph.

"Do you know who this is?"

"Yeah, it's Phillip Hardesty. Even without the moustache, I'd recognize him. Where'd you get it?"

"I found it in the trunk of a dead woman. Her name was Adele Belden. Do you know a prostitute by that name?"

"Now that you mention it, the name sounds familiar. There was a high-class whore back in Telluride maybe had a name like that, or it coulda been something like that. I went to see her once–couldn't afford but the one time." Frank saw Morgan's frown and misinterpreted it as disapproval. "Hell, you know how it is, Morg, a man's gotta get laid now and then just to stay fit. Besides, there ain't any proper women in a mining town, or at least none a miner is likely going to have a chance of meeting."

"Did Hardesty know her?"

"He must've. Hell, most of the men knew who she was even if they couldn't afford her. She was expensive, but goddamn, she sure was worth it."

"Do you know if Hardesty had any special arrangement with her?"

"It's possible," he replied, looking away.

"By any chance is she the reason you and Hardesty fell out?"

"Goddamn, how come you know that?"

"A lucky guess. How about telling me about it?"

"Well, one morning I was shooting my mouth off about the expensive whore I spent the night with and how it was about the finest time I ever had with a woman when all of a sudden he hauls off and lets me have it without any warning. He went plumb crazy and beat the hell out of me before I knew what was happening. Shit, at first I thought it was because he was a damn fool for falling in love with a whore, and I told him so. He didn't say anything and just walked away. I tried to apologize even if I didn't exactly know what the hell I was apologizing for. He wouldn't talk to me. From that point on, whenever he got a few drinks in him, he'd find some reason to pick a fight, and it was usually with me. Pretty soon it got so's I'd go out of my way to avoid him. By the time we came here, we weren't exactly lookin' for each other's company. We made a point of stayin' away from each other as much as we could, then damned if we didn't both end up in the same goddamn mine and on the same goddamn shift."

"Did you know she was here in Adobe Wells working in a crib out behind the Arabian Club?"

"Nope, I didn't."

Morgan changed the subject. "Why didn't you tell me you saw Hardesty at his hotel the night before he was killed?"

"I didn't think it was important."

"Jesus Christ! Frank, how many times do I have to tell you I'll decide what's important. You've got at least one, possibly more, potential witnesses for the prosecution ready to swear you were causing a disturbance late at night. Now quit wasting the little time we have and tell me what you and Hardesty were arguing about."

"Morg, you got it all wrong. It wasn't like that at all. For once we weren't havin' an argument. You remember when I told you about the union man that tried to get me to sign up?"

"Stockwell?"

"Yeah, well, Stockwell told me Hardesty had already signed up. There'd been some talk down in the mine that maybe he had. When I heard someone talkin' that way, I went over to see Hardesty and warn him to watch his ass if it got around in the TJ&M mines. At first, he was mad for wakin' him up and yelled at me after I told him why I was there. He told me he could take of himself and to quit interferin'. I guess I got a little bit pissed myself for takin' the trouble to come there. We both finally calmed down and had the first decent conversation we'd had since the fight in Telluride. It's a damn shame it was the last one we ever had. Anyway, he tried to get me to come over and join too, but I wasn't ready to do somethin' like that. He hinted the union was fixin' to call a strike and there was going to be trouble. Hardesty warned I'd better end up on the right side. Shit, I told him the same thing. We shook hands, and I left. So help me, Morg, that's what happened."

"Tell me about Willard Merrick."

"Not much to tell. He ain't particularly liked. He mostly keeps to himself. He and Hardesty seemed to get along; I'd see them occasionally drinkin' together. I heard he wasn't all that good with a drill."

"Was he in Telluride before coming to adobe Wells?"

"If he was, I never saw him there. He came in after most of us got here."

"Any reason you think it was Merrick you found and not Hardesty?"

"Not a chance. Where'd you come up with that idea?"

"No particular reason except it was dark in the tunnel, and the dead man's face was hardly recognizable."

"Nah, I'm pretty sure it was Hardesty." Morgan had the impression his brother was less certain than before.

"Merrick was one of the men Cardwell told to take the body up out of the mine. He then disappeared right after and no one has seen him since. Cardwell said he didn't collect his wages for the week. Do you have idea why Merrick would go away, particularly without even collecting his pay?"

"I didn't know he was gone, and if he is, I sure don't know why he would. It don't make no sense."

"Did Merrick know Adele?"

"I don't know, maybe he did if Hardesty told him about her. Like I said before, the last couple of months Merrick and Hardesty were friendly."

"Why would Hardesty drill toward the Imperial when the vein was beginning to shift away from the boundary between the two mines?"

"No reason at all, particularly after I told Cardwell it was just a matter of time before that drift was going to have a major water problem."

"You told Cardwell that? How did you happen to know there was water in there?"

"Hell, I guess I oughta know since I'm the one drilled most of that drift."

"I thought Hardesty was assigned to work that drift?"

"Nah, you got it all wrong. It was me up until a few days before Hardesty was pulled out of another drift and put in there. I got moved over and Merrick was sent farther down the tunnel."

"Did you mind getting switched?"

"Why should I? Didn't make any difference to me which drift I work as long as I get paid" Morgan was surprised to hear the reply. Cardwell had made a point about keeping the drillers working the same drifts. Then why had the shift boss moved three of his drillers to other locations?

Frank continued. "One drift is pretty much like the next unless you run into hardrock. Hardrock takes longer to drill the round, although workin' hardrock is safer. The drift I was workin' that night was hardrock, and it took longer to finish up. The drift Hardesty was in that I drilled before was real easy to work, but the rock around the vein was soft. That's why the water was seepin' so much. I drilled into one of the seeps just to see how bad it was. I only went in maybe ten feet and sure enough water come pourin' out."

"How many holes did you drill?"

"Just one. Didn't see any point in drillin' more. What for? It was only goin' to make things worse."

"Frank, I found at least six holes drilled in that wall. Are you sure you didn't drill more than one?" Morgan saw the irritated look on his brother's face. "All right, so you only drilled one. Can you think of a reason why Hardesty would have drilled more?"

"No, and if he did, he was a damn fool for doin' it. I told Cardwell after I drilled the one hole, it would be safer to close up that drift and put cement in there to strengthen the wall else there'd be no chance to mine the vein much longer before the tunnel flooded."

Morgan recalled Cardwell's look of surprise when he told him about the drill holes he'd discovered. Either Cardwell or Frank was lying. This time he thought Frank was telling the truth. Why the shift boss would lie about something like that was curious. Another discussion with Tate Cardwell was required.

Before he left Frank, Morgan cautioned his brother to tell Myron or Truesdale to contact him if he thought of anything else. He considered telling Frank the judge had turned down the petitions for a change of location and a trial delay and rejected the impulse; Frank didn't need another reason to be discouraged.

By the time he came downstairs, the marshal was walking in the front door. A deputy followed pushing ahead of him two disheveled and scowling men handcuffed together. One of the men had a bloody cut on his forehead.

Thumbing toward them, Truesdale said, "This is only the start of it. Frank's gonna have a lot of company, and Judge Breen is gonna be busy."

"How bad is it, Dan?"

"It's settled down some, mostly just shoutin' and shovin'. These two got into it so I'm gonna cool 'em down for a time. I'd be careful if I was you and stay away from the mines where most of the trouble is. It'll get a lot worse when the scabs start showin' up. Then things are gonna get out of hand real quick. You want a pistol now you got a badge?"

"I've got my own if I need it."

"If I were you, I'd strap it on. If this strike goes the way of the last one, it's gonna be real bad."

Chapter Fourteen

Before he left the jail, Morgan made a phone call to the offices of TJ&M in the faint hope of getting another appointment with Victor LaTrobe. One of the secretaries informed him Mr. LaTrobe had gone home for the day and was not expected to return. With the strike gathering steam, he was surprised LaTrobe would leave the office. He had nothing to lose by accepting LaTrobe's invitation to bypass the main office and come to his home. One of the deputies offered to give him a lift on his way back to town. After seeing the vehicle was actually a panel truck with barred doors on the back and designed to carry prisoners, Morgan had the deputy let him off a block away from the winding gravel drive leading up to the superintendent's home.

The two-story territorial with a low gable roof and wrap-around porch completely surrounding the first floor was perched on a hill overlooking the town. The location alone made it imposing. A carriage house converted to a garage was located off to one side of the main house, and through the open doors, he glimpsed the large black touring car he had seen Olivia LaTrobe leave the TJ&M office building. A small, cream-colored roadster was parked next to it.

Before lifting the brass door knocker, Morgan paused to mop the perspiration off his face and to catch his breath after the steep climb up the hill. He heard a loud angry voice from somewhere inside and wondered if coming unannounced was a mistake, especially if he was about to interrupt a domestic dispute. He took the risk and brought the knocker down several times on the metal striker.

The door was opened by a middle-aged woman wearing servant's livery. "May I help you?"

"My name is Westphal, and I'd like to see Mr. LaTrobe."

"I'm afraid this may not be a good time to call on Mr. LaTrobe. He's not feeling very well and doesn't want to be disturbed."

"Who is it, Celia?" Morgan recognized LaTrobe's voice.

"It's a gentleman to see you, Mr. LaTrobe. He says his name is Mr. Westphal."

"Please take him to the study. I'll join him there."

"Very good sir," she replied and stepped aside to allow him to enter. Morgan followed her as she made her way down a hallway and stopped in front of an open doorway then motioned him inside. Dominated by a large mahogany desk positioned under the window, the room was spacious and elegant. Floor to ceiling bookshelves lined the walls.

Morgan walked over to the nearest bookshelf and casually scanned the titles. Apart from a few volumes clearly related to mining and geology, the vast majority of the books were classics many of which were printed in French, Italian, and a few in Latin. He was surprised to see such an extensive library and wondered if LaTrobe had ever taken the time to read any of them or if they were merely decorations. As if reading his mind, Latrobe said from the doorway, "I'm afraid my wife is the one who gets the credit for the library. She has a passion for fine literature. It's good of you to come, Mr. Westphal. How did you find the Emily?"

Morgan watched LaTrobe limp into the room, left hand thrust in the pocket of his lounging jacket. He was surprised by how ill he looked. Pale and favoring his left leg more than he had the first time they met, Morgan could scarcely believe the physical change. He did not offer to shake hands and instead walked directly to the desk and sat down in the high-backed leather chair. LaTrobe was controlled but tense.

"The mine was interesting, Mr. LaTrobe, very interesting. Mr. Cardwell was most helpful and instructive. The Emily is a remarkable example of engineering and the efforts the human being will go to extract the riches of the earth."

"Mr. Westphal, your description is not only accurate but quite expressive. Did you learn or find anything of interest?"

"Why would anyone be drilling toward the Imperial mine from the easternmost drift?"

LaTrobe looked startled. "I can think of no reason at all. The vein doesn't go in that direction. Why do you ask, and what does this have to do with the miner that was killed?"

"I found a number of drill holes 90 degrees to the left of the working face. Water was coming from them. Cardwell didn't seem to know anything about them when I told him."

"I'm completely mystified why anyone would be drilling on the east wall for two reasons. You may not know that TJ&M is under lawsuit filed by Louis Sandusky for allegedly encroaching on the Imperial. Although the suit has no merit, I would be a fool to authorize an expansion in that direction at a time when the matter is under litigation. Furthermore, I have enough seepage problems in that part of the Emily without causing more by drilling in a wall that is inherently unstable and made more so by unprofitable extraction. The vein in that drift does not extend in that direction. Quite the contrary, the ore vein goes almost due north, and that is the direction the drift is moving. No, Mr. Westphal, there is no rational explanation for any drill holes as you described. I fail to see what this revelation, strange as it may be, has to do with the miner's death."

"Murder, Mr. LaTrobe. The man was murdered. There is always a motive for murder. Someone had a reason to kill Hardesty, and when I find out what that reason is, I will know who killed him. It's possible the holes I found were deliberate attempts by someone to sabotage the Emily, and perhaps Hardesty found out and was killed to prevent him from reporting it."

"A somewhat fanciful theory at best, but I concede it's possible. I'm curious, you seem unconvinced the man now in custody is guilty of the murder. Surely he is. I'm told he and the dead miner did not get along. If that's true, why wouldn't that be the motive you're looking for?"

"I agree, except the extent of the disagreement between the two men has not been well-substantiated. It is also a fact that at one time they were good friends; consequently, I'm obliged to keep an open mind for other possibilities."

LaTrobe glanced at the bookshelves and said softly, "It wouldn't be the first time two people with some regard for each other eventually become estranged. Friendship, love, can easily turn to something else."

Morgan was struck by the words and LaTrobe's bleak expression. He had the feeling the comment had nothing to do with Hardesty and Frank.

"Mr. LaTrobe, in our previous meeting, you seemed convinced Hardesty was working for the WFM. Is that true?"

"A fair question, but one I'll have to give less than a complete answer. Suffice to say, I have my sources. I would not be successful in running the largest mining enterprise in Adobe Wells if I had to rely solely on contracts and the good intentions of my employees. Mining is not only physically dangerous, it's a rough business. My competitors will stop at nothing to increase their production at great cost to me. Since TJ&M shares are the only publicly held positions in Adobe Wells, the stakes are high. Even if our production is high in the TJ&M mines, which I'm happy to report it is, shares can fall in New York on the merest hint of scandal. This gives my competitors an edge I do not have against them. It is something that can be easily exploited. For that reason, I must keep a vigilant eye, and I pay a great deal of money to keep that eye open. It is more profitable to solve a problem when it is at the stage of only being a potential problem. When small things are allowed to escalate into larger issues, stockholders become concerned, and when that happens, board of directors become nervous and look for someone to blame. That makes me vulnerable, even expendable."

"If you don't mind my saying so, such a philosophy would seem to offer some justification for TJ&M to have Hardesty killed. That is, if there was a strong reason to believe he was working for the WFM."

"Don't take me for a fool, Westphal," LaTrobe said, obviously nettled. "You miss the point entirely. If I knew Hardesty was working for the WFM, why on earth would I want to harm him? For practical reasons, I wouldn't want anything to happen to him while he was on TJ&M property. I can't think of anything more problematic if the public learned of some ill-conceived plot hatched by TJ&M to prevent the union from being established in our mines. TJ&M shares would plummet. That you have even voiced such a theory is troubling if it should be bandied about in public." Morgan thought LaTrobe's explanation was valid. "I suggest in finding your motive, you look to my competitors starting with Louis Sandusky. Since my expertise is limited to other areas, I don't want to tell you how to run your investigation; however, if you find a link between the man now in custody and one of my competitors, then I think you will have the motive you're looking for."

"Mr. LaTrobe, your point is well taken, and I'll keep it in mind."

LaTrobe gave Morgan a penetrating look, and his voice had an edge when he spoke. "I have the impression your reason for coming here wasn't to report what you have so far discovered, which I am disappointed to say, appears to be very little more than when we last spoke. Am I correct, Mr. Westphal?"

Morgan nodded. "You're very perceptive, Mr. LaTrobe, and I'll not deny it. In my business, I've found it is usually the detail left out rather than the ones revealed that become significant to finding the truth. In a way, an investigation is not unlike the mining business. You may have to dig through worthless material before you mine something productive.

For that reason, it may be necessary in the future to talk to you again."

"In keeping with your metaphor, I don't relish being subjected to needless and, I might add, pointless scratching away in the forlorn hope you'll find some reason to think TJ&M is somehow responsible for that miner's death. For that reason, I withdraw my invitation to seek me out in the future as I see nothing to be gained for either one of us."

"On the contrary, Mr. LaTrobe, I'm not really here at your invitation. Because of the trouble in town, Marshal Truesdale deputized me this morning. I'm no longer a private citizen performing a service for a friend. If I find it necessary to contact you again, it will be in an official capacity as I am here now."

LaTrobe's surprise rapidly changed to anger. "I see, then in the future make arrangements to see me in my office."

"Mr. LaTrobe, I really don't wish to be confrontational. I will see you when and where it is necessary and not to accommodate your schedule as busy as it may be."

Thoroughly perturbed, LaTrobe struggled to control his temper. Morgan noticed he was again unconsciously kneading his left hand. Whatever he was about to say was interrupted by the telephone ringing. LaTrobe reached for it and Morgan moved back from the desk a few paces to keep from intruding. The conversation was brief and ended when LaTrobe snapped, "All right, I'll be right there." LaTrobe stood up and said coldly, "We will have to continue this conversation another time; that is, if there is another time. I'm sure you're aware of the strike and what is happening in town. It seems I must return to the office. I'll have Celia call a taxi for you." He pressed a button at the side of the desk and the same woman who met him at the door appeared in the doorway. "Celia, have Stevens bring the car around. I'll be returning to the office, and call a taxi for Mr. Westphal."

"Would it be possible to get a lift into town?" Morgan asked.

"I'm afraid not," LaTrobe responded and left the room.

Morgan wasn't surprised at the petty gesture. He had already concluded from his first visit LaTrobe was used to getting his own way. He thought LaTrobe was probably a tyrant to work for and sympathized with the employees of TJ&M whose jobs depended on getting along with him.

Morgan looked out the window and saw LaTrobe being driven off in the limousine. He was still standing at the window admiring the mountain vista when Celia entered the room.

"I'm terribly sorry, Mr. Westphal, it seems there are no taxis available at the present time." Morgan remembered what the taxi driver said during the trip from the hospital to the jail about going home. Apparently, he wasn't the only taxi driver looking to avoid trouble.

"It's all right, Celia. It probably has to do with the strike. I'll walk back to town."

Morgan glanced at the desk and saw a photograph of LaTrobe and his smiling wife. He picked it up for a closer examination. From the clothes they were wearing and the bridal bouquet she was holding, it was obviously a wedding photograph. Dressed in a morning suit, an unsmiling Victor LaTrobe stood serious and stiff in contrast to his wife's relaxed stance and smiling face. She gave every indication she was a happy, contented bride. The photograph reminded him of the one he and Lydia had made a few days after their marriage. The only thing that made the two pictures similar was the same warm smile on each bride's face and the more serious faces of the grooms. Morgan smiled at the memory. He had been dressed in a second-hand suit, and Lydia had made the dress she wore. He wondered why brides found it easier to smile on such occasions when grooms more often than not looked like they wanted to be somewhere else.

Morgan put the photograph back on the desk just as Olivia LaTrobe came into the study and gasped in startled surprised.

She was elegantly although somberly dressed in gray silk. Her jewelry consisted of black onyx earrings with matching bracelet and brooch. There was no trace of color to brighten the somber tones of her attire. Her make-up was minimal. She had a complexion most women would have wished for or paid a fortune to get. She was even more beautiful than he remembered from the brief glimpse of her in town. She had an ethereal beauty that reminded him of a remote, crystalline statue, aloof and indifferent to those who admired her. In spite of her husband's wealth and lavish surroundings, he had the impression she was a deeply unhappy woman. There was a distant, lonely sadness about her bearing little resemblance to the vibrant, smiling woman pictured in the photograph.

"My name is Morgan Westphal, and I came here to see your husband. I apologize for startling you."

"I'm Olivia LaTrobe," she replied in a low, pleasantly modulated voice.

"Yes, I know." When she raised her eyebrows, he added, "You were pointed out to me, and there is more than a slight resemblance to the photograph," he added, gesturing toward the desk.

"Ah, yes. It was taken seven years ago when I married Victor. As I recall at the time, it was a happy occasion." Morgan thought the comment strange and had the impression there may not have been many happy occasions since.

"I thought you had left with my husband. May I help you?"

"Unfortunately, your husband was in a bit of a hurry and declined to give me a lift back to town. And since Celia just informed me a cab is not available, I was about to walk back to town."

Lips curving down in disgust, she said. "At times, Victor can be very disagreeable."

"I'm afraid your husband is a trifle upset with me, and that probably contributed, if not justified, the reason."

"Why on earth for?"

"I happen to be investigating the murder that took place in the Emily a few days ago. Your husband seems to have taken offense that I do not share his views concerning who may have committed the murder or under what circumstances the murder took place."

Olivia LaTrobe nodded, "I knew the man who was killed and the one they say who did it."

Morgan was struck by both her detached manner and the admission. "You knew both of these men?" he asked, unable to imagine the circumstances where Hardesty and his brother would have had the opportunity to meet Olivia LaTrobe.

"Actually, we met quite by chance. I was out for a drive in Colorado near the town of Telluride. Mr. Hardesty and the other man now in jail were kind enough to assist me when I had some difficulty. To be perfectly truthful, I was driving too fast and went off the road. I'm not a very good driver as Victor has told me many times. The two men were fishing in a stream nearby and heard the noise. They came over and managed to get the automobile out of the ditch. I told them to go to the TJ&M office, and my husband would be happy to reward them for coming to my aid. Later my husband learned they knew something about carpentry and building. He hired them on their days off on a number of occasions to complete some improvements to the house we were living in at the time. Mr. Hardesty did a few things to this house after TJ&M shifted most of their miners and staff from Telluride to Adobe Wells. Even though I had little contact with the two men, I was under the impression they were apparently close friends. Mr. Shaw does not seem to me someone who would commit such a terrible crime."

Olivia LaTrobe's presence and beauty was a distraction, and Morgan had difficulty concentrating on what she was telling him. He suspected she was fully aware of her effect on men, but he was equally certain she was so used to the attention it no longer made any impression. It was a moment before he realized he was staring so intently at her he had yet to respond to a question she had just asked.

Morgan flushed self-consciously and belatedly replied, "Apart from being convinced Frank Shaw did not murder Hardesty, I also have no proof someone else did."

"If you don't mind me asking, how can you be so sure?"

"Frank Shaw happens to be my half-brother. He has a wild streak, and I'll admit he has been a trial to me in the past. Even so, I don't believe he would kill anyone, at least not in cold blood. And there are other factors involved that make it extremely unlikely my brother killed Hardesty. Marshal Truesdale is of the same opinion. I doubt you would have heard, but a prostitute died, possibly murdered, sometime late last night or early this morning. She knew Hardesty, and I believe her death has something to do with his. I have reason to think she and Hardesty were," he caught himself and amended, "shall we say friends."

Morgan saw her brows lift, and her expression was one of interest. "You need not be polite, Mr. Westphal, I know full well what prostitutes do. After all, it's 1915, and women are now seldom shocked or surprised that men often hire women for sex. Do you, Mr. Westphal?"

He felt his face burning at the blunt question. "Mrs. LaTrobe, I hardly think—"

"Oh, never mind, you needn't answer. It was quite unforgivable of me to embarrass you like that. But I'm confused, Mr. Westphal. If you and the marshal are so sure your brother is innocent, why is he still in jail?"

Morgan was reluctant to tell her it was largely because of her husband. She noticed his hesitation. "It's because of my husband, isn't it?"

"I believe so. Your husband has a great deal of influence, and he's convinced Frank is guilty for reasons of his own. Regrettably, there was and still is just enough circumstantial evidence in the case to convince the judge to sign a warrant for Frank's arrest."

"Unfortunately, Victor has always held strong opinions on just about everything and seldom changes his mind once it's made up. He's fixated on proving he's always right no matter what facts might be presented to the contrary. He's a skilled and gifted engineer. It's unfortunate he is considerably less so when it comes to dealing with people."

Morgan was struck by her cold expression and toneless voice. His impression she was a prisoner in a loveless marriage was reinforced. He wondered what had happened to have brought her to such an embittered state. He recollected Truesdale's comment to the effect he didn't understand what a woman like her saw in Victor LaTrobe; it was an opinion he now shared.

"Mr. Westphal, I wish you well in finding the man who killed Mr. Hardesty. I'm certain he was a decent man and didn't deserve his fate, nor does your brother. Now let's see what we can do to keep you from having to make a long, hot walk back to town. If you will come with me, I'll drive you back."

"Mrs. LaTrobe, I don't wish to put you to any trouble. I assure you I don't mind walking particularly when most of it is downhill." He expected her to withdraw the offer and was surprised when she didn't.

He followed her down the hallway and out a side door leading to the garage. He helped her into a linen duster then opened the door for her. The small automobile's interior was small enough their shoulders touched. He hoped her driving had improved since Colorado. It didn't take long to find it had not. She drove with reckless abandon. The worst part of the drive was descending the steep, gravel drive. Morgan concentrated on not paying attention to the thirty-foot drop whizzing past a foot or so from the running board. He stole a glance at her on the pretext of looking at the view. Her profile was classic and reminded him of an ivory cameo. She seemed completely indifferent to the risks she was taking as she skidded around the tight turns.

A few minutes later, they came to the outskirts of Adobe Wells. Ahead, Morgan saw a crowd of men standing around the entrance to one of the mines.

"Mrs. LaTrobe, I think you'd better stop here. I can't allow you to drive back through town alone. It isn't safe."

She slowed down and pulled to one side of the road. "You may be right at that. I'm sorry I can't take you farther."

"Don't be," he replied, disappointed his time with her was cut short.

He got out of the car and stood with his hands on the closed door searching for something to say more than a simple goodbye. She extended her hand, and he held it briefly. "Goodbye, Mr. Westphal, and good luck."

"Thank you, Mrs. LaTrobe, for your trouble and your wishes. I hope we meet again." Their eyes met, she smiled and for a brief moment, she looked like the woman in the photograph.

"It's a small town." She paused and looked closely at him, "I rather think we will."

Morgan was still thinking about her enigmatic comment when he saw Elias Stockwell separate himself from the mob ahead and come toward him.

Chapter Fifteen

"If it isn't the Pinkerton Man," Stockwell sneered. Except for the unmistakable air of authority he conveyed, Stockwell was indistinguishable from the surly miners crowding the gated mine entrance. All were coatless with their sleeves rolled up, and each man had a small black and red ribbon pinned to his chest. Morgan noticed Blaylock farther up the road standing impassively with his arms folded leaning on the side of a truck.

Morgan crossed to the other side of the road with the intent of avoiding a confrontation, but the burly union representative moved to block his way. He wished now he hadn't been so cavalier in ignoring Truesdale's advice to carry a sidearm. Although Stockwell was no taller than Morgan and at least ten years older, he had the physique of a man accustomed to hard physical labor and was easily fifty pounds heavier. He doubted if things got nasty, Blaylock would lift a finger to help.

Unable to ignore Stockwell any longer, he greeted him. "Good afternoon, Mr. Stockwell. I see you're on the job even if the other men aren't."

Stockwell scowled and blocked Morgan's progress with an outthrust hand. "Not so fast, Pinkerton Man. I'd like to introduce you to some of my friends. Hey, boys, look what we got here, a weasel. I saw him in Colorado a few years back pretending to be an honest union man, but all that time he was working for the Pinkertons and the mine owners." There was an angry mutter among the men now standing motionless watching the unfolding drama. "Where I come from, we skin weasels, and I'm willing to bet if I skin you, I'd find nothing but yellow meat. What do you say to that, Pinkerton Man?"

"Stockwell, I'd say if your words were horseshit, you'd be able to fertilize five acres with them." A few of the onlookers laughed.

Stockwell's face reddened. "Watch your mouth, weasel. In case you haven't noticed, I'm not alone. All I gotta do is wiggle a finger and some of my friends will come on over here and see how smart you can talk after they're through with you."

Morgan stepped back and adopted the same mocking pose as Stockwell's with his hands on his hips. He directed his attention to the crowd.

"It appears Mr. Stockwell is going to need your help. He's got something started he can't seem to finish by himself even if the odds don't look like they favor me much. In fact, the odds of me taking on Mr. Stockwell by myself and succeeding are so bad that if any of you are thinking of betting, I'll put a few bucks on Mr. Stockwell myself." Morgan took out his wallet and held up a dollar bill. "Any takers?" He was relieved to see open amusement or curiosity on most of the faces.

"Hey, mister," one of the burly miners called out belligerently, "is what he said about you working for the Pinkertons true?"

"I'm afraid at one time it was true," Morgan replied and held up his hands to quell the noisy response. "Now, boys, let me explain what happened, and if Mr. Stockwell had stayed around long enough the other night to hear what I'm about to say, we'd probably be having a drink by now instead of standing out here under a hot sun trying to figure out who can piss farther." Now that he had their attention, he summarized his brief work with the Pinkerton Agency and why he broke the contract. He ended by saying, "I'll level with you boys. I'm not for you, but I'm damn sure not against you. The name's Morgan Westphal, and my father was killed in a mine here in Adobe Wells. If you don't believe me, you'll find the name Mason Westphal—that's

Westphal with a 'phal'—on a monument over on Jefferson Street. My father along with a dozen other miners died in a cave-in almost thirty years ago. I was ten years old when it happened. Later, I did some hardrock mining long enough to know what it's like to go underground and work for low pay, long hours, and for people who don't care about anything except how much ore you can get out during your shift." The men nodded and voiced their agreement. "Now, if what I said so far isn't enough then take a look at this," Morgan pulled open his coat and displayed the badge. "I've got only one reason to be here in Adobe Wells, and it has nothing to do with interfering with your strike. I'm investigating the murder of Phillip Hardesty. Maybe you know or heard of him. He was the miner who was killed a week ago down in the Emily. It seems to me from what I've heard about Phillip Hardesty, he deserves to have whoever killed him brought to justice."

Morgan was gratified to see most of the men were regarding him with open interest. He turned around and faced Stockwell whose expression had changed from open hostility to curiosity. "Mr. Stockwell, I would prefer to talk to you about Mr. Hardesty than fight about what I did or did not do in Colorado over ten years ago. What do you say?"

"All right," you've made your point. I'll listen to what you've got say. I was just getting ready to go back into town. I reckon we can talk on the way."

"Before we go, I'd like to ask these men if they know someone I'm trying to find." He turned back to the miners. "Does anyone here know a driller by the name of Willard Merrick?"

Several men admitted to knowing him. A miner chewing a plug spat a stream and stepped forward. "Yeah, I do. What about him?"

"He was a good friend of Hardesty's and working the same shift when Hardesty was killed. Merrick helped carry the body to the surface then disappeared right after he came up. I'm hoping to find someone who can tell me where he lives or where I can find him."

"Probably at the Arabian is where you'll most likely find him. He was real friendly with Adele; she's a whore works over there." Morgan said nothing about Adele's fate for fear they would think he was looking for him as a suspect in her death.

"When he was workin' the Imperial, he was livin' at a boarding house over on Pierce–Ballinger's, I believe. If he ain't still there, he's probably left town."

"Thanks for the information."

He and Stockwell struck off down the road toward town. They passed Blaylock still leaning against the truck with a sardonic smile on his face. Stockwell hawked and spat conspicuously in the direction of the deputy and then asked, "What you said back there, was it true about your father and you being a miner and all?" he asked, glancing at Morgan.

"Every word of it."

"You talk real good, Westphal. You had them men eatin' out your hand. If you'd kept on, they might've turned on me instead. I wish I could talk like you."

"Mr. Stockwell, persuasion depends more on truth than eloquence. They understood what I told them had the ring of truth. I also didn't try to tell them I was one of them. If I had, they would have known I was saying it to save my neck."

"And were you talkin' to save your neck?"

"I must admit the thought crossed my mind,"

Stockwell's face softened. "What about Hardesty? Were you tellin' the truth about that, too?"

"I was."

"I thought Shaw was the one who done it."

"I don't think so, and I intend to find the man who did. Was Hardesty a union man?"

"Hell, he was more'n just a member. He'd been working for the WFM for maybe two years or more. We put him undercover with TJ&M back in Telluride. We've been trying to get TJ&M to go union for a long time with no success."

"What was Hardesty's job, recruiting?"

"Nah, I got people to do that, me included. We wanted someone on the inside of TJ&M to keep his eyes and ears open."

"What for?" Morgan asked, not understanding the point of Hardesty's role.

"In a non-union mine, if a man is suspected of being union, he might have an accident, and the rest of the men at least ain't gonna talk to him. Hardesty kept us informed of what the men were sayin' and what the conditions were like. The reason I come here was because Hardesty said things was about right for a strike."

"Why do you think Hardesty was killed?"

"I think someone found out what he was doing and killed him for it. If that fool Shaw done it, it's because LaTrobe paid him to do it."

"So you're convinced Shaw really did kill Hardesty?"

"I don't care what you told them back there, it sure looks like it to me."

"Didn't you try to recruit Shaw?"

"How'd you know that?" Stockwell said in surprise.

"Shaw told me. I also came away with the impression he was considering becoming a member of the WFM."

"Yeah, I think so, too. A little more time, and I woulda had him signed up."

"Shaw suspected Hardesty was union," Morgan said.

"I don't believe it. Hardesty knew better than to let on he was union."

"At one time back in Telluride, they were good friends. Maybe Hardesty slipped up after a few drinks and gave Shaw a reason to believe he was a union man or at least sympathetic to the cause. They had a falling out for reasons I'm still not sure about. They still remained close enough.

Maybe Shaw tried to warn Hardesty the TJ&M people were on to him."

"Sounds like a lot of speculation," Stockwell said.

"I know Shaw went to see Hardesty a few hours before their shift started. Hardesty had his bags packed some time after that meeting as if he was going somewhere, possibly after his shift was over. Do you know if he was planning to leave?"

"No. He didn't say nothing about it the last time I saw him about five days before he was killed."

"Did you meet regularly?"

Stockwell shook his head. "Nah, it was too dangerous. Occasionally, he'd send me a letter. In Telluride there was a high-class whore who had a small house; we met at her place a few times where we were able to talk in private."

"Was her name Adele Belden?"

"I wouldn't know. Hell, she was just a goddamn whore 'though not bad lookin.' If I ever knew what her name was I don't remember it. I do know she's here in Adobe Wells 'cause the last time I met Hardesty was in her place over behind where the private clubs are."

"Is there anything else you can tell me about the whore?"

Stockwell flashed, "Why're you askin' me about some whore? I thought you was interested in Hardesty. If you want to get laid, that's your business, but I ain't interested in helpin' you. Maybe I got nothin' more to say to you."

"Adele Belden was murdered sometime last night or early this morning. She's now part of the investigation. I knew she was somehow linked with Hardesty, but until now I thought he was just buying some of her time. There may be more to it than that."

"Jesus Christ! All right, what else do you want to know?"

"Is there anything else about Hardesty or the woman you can tell me?"

Stockwell pursed his lips. "I always had the impression the woman was more to Hardesty than a convenience, if you know what I mean."

"Possibly a mistress?"

"Yeah, somethin' like that, I suppose. It was the way they looked and treated each other. You know respectful like, and they seemed real friendly, not like he was payin' for her time. It was none of my business, so I didn't care one way or the other."

"Was she ever present during the occasions you met with Hardesty?"

"Yeah, didn't talk much, mainly just listened. She was the one told us TJ&M was pulling out of Telluride and planning to concentrate most of their interests in Adobe Wells. Damned if she wasn't right. A month later, the company sold out and left."

"What can you tell me about Hardesty? Did you trust him?"

"I had no reason not to."

"How and where did you meet?"

"It was in Telluride almost two years ago. I was in my hotel room one night, and I heard a knock on the door. It was Hardesty. Said he wanted to talk to me, and I figured maybe he wanted to join up. I was a little surprised since it ain't often a new member comes lookin' for me although once and awhile it happens. Anyway, he comes in and tells me he knows how hard I been workin' to get TJ&M to go union, and he thinks he can help. He says he's willing to do some things to maybe encourage LaTrobe to consider changing his mind. I asked what he had in mind. He suggested maybe a few dynamite charges here and there would do the trick. I almost threw him out; I told him that was the last thing I wanted."

Morgan was surprised at Stockwell's comment and said, "That's what the union was doing in Cripple Creek and the reason the Pinkertons went in undercover to find out who was doing it."

"Yeah, there's some truth to it," the union representative's candid admission surprised Morgan. "I don't deny some of that was goin' on although it was the Pinkertons who was behind most of it. They put some of the men up to it."

Morgan knew much of the sabotage done at the Cripple Creek mines and smelters had been instigated or committed by Pinkerton undercover operatives to demonstrate their union support. The revelation made his decision to go back to Albuquerque an easy one.

"I'm not sayin' we didn't do a few things I've since come to regret, but the only goddamned thing all that shit accomplished was to reduce our chances for getting the mine owners to support the union. It also brought in the army, and got some of the miners and their families killed. I told him to get his ass out of my room. He said maybe there was another way he could help, and that's when he had the idea about working on the inside to tell us what was going on inside the TJ&M. We talked some more, and that's how it came about."

"Was Hardesty a union member then?"

"That's the funny thing about it. At the time, no, but he was by the time he left my room."

"Didn't you wonder at the time why he was volunteering to help the union, and he wasn't even a member?"

"I did, and I asked him why he was willing to do it. He said it was personal, and that it was his business. Hell, it wasn't like what he was offering was gonna cost the union very much so I let it go. We never talked about it again."

"Was the information Hardesty gave you significant?"

Stockwell did not respond right away as if considering his answer. "Maybe not significant, more like helpful. To tell the truth, the risk he was takin' for what he ended up telling me was hardly worth it. If some of those TJ&M people had ever suspected him of being a union man, he woulda had an

174

accident as sure as I'm here talkin' to you. I'm bettin' they did find out, and he paid for it."

Morgan was inclined to agree with Stockwell's assessment. It still left unanswered why Hardesty had put himself at such risk for so little return. Perhaps if Hardesty had confided his reason to Stockwell, he'd have a better idea who murdered him and why.

The Territorial Hotel was a virtual palace compared to the boarding house where Merrick had been living. For twenty-five cents a day, a miner had a roof over his head, a room he shared with four other men, and not much else. A common room with a wood floor contained a long table with benches on either side. There was a woodstove where the boarders prepared their own meals. A sign over a large box with a lock advertised wood for sale in the office.

His visit didn't take long. Horace Ballinger identified himself as the owner and manager. He was cooperative but had little to say of significance.

"Does Willard Merrick live here?"

"He did up until a couple of days ago when he woke me up about two in the morning. He paid me what he owed and then left with his bag in a big hurry." Ballinger's answer was enough to finally convince him the dead man wasn't Merrick. The driller must have come directly here after helping Davies carry the body to the surface. Merrick's sudden disappearance right after the shift ended was more suspicious than ever.

"Did he say why and where he was going?"

"Nope, and I didn't ask, but I sure wondered about it."

"How did he seem, afraid, angry?"

"Well, now you mention it, he looked a mite scared–kept looking behind him and seemed real nervous-like. Never saw him acting so skittish before."

"How well did you know him?"

"Well enough, I reckon, and better'n most 'cause he'd been here awhile. Didn't talk much, but I didn't hold that agin him. Don't talk that much myself. You got nothin' to say, I always say better not to say it. Anyways, he was a decent sort and always paid on time, not like some others here I got to stay on 'em before they drink up all their wages."

"Has anyone else been here looking for Merrick before me?"

"Yeah, there was a man come here a few hours after Merrick left. He claimed Merrick owed him for money he lost in a card game. Thought there was somethin' strange about that."

"Why strange?"

Ballinger shook his head in wonder and replied, "Merrick was one of the few miners I ever knew who didn't smoke, chew, drink, or gamble. I never asked but figured he was one of them Mormons."

"Do you recall the name of the man who came looking for him?"

"Nope, if he said, I don't remember."

"What can you tell me about him?"

"He was big. Not so much tall as, you know, well stood up. Don't reckon too many men would be messin' with him even if he did wear spectacles. And he had a badge just like yours. What's the matter, don't you law fellers talk to each other?"

It was a reasonable question. A better question was why Blaylock had concealed the fact he knew where Merrick lived and that he wasn't married. The deputy had some explaining to do.

Chapter Sixteen

Morgan reviewed the proposed telegram to his partner, crossed out another unnecessary word, and handed it to the young lady behind the counter. She quickly read it aloud to be certain of the content:

To W. Cosgrove, Westphal & Cosgrove
Investigations, 1414 West Palmer Street
Albuquerque, New Mexico

Frank accused of killing Phillip Hardesty. Find what you can re victim. Victim aged 32-37, 190 lbs, approx 5 feet ten inches, fair skinned, and reputed to be very handsome. Last known residence Telluride Colorado. Arrived AW approx 6 months ago. Also interested in Adele or Adelaide Belden aged 28-33 murdered yesterday and known associate of Hardesty in Telluride. All info regarding subjects such as previous residences, other possible names, relatives, and associations critical to ongoing investigation. Wire results to local jail or phone AW S. Spencer at Ext 19 or Truesdale at Ext 4. Morgan

With only three days left until the scheduled trial, the odds Cosgrove would uncover any useful information in time were slim, but he couldn't afford to leave any avenue closed. He was counting on Adele's murder to help convince Judge Breen there was another reason to delay the trial. Samuel Spencer wasn't confident the judge would relent unless a closer tie between the murders was established.

Before he left, he called Truesdale and told him he was going to visit his father's memorial before going on to the lawyer's office. He felt guilty he hadn't taken time before now. He also needed time to think and the memorial away from the turbulence of the strike might be a quiet place to spend some time.

Morgan turned down Monroe and headed to where it crossed Jefferson. A few minutes later, he stood in front of a large rock flanked by two metal benches situated in a small park. It had been more than three decades since he had been here. He was surprised to see it was well cared for. The only debris was a cluster of withered flowers near the base of the rock. The last and only time he had been here, the memorial was no more than a cleared lot with the large boulder in the center; the plaque had not been finished for the dedication. He mainly remembered during the ceremony his mother had not cried as the other wives had. A bronze plaque was now fastened to the side of the rock below a bas relief of a miner holding a pick. Underneath were the words:

In Memory of the men who lost their lives in the
Emperor Mine, August 11, 1887.

Below the figure and listed in alphabetical order with each man's job identified were the names of the thirteen men who had been killed. The name Mason Westphal was last. He noticed next to the sixth name down was the word 'Owner.' He had no recollection of a Robert McClendon, nor had he known he was among those who perished in the disaster.

He sat down on one of the benches and removed his hat to mop his brow. The late afternoon sun was hot enough for him to miss the cooler temperatures in Albuquerque. A half hour later he felt the bench shake as if caused by underground blasting and decided it must have been a mild earthquake since the mines were always closed on Saturday afternoon. His attention was distracted by the chugging of an automobile engine growing louder.

Morgan looked up the street and saw Victor LaTrobe's black touring car approaching. He was more curious than surprised when the sleek machine pulled to a stop at the curb. Stevens leaped out and opened the door to allow Olivia LaTrobe to exit. She was carrying a spray of flowers. That she was not surprised to see him made it clear her visit to the monument was no coincidence.

Morgan stood up and greeted her. "Good afternoon, Mrs. LaTrobe, I see you found me."

"How do you know I was looking for you?"

"Adobe Wells is small but big enough that it seems a little too coincidental for us to meet accidentally," indicating the flowers, "I think you've been here before."

"You're very observant, and correct on both points. Marshal Truesdale told me where you might be," She added, taking seat on the opposite bench. "I thought I recognized your name yesterday when you introduced yourself. It wasn't until after we parted when I realized where I'd seen it. Was he your father?" she asked, pointing to the plaque.

"Yes, he was. We didn't get a chance to know one another very well. And you?" Morgan raised a quizzical eyebrow. "What brings you here?"

She nodded toward the plaque. "Robert McClendon was my maternal grandfather. Of course, I never met him. My mother often talked of him with great fondness. She told me what happened to him. When I came to Adobe Wells, I made a point to find the monument. Since my mother is no longer alive, I come occasionally and bring flowers for her. Does that seem a pointless and foolish thing to do?"

"Not at all. It seems a good thing to do."

"Yes, a good thing," she mused softly almost as if she had been talking to herself and not to him. "I wonder sometimes if he had simply been one of the miners instead of the owner how different my life might have been." Her expression was bitter as she continued, "Certainly less privileged and

179

without Victor. That alone would have been worth a life of poverty. I suppose you're surprised to hear me say that?"

"Not entirely. It occurred to me yesterday your marriage might have started out happy, but it doesn't seem that way now."

"Is it so obvious?"

"Yes. In my business, I study people. Most people are not good actors. It isn't their words that give them away, it's their faces."

"What do my face and words tell you about me?"

Morgan thought about it for a moment, wondering why she asked and whether he should answer. She must have a reason, and if he avoided answering, he would never know why she wanted to see him.

"Mrs. LaTrobe, you're a puzzle to me. You are one of the most beautiful women I've met, or possibly ever seen. On the surface, you seem to have everything a woman could possibly want, wealth, a successful husband, the envy of other women, and the admiration of any man who sees you. In spite of all that, you seem to be an extremely unhappy woman."

"Apparently, I'm more transparent than I realized. Would you care to venture a guess why?"

"I think it would be better if I did not. I'd like to know why you wanted to see me."

She ignored the question and looked at him intently before speaking. "You said men find me attractive. Believe me when I say that is more a curse then a blessing. I'm not naïve, and I'm not blind when men stare at me. It may surprise you to know I neither encourage nor welcome such attention."

"I really don't know you well enough to have an opinion one way or another. Mrs. LaTrobe, I fail to see why you're telling me this or what it has to do with my investigation."

"Regrettably, it has everything to do with it. You may recall I told you yesterday Mr. Hardesty and Mr. Shaw did some work on our home in Telluride. After we came here, Mr. Hardesty continued to do so. Mr. Westphal, my husband is insanely jealous of any man who looks at me. I have reason to believe Victor thought Mr. Hardesty and I were having an affair. Of course, we were not although it became obvious that is what Mr. Hardesty wanted. As soon as he made his intentions known, I told him his services would no longer be required. Soon after that, Victor and I quarreled. He accused me of having an affair, and I made the mistake of allowing him to believe it. When he asked if it was Mr. Hardesty, I denied it. Phillip Hardesty was an extraordinarily handsome man. If I had ever been inclined to infidelity, it would have been easy to give way with a man who was as physically attractive as he was."

"Did your husband believe you?"

I'm afraid Victor did not believe me, and the quarrel escalated until I finally lost my temper. Then I did something unforgivable. I taunted him by asking him why he should care at all when there was so little left between us. This only convinced him more than ever his suspicions were justified. After I heard your brother had been arrested for murder, I suspected my husband had something to do with it. I did not know your brother well, but it was difficult for me to believe he would do anything like that unless Victor had somehow persuaded him to do it. Victor is a ruthless, unforgiving man. He also has the wealth and position to be very persuasive."

"Why didn't you tell me this yesterday?"

"I should have. Let's just say I had time to think over our conversation."

"What you've told me hardly convicts your husband of the crime, although it suggests a motive for Hardesty's murder."

"I quite understand enough about legal matters to agree with you. I only thought by telling you this it might give you an insight you might not otherwise have discovered had I remained silent."

181

"If you dislike your husband so much, Mrs. LaTrobe, why don't you simply divorce him?"

"I believe the word 'dislike' may understate my feelings for Victor, and while a divorce might seem an easy solution, it would be entirely too easy. It's a complicated problem that can't be solved by a divorce even if divorce was possible. I am the product of a family with its share of scandals and improprieties. Unfortunately, divorce is not among them." Her bitterness once again reflected in both her face and what she said next. "It's unthinkable that a Thurlowe would accept the social consequences of a divorce."

She remained silent for a time looking thoughtfully at the monument, and Morgan took the opportunity of studying the strange woman. He had the impression there was something else on her mind and perhaps the real reason for seeing him rather than what she had said about her husband. She surprised him by asking, "Have you yet reached any conclusions about the prostitute's death?"

"I'm afraid not; however, I expect in time we will."

Without another word, she stood up and placed the flowers on top of the monument. After bending down to retrieve the withered bouquet on the ground, she nodded to Morgan and walked toward the touring car where Stevens was waiting with the door open. She did not look back when the car drove off.

Morgan watched the automobile until it disappeared out of sight. He was still speculating why Olivia LaTrobe had gone out of her way to tell him the things she had when a loud explosion rattled windows and roof tiles in the nearby buildings.

Chapter Seventeen

The explosion reverberated like rolling thunder in the surrounding canyons. Before the echoes of the first explosion faded away, a second explosion followed soon after. Moments later, there was a third explosion. The piercing and prolonged shriek of a steam whistle needlessly signaled a mine disaster. Twenty minutes later, the deafening roar of a fourth explosion boomed at the other end of town.

The sharp crack and deafening volume of the explosions reminded Morgan of bursting artillery shells he experienced in Cuba. The absence of ground tremors and the sharpness of the explosions indicated surface rather than underground detonations. He remembered the tremor he had felt a half hour before and wondered if the surface explosions had been preceded by one underground. The direction of the smoke columns made him think the TJ&M mines were the sources of the explosions. A third smoke column in the opposite direction appeared to be in the vicinity of the Territorial Hotel and the equipment yards. He remembered Stockwell's claim the union wouldn't resort to sabotage to further their objectives, and it occurred to him the union representative may have lied. In any case the union would get the blame.

Morgan set off at a half-trot toward the lawyer's office. By the time he got there, he heard the clanging of bells, and a fire engine went racing past him heading in the direction of the first explosions. He saw Miss Ottmier, one hand pressed to her cheek, standing on the sidewalk talking to several bystanders. They were looking up at the dark smoke drifting across the sky. She saw him coming toward her and asked, "Mr. Westphal, what's happened?"

"I don't know, but I can make a guess the peaceful stage of the strike is over. One explosion could be an accident, three tells me it's something else."

"Oh, I do hope you're wrong. I pray it doesn't turn out the way the last strike did. It was simply awful!"

Not caring to engage in a lengthy conversation over past events, he asked, "Is Mr. Spencer in?"

Just as he spoke, Spencer appeared in the doorway and after peering in the directions of the explosions, shook his head, and motioned Morgan inside. The lawyer dropped heavily into a chair in the reception area. He didn't waste any time telling Morgan that Judge Breen had changed his mind and granted a week's extension for Frank's trial date.

"What made him change his mind?" Morgan asked.

"I don't really know. His clerk called me an hour ago to tell me the judge had reconsidered the petition and set a new trial date. It wouldn't surprise me if the prosecuting attorney had something to do with it. I imagine the court docket has become rather crowded now with the miners on strike. I should imagine if I'm right and the union is responsible for those explosions, there might be another postponement."

"What's the chance of getting Frank out on bail?"

The lawyer shook his head. "Any other charge but murder I might be able to convince the judge to grant it. I wonder even if he did whether it would be a good idea. For your brother's safety, he's better off where he is. The judge's clerk told me there's quite a mob out front of the courthouse and jail protesting the arrests made so far. Have you learned anything else that might help Frank?"

Morgan briefly summarized what had happened to Adele Belden and his conversation with Elias Stockwell. He avoided any mention of being sworn in as a deputy for fear the lawyer would withdraw because of a perceived conflict of interest.

"Apart from being convinced Adele's murder is somehow tied to Hardesty, I can't prove it or come up with a theory why they are. Stockwell told me, the prostitute was present during the meetings he had with Hardesty. I've asked my partner to check on her and Hardesty's background. Now the trial date is delayed, there's more time to come up with something useful. If I can find Willard Merrick it could be the breakthrough I need. On the surface, the strongest motive for Hardesty's murder is his connection with the WFM."

"Maybe someone in TJ&M found out Hardesty was working for the union and killed him for it," the lawyer proposed.

Morgan's doubt was evident. "It's possible, however, I'm beginning to believe what happened to Hardesty may not have been planned, particularly if no one in TJ&M ever knew Hardesty was working for the union. I believe they didn't or else they could have killed him somewhere other than inside one of the TJ&M mines. It would have been just as easy and safer to shove a knife in him in a dark alley on a Saturday night. There's another thing that bothers me—the probable murder weapon. Even if you were planning to kill someone in a mine, wouldn't it be logical to simply hit him over the head? According to Chambliss, the wound in the back may have come before the head wound. I also can't figure why someone would use a candle-pick for the murder weapon?"

"It would seem a perfect weapon to use if the assailant wanted to make the murder look like an accident," Spencer said. "Apparently at first everyone thought the death was accidental. You said Hardesty's face had been crushed by a sizable object. Why go to that much trouble to try and conceal his identity?"

"Perhaps the killer wasn't trying to conceal his identity at all and was just taking extra care to make the death look accidental."

"Well, you've given me a plausible explanation of what may have happened without answering the important questions who it was and why he did it."

"I might have an answer to both. There was only one man on that shift who has a reason and the capability to come and go when and where he wants because it's his job to inspect and supervise. Tate Cardwell, the shift boss, could be the man I'm after."

"What makes you think it's him?"

"Partly for the reason I just gave and because he would have known the significant consequences of what Hardesty was doing if he caught him drilling into the east face. Cardwell denied knowing anything about any drill holes when I told him what I'd found. Frank told me later he'd worked that drift and drilled at least one hole to check out a seep. He said he told Cardwell about it."

"That hardly explains why he killed Hardesty instead of just firing him. Let's not forget, we don't know why, nor can we prove it was Hardesty who drilled the holes. Maybe Cardwell drilled the holes after he killed Hardesty."

Morgan had to admit everything the lawyer said was possible if not factually correct. Following a moment of reflection, Morgan asked, "Do you know Olivia LaTrobe?"

"Not really. I've talked to her a few times at charity events for the hospital. I knew her father better when I lived in Virginia. Why do you ask?"

Morgan told him about meeting her the day before and their strange encounter an hour ago. "I wonder why she dislikes her husband so much to suggest he might have been responsible for his murder. It isn't because I think LaTrobe is incapable of hiring someone to do it; rather, my impression of Olivia LaTrobe is she isn't the type to have an affair with a common miner."

"If she did, it wouldn't be the first time a married woman of her social class had an affair with someone well below her station."

"I agree, although my point isn't about class differences. She strikes me as someone who is emotionally dead. As beautiful as she is, she has the warmth of a marble statue. I don't doubt for a minute Hardesty may have made advances. He had opportunities. I just find it difficult to believe she would encourage him."

"If she dislikes her husband as much as you seem to think, wouldn't it be just as logical for her to have an affair if only to make her husband jealous?"

"I suppose it's a possibility," Morgan agreed. "You said you knew her father in Virginia. What can you tell me about her?"

"She's the only daughter of a wealthy widower by the name of Henry Lancaster Thurlowe. The Thurlowe name is old Virginia and 'old money'; however, Henry Thurlowe didn't rely on the family inheritance. He had the Midas touch, and his considerable investments were always profitable. I did some legal work for him once and swore afterward I'd never do it again. I've never met a more unpleasant and domineering man before or since. I understand LaTrobe also came from a socially prominent family although the financial resources of the LaTrobes were far more modest in comparison to the Thurlowe fortune. The marriage of Olivia Thurlowe and Victor LaTrobe in Richmond was the social event of the year. A few years later a child was born. I understand the boy was sickly and died less than a year later. Soon after the baby died, Victor and his wife went to Colorado where he took a position with Thurlowe, Jansen & McCormick better known as TJ&M. From all I've heard, Victor LaTrobe has done well enough as superintendent of the TJ&M mines. It does seem strange Thurlowe didn't find his son-in-law a position closer to Richmond. Rumor has it she's estranged from her father, and that may have something to do with it."

"Perhaps the child's death may be the reason for the hatred she evidently has for her husband," Morgan said.

"I wouldn't know about that, but if it is, I can't see whatever problems there are between them have anything, to do with your brother's case."

"You're probably right. It's also possible she had a reason to see me that had nothing to do with helping me or Frank."

The phone rang. After a brief conversation, Miss Ottmier hung up and announced, "Mr. Westphal, Marshal Truesdale would like you to meet him at the Pearl Mine."

The Pearl and Dorothy Mines situated a hundred yards apart looked very much alike in the way the head frames lay in smoldering heaps of blackened timbers and twisted metal. Some of the burning timbers from the collapsed head frame of the Pearl had crashed through the roof of the small adobe building housing the explosives. Now there was nothing but a deep crater. The Emily head frame was badly damaged and leaning precariously.

Morgan saw the marshal talking to Victor LaTrobe. The two men were surrounded by a dozen men he assumed were probably TJ&M supervisors and shift bosses. Tate Cardwell was among them. Face livid, LaTrobe was jabbing his finger in the marshal's chest.

"You know goddamned well it was Stockwell who's responsible for this," Morgan heard LaTrobe say angrily. "I want him and every goddamned man who has the guts to admit to being a union member arrested, or else I'll call the governor and have the National Guard in here to do what you won't."

"I can understand how you feel, Mr. LaTrobe, but—"

"You two-bit peckerwood, you have no goddamn idea how I feel. The last of your kind faded away twenty years ago. You've got about as much chance of finding out who did this as I have of getting these mines back in operation tomorrow. Now why don't—"

To Morgan's delight, it was Truesdale who cut LaTrobe off. "LaTrobe, you're a jackass, and I think I've heard about all I want from you. For your information, the governor just happens to be a friend of mine and before he sends the guard in here, he's gonna call me first. He's gonna ask me, 'Dan, why in hell do you want the guard in Adobe Wells?' Then I'm gonna tell him it ain't my idea. In fact, I'm gonna say, 'Paul, that would be about the stupidest thing you could do, and it'll only make things a lot worse than they already are'. I might even add, 'I got a turd here by the name of LaTrobe who is interfering with my investigation.' Now, Mr. Latrobe, I'm askin' you about as polite as I can to piss-off and leave these premises."

LaTrobe, face drained of all color, sputtered in a hoarse whisper, "The mayor will have your badge for this. You can't order me off my own property. This time tomorrow you'll be nothing but yesterday's joke."

"Well, it's like this, Mr. LaTrobe, what you say could be right. In the meantime, I'm still marshal and you ain't, and right now you and your yammerin' are gettin' in my way and on my nerves." Truesdale rested his hand on the butt of his revolver and added, "Therefore, I would hate to have to arrest you in order to proceed with my investigation. Do you hear what I'm sayin'?"

Without another word, LaTrobe growled to the other men standing nervously and uncertain, "Come with me. I'm going to see the mayor."

"No, Mr. LaTrobe, these men will remain here. Unlike you, I think they may be able to help." Without a backward glance, LaTrobe stalked off.

"That might not have been the best way to handle LaTrobe," Morgan said. "What if he goes to the mayor?"

Amused, Truesdale laughed. "It won't do him no good. Thomas Cunningham will listen all polite, concerned, and sympathetic until LaTrobe is done. He'll thank him for his comments and tell him he's gonna give the matter careful consideration. Cunningham ain't never made a decision in his life he couldn't find a dozen ways to avoid makin'. Don't you fret none, this time tomorrow I'll still be marshal. Now, gentlemen, anyone here got some idea how someone in broad daylight can come up here in plain sight and do all this?"

After a moment of silence and exchanging blank looks, it became obvious no one was willing or able to voice an opinion. Morgan was the first to speak.

"It's possible whoever did this was never in plain sight or, at most, only here long enough to set and light the fuses."

"What do you mean?" Truesdale said.

"While most of the head frames are as visible from the town as the tops of the tailing slides, where we're standing now isn't visible to anyone in town below. Also, notice how the ground slopes down slightly from here before it starts to go uphill to the ridge above? Someone could have come over from the direction of the Emily and after finishing here went on over to the Dorothy. From the Dorothy, he would have had plenty of time to continue west where the third explosion occurred."

"There were five explosions," Cardwell said. "The first was in the Emily below ground and almost likely in the drift you visited; three were on the surface and as you can see damaged or destroyed the head frames; the fifth destroyed the TJ&M storage yard in town. The Emily's bottom tunnel is completely flooded, and the water is already starting to flood the one above."

Morgan thought back to the tremor he had felt sitting on the park bench and now realized what had caused it.

Cardwell continued, "There may be another way different than what Mr. Westphal described. It's possible he, or they, went down into the Emily and planted the charges on the east side of Tunnel 3. If they used a candle fuse, there would be plenty of time to reach the Pearl and Dorothy underground to do the same. Or, as Mr. Westphal suggested, they may have stayed on top and used the slope to hide their movements."

Morgan thought Cardwell's contribution was both helpful and plausible. He may have to reconsider his opinion of the blunt-speaking shift boss.

"The mines are connected?" Truesdale said in surprise.

"They are," a small man wearing suspenders and a brown derby responded. "The name's Dunwell. I'm the foreman of the Dorothy. What Cardwell says is true. In fact, most of the mines around here connect; some even share the same head frame. It could have happened the way Cardwell described."

"What about the watchman?" Morgan asked and was shocked at the reply.

Dunwell shook his head. "On Saturday, he don't come on until dark, and then he leaves at sunup. One of LaTrobe's cost-cutting ideas," he added. "I expect it's the same with the Emily and here at the Pearl." The disgusted nods from some of the other men confirmed the statement.

"Whichever way he or they gained access he, the result indicates experience with explosives." Morgan said. "Mr. Cardwell, in your opinion do you think the water flooding the Emily came from the east side?"

"I don't doubt it for a second."

"Was there any additional drilling done on the east wall since I went there?"

"Not likely. I closed down that drift after you told me about the drill holes you found. I hated to do it considering the wide vein there, but it wasn't safe."

"Was the drift sealed?"

"No, LaTrobe wouldn't approve it, instead he wanted to reinforce the east wall with concrete and keep on drilling. I told him he'd have to get himself a new shift boss for Tunnel 3 if he was gonna fiddle around in there."

"Who else besides you, Shaw, and Hardesty knew about the water problem in that drift?"

"Merrick probably knew since he worked in that drift," Cardwell replied.

"And Merrick hasn't been seen or heard of since the night Hardesty was killed," Morgan said. "Anyone have an idea why Merrick would do something like this?" Morgan looked around and saw only shaking heads. "Mr. Dunwell, were you

191

employed with TJ&M in Telluride before coming to Adobe Wells?"

"I was."

"Were there any incidents of sabotage against TJ&M holdings in Colorado?"

"Now that you mention it, there were. It was nothing like this," gesturing to the blackened wreckage. "It was more like little things, cables cut, pulleys getting jammed, blasting caps placed in switch panels."

"Did any of the other mines besides TJ&M report similar incidents?"

"Not that I know of, but then like here in Adobe Wells, TJ&M was the largest non-union syndicate in Telluride, and we figured it was union doings. At least, that's what LaTrobe thought then and now here. I think he's probably right."

"Possibly, but I don't believe the union is behind this. Stockwell, the senior union representative for the union here in Adobe Wells, doesn't want any trouble like this. He knows the union will be blamed, and it would give the mine owners the excuse to bring in the National Guard and have another incident like what happened in Ludlow. Some of you may remember what happened around Cripple Creek Colorado about twelve years ago when the mine owners just about broke the union. If you've forgotten, I can assure you Stockwell hasn't. The last thing Stockwell wants is for anything like this to happen and risk exactly what LaTrobe threatened to do. I think since the other non-union mines haven't been affected, at least so far, it could be someone with a grudge against TJ&M." Morgan looked at Cardwell, "Did Merrick work in Telluride, or did he sign on here?"

"He was already here when I got here. We hired him away from Sandusky."

"Did you ever have any reason to suspect Merrick was a union member?"

"If I'd thought that, he wouldn't been around longer than the time it took to collect his wages."

"Do you know of any reason why he might have a grudge against TJ&M?" Cardwell shook his head. "How about any other drillers on your shift dissatisfied with TJ&M?"

Cardwell bristled, "Why're you singling out my particular shift? It could've been someone from another shift."

"Whoever set that charge in the Emily was familiar with the conditions on the east side of Tunnel 3 and knew exactly where it would cause the most damage. He also had to be experienced in handling explosives. Hardesty is dead, Shaw has been locked up for five days, and Willard Merrick is missing. If we can find Merrick and establish he had nothing to do with it, then every other driller or man on your shift who knows anything about explosives is open to suspicion."

"I suppose that includes me," Cardwell responded, his voice flat, eyes hard as flint.

"I suppose it does at that, Mr. Cardwell. Would you care to comment?"

"Are you accusing me?"

Morgan held up a restraining hand, "Easy, Mr. Cardwell. No one is accusing you of anything, at least not yet, and no one will if you can account for your movements today."

Cardwell took a step toward Morgan, his hands balled into fists. Truesdale quickly stepped in front of the shift boss and ordered, "Hold it right there, Tate, no need to get riled. Best just answer the question, and then we can move along here and see if maybe we can find out who really done this."

The shift boss slowly relaxed and with effort controlled his temper. "All right, but one way or the other Westphal I'm gonna look you up when this business is cleared up."

Mr. Cardwell, "Do you know of any driller or worker on your shift that might have something against TJ&M?" Morgan continued

"If I did, he wouldn't be working for me."

"What about anyone you fired or the company let go recently that has a reason to have hard feelings for TJ&M?"

Cardwell shook his head.

"How about in Telluride?" Again, Cardwell shook his head. What about anyone in the Pearl or Dorothy?" Morgan asked the other two foremen and received similar responses.

An hour later, Truesdale excused the foremen and shift bosses including Cardwell to attend to the damaged mines. Even to Morgan's untrained eye, it was obvious, TJ&M was going to be out of business for some time to come.

Chapter Eighteen

The one night Mrs. Johansen did not serve an evening meal was Saturday night, leaving few options other than the Fremont Hotel. The hotel's dining room was the only place in town to boast of linen tablecloths and napkins and the only respectable alternative to the private clubs or shabby restaurants frequented by the miners.

Morgan finished attaching the collar to his best shirt and was in the act of pulling on his coat when he hesitated. Saturday night in a typical mining town was usually a lively affair. The tensions caused by the strike might very well add a dimension beyond the usual revelry caused by hardworking miners celebrating a night off with rye whiskey and beer. He tossed the suit coat on the bed, pulled open the bottom drawer of the bureau, and withdrew the Colt. Automatically, he checked the cylinder before thrusting it back into the shoulder holster. He fastened the shoulder holster on, donned his coat, and left the room.

As he reached the down stairs hallway, he heard Cady Flynn call his name.

"Morgan, by any chance are you going into town?"

"As a matter of fact, I am. I'm going down to the hotel for dinner."

"In that case, would you mind terribly if I came with you? I tried to call a cab, but I can't seem to get anyone to answer. I suppose it's because of the strike."

"I'm afraid you're right, and I would be delighted to walk with you on one condition, that you be my guest."

"That's very kind of you, but I simply can't allow you to do that. It's enough you're willing to escort me."

"I'm sorry but the escort service is conditional and must include dinner. My terms are non-negotiable."

"Morgan, I believe you're taking advantage of me. All right I accept since it seems I have no other choice."

When she joined him, he silently took in the dark burgundy dress she was wearing and matching black-beaded handbag hanging on her arm. Cinched tightly at the waist, the ankle-length dress called attention to a figure any woman would have envied. The garment was alluring and yet at the same time chastely feminine. In style, it was a dress Olivia LaTrobe might have worn. There the comparison ended, for in contrast to the superintendent's wife, Cady Flynn was warm and vibrant.

"Well, what do you think?" she said, pirouetting to give him a full view. He caught a trace of her perfume and liked it. In his opinion, most perfume was too strong to suit him. The delicate scent she was wearing was subtle and pleasing.

"I think you'll light up Adobe Wells in a way it has never been before," he replied in admiration. He would have liked to say more but did not. He was unaccustomed to voicing sentiments and even more so when it came to praising a woman. He was pleased with himself for saying what he did. She rewarded him with a smile that made him feel fortunate for the chance encounter. Cady took his arm and they went downstairs.

As they passed by the parlor, Mr. Dahlgliesh glanced up from the newspaper he was reading. His face registered a range of emotions starting with surprise, open admiration, and finally, visible disappointment as his eyes followed Cady all the way to the door.

On the porch, they encountered Hanson Markham coming up the steps. He lifted his hat automatically to acknowledge Cady then gave no further notice of her as he focused his attention on Morgan. "Mr. Westphal, I trust you are making satisfactory progress in your investigation."

"I think well enough at this point. I'm optimistic there is sufficient evidence already to absolve my brother even if we're unable to identify the murderer." He hoped he sounded more confident than he was.

"I'm delighted to hear you say as much. I find the entire matter fascinating. I feel as if I'm a bystander to something I may eventually read about in the newspapers. I don't suppose you're at liberty to give some hint who you think may have done it." The comment was made with a studied casualness that aroused Morgan's suspicions. He knew there was more than idle curiosity behind the question.

"I'm really not at liberty to say more than I already have."

"I understand, and I apologize for even asking. Of course, you're entirely correct in not saying more. Well, I won't detain you since it's apparent you and Miss Flynn are on your way somewhere. Do be careful. There's more unrest in town tonight than usual, particularly on Main Street. Since taxi service seems to be unavailable, you might consider taking a longer but safer way to get to the hotel."

"Thank you, Mr. Markham, and good evening," Morgan replied.

Markham's suggestion confirmed his decision to carry the pistol, but it was also giving him second thoughts over the wisdom of escorting Cady Flynn into town on a Saturday night during a labor strike. His better judgment told him to turn around and go back to the boarding house. That she had gone to such pains to prepare for the outing prevented him from doing so.

The sun was well down by the time they reached the center of town and saw men standing on each corner under the street lamps. While most were talking quietly, a few of the strikers were clearly restless and spoiling for trouble, rudely approaching pedestrians walking by trying to enlist their support. They heard loud voices shouting obscenities and trading insults, and the sound of a bottle breaking.

"Perhaps we should turn back." Cady said.

"We will if it gets any worse."

Fortunately, the remaining few blocks to the hotel proved uneventful and even pleasant as the two talked comfortably along the way.

Cady drew admiring stares as they entered the lobby and made their way toward the dining room. Morgan saw Elias Stockwell standing near the front desk facing the front door, an unlit cigar in his mouth and a frown on his face. The union representative's attention was on a lean, swarthy-faced man who punctuated whatever he was saying with vigorous hand gestures. To Morgan's chagrin, he saw Stockwell break off the conversation and come toward them.

"Miss Flynn, you are an object of perfection," Stockwell said in open admiration. "If I were twenty years younger, I'd envy Mr. Westphal even more than I do now." Morgan never would have expected the rough-mannered man was capable of such eloquence.

"Why, thank you, Mr. Stockwell," she responded with a smile, visibly pleased and added, "What a nice thing to say,"

Stockwell turned to Morgan and said with a note of urgency in his voice, "I'm sorry to intrude, Mr. Westphal, but it's important we talk in private."

"Perhaps we could meet in the morning at the boarding house." Morgan responded. "This isn't the best time."

"I understand, and I don't want to leave out the lady. But what I have to tell you is something I don't want to say in a public place. I have a room upstairs, and if you would come with me, we can talk in private."

Morgan concealed his irritation and looked at Cady. "Morgan, go with Mr. Stockwell, and I'll wait in the dining room." The protest from both men was immediate, and a moment later, all three were standing in the elevator waiting for the operator to take them to the third floor.

The elevator drew to a halting stop as the operator pushed back the cage door. Cady and Morgan followed Stockwell to a room halfway down the corridor.

Stockwell wasted no time. "Mr. Westphal, the union had nothin' to do with what happened today."

"I agree with you, Mr. Stockwell. I never really thought it did, or else we would have been talking before now."

The union representative's surprise was evident. "I'm glad to hear that. I was sure someone would try to pin it on me and the union."

"My comment doesn't necessarily apply to the union as a whole. It's still conceivable you have union members involved, men who are on the TJ&M payroll and unwilling to wait any longer for a more measured approach to resolving their pay and safety concerns. It's no secret Victor LaTrobe will resist any accommodation to union demands or agree to unionize."

Grim-faced, Stockwell replied sharply, "It also gives LaTrobe a chance to use the same kind of underhanded tactics the TJ&M used to bust the union at Cripple Creek twelve years ago including Ludlow, Colorado last April when men, women and children were massacred!"

The mention of Ludlow evoked a quick reaction from Morgan. "I didn't realize TJ&M was working in Ludlow?"

"Hell, TJ&M was behind the whole thing. TJ&M brought in people posing as union members to stir up trouble and put the blame on the union. When things got bad enough, it was Victor Latrobe who called in the National Guard. I'm not saying the union didn't cause some of the trouble, but things went from bad to worse when the soldiers showed up. Most of them Sunday soldiers were non-union and looking for ways to help the mine owners kick the union out of Colorado. Ludlow was even worse than what happened at Cripple Creek."

Morgan considered Stockwell's comments. Although he didn't believe LaTrobe had engineered the destruction, he had been quick to threaten calling in the National Guard earlier that day. There was the equal possibility someone with a grudge against TJ&M had done it. He made a mental note to find out more of what had happened in Ludlow.

"I'll be certain to inform Marshal Truesdale of your concerns. You must realize my main interest is to determine who killed Phillip Hardesty to exonerate my brother."

"I understand, and I've got information that may be useful to you and your brother. It may also have something to do with what happened today."

"I'm listening, Mr. Stockwell."

"One of my union members working in the Imperial next to the Emily heard some talk about how the lowest levels of the Emily can be flooded out by blowing out part of the west wall of the Imperial."

"But that would flood the Imperial as well."

"Not necessarily. The Imperial's lowest tunnel is a few hundred feet above the lowest tunnel in the Emily. Any water coming into the Imperial will flow down the ventilation shaft connecting the surface to the Emily's lowest level; that shaft crosses over into the Imperial claim."

"Why can't LaTrobe pump out the water as he's been doing?"

"He can, but it means closing down Tunnel 3 and possibly even the level above if the water can't be pumped out fast enough. Even if LaTrobe is able to pump the water out, he may still have problems."

"What do you mean?"

"The rock around here is unstable enough without adding the effects of water to make it worse than it already is. Take a closer look around Adobe Wells tomorrow in the daylight, particularly on the south side of the canyon and east of the Imperial. You might notice a couple of head frames leaning north. There's one shaft belonging to Sandusky where the lifts can't even operate anymore. Sandusky is taking the ore out of that mine through the Imperial. It's only a matter of time before Sandusky will have to close it down. Already the union is taking the position it ain't safe to go into some of the mines, especially on the east side.

Morgan realized the geological condition Stockwell was describing was probably the cause of the mine collapse that killed his father.

Stockwell continued. "The main point is TJ&M can't afford to lose a few months of production.

"What would Sandusky gain by sabotaging TJ&M?" "They couldn't possibly outspend and outwait TJ&M before they'd go under."

"Maybe Sandusky is financially better off than TJ&M," Cady said.

"That's hard to believe," Morgan said.

"Perhaps not," she responded, lips pursed in thought. "I had lunch with one of the secretaries working for Mr. Warren—he was the one who escorted you in to see Mr. LaTrobe. He said TJ&M's balance sheet is a little on the thin side. The buy-out of the railroad to Mesquite Flats may have put the company dangerously close to receivership. If so, Mr. Stockwell may be right concerning TJ&M's shaky financial condition."

"Until now, I've been concentrating on what happened as internal to TJ&M. What's the chance Sandusky is involved? What if Hardesty was working for Sandusky?"

"It's possible," Stockwell replied. "If Hardesty had been trying to sabotage the Emily, LaTrobe still doesn't know it, or he would have been the first to raise the point and use it against his competitor."

Morgan recalled Cardwell mentioning Willard Merrick had once worked for Sandusky. If true, finding Merrick was becoming even more critical. It occurred to him Merrick may not be alive. With so many abandoned mine shafts around, it would be easy to dispose of a body.

He turned to Stockwell. "I don't suppose your source working in the Imperial might know more?"

"I think he told me everything he knew."

"Could he identify the men talking?"

"One of 'em was Dandridge, foreman of the Emily. The other was an engineer whose name he doesn't know; he recognized him because of the funny way he talks, like one of them Britishers, you know like Markham."

Morgan thought it was a lead worth following in spite of his difficulty in believing Markham would be involved in anything underhanded.

"Thanks for the information. I'll make a point of looking into it." Morgan took Cady's arm and started to head for the door, thinking Stockwell had finished. Stockwell held up a restraining hand.

"Wait, there's another reason I wanted to talk to you. I heard a man with a few drinks under his belt talking in one of the saloons tonight about how he was going to teach you a lesson. At first, I didn't know it was you he was talking about until he mentioned how he was going to arrange to pull the trapdoor at your brother's hanging. I knew then it was you he was talkin' about."

"Do you know his name?"

"No, but I know what he does. He's a deputy marshal and works for Truesdale."

"That would be Kincy Blaylock. In the short time I've been in Adobe Wells, Blaylock and I have managed to avoid friendship. I suspect Blaylock is more talk than action, but I appreciate the warning all the same."

Stockwell shook his head dubiously. "I'd be careful if I were you. He's a mean bastard and strong. You wouldn't think so on account of the spectacles he wears. He hit a man as big as him for bumpin' his arm while he was taking a drink; he decked him then kicked the hell out of him. A couple of fellas drinkin' with him just stood there and laughed."

"I'll talk to Blaylock tomorrow. Maybe we can settle our differences and prevent something we'll both regret."

Morgan paused and looked closely at Stockwell. "I'm a little surprised you've gone out of your way to tell me all this."

"I heard about what you told them TJ&M people over at the Dorothy this afternoon, about how you were pretty sure the union wasn't behind the trouble. I figured I owed you for sayin' it. I also wanted to apologize for what I said the other night. I was wrong. Maybe you and I got more in common right now than not. The way I figure it, I got just as much interest as you do, maybe more, in finding out what's going on with LaTrobe's mines even if our reasons might be different. If I hear anything else, I'll let you know."

After thanking Stockwell again, Morgan took Cady down downstairs to the dining room. However well-intentioned the union representative's impromptu comments were, they had cast a shadow on what otherwise had promised to be a pleasant evening.

Chapter Nineteen

Early the next morning Morgan went downstairs for a cup of coffee, and saw Hanson Markham carrying a suitcase in each hand toward the front door.

"You're leaving?" Morgan asked.

"I'm afraid so, Mr. Westphal. I'm glad to see you again. I was hoping for the chance to say goodbye before I left. I'd like to apologize again for what must have seemed a rather clumsy attempt to learn how you were coming along on your investigation. I believe I owe you an explanation."

"I took no offense, although I did wonder about it. Is this a sudden decision to leave Adobe Wells?"

"Yes and no. I've been considering it for the past week or so."

"What made you decide?"

"You might say what happened yesterday to the Emily and the other TJ&M mines firmed up my decision. Louis Sandusky is a tough, shrewd man whose business practices I believe border on being unprincipled. That is part of my decision for not renewing my contract with SMC. The main reason is that I believe Louis Sandusky may have been planning to ruin TJ&M by using methods I cannot condone.

"I'm afraid I don't follow."

"As you may already know, I was under contract to Sandusky. I'm an engineer specializing in hydrology. I met him almost a year ago in England while he was touring a coal mine where I was employed. Mr. Sandusky visited the mine to see how we were coping with water problems not unlike those found in some of the mines here in Adobe Wells. He convinced me to come here to advise him concerning the water problem and what could be done about it. I've fulfilled the terms of my contract and feel it's time to leave and go back to England. Before I left I wanted to give you information that might assist you in your investigation. I didn't want to find out some day your brother was executed and my silence may have been partly to blame."

"I appreciate anything you can do to help."

"I'll begin by telling you something about the geology of the area to explain the flooding in the Emily Mine. First I have to give you a non-technical understanding of the nature of the hydrological problem affecting both the SMC and TJ&M mines. Subsurface water pressure is the cause of flooding in both the Imperial and the Emily. A mile or so to the south and above where the mines are located, there are several springs. The springs are created by subsurface pressure forcing water upward through porous limestone and sandstone between near vertical folds of Precambrian rock. The porous layer between the volcanic folds is inherently unstable and made more so by subsurface blasting in the mines. Since my arrival a few months ago the springs have continued to decrease in size. The reason for the decrease is the pressure below is forcing the water into a horizontal than a vertical direction along a fault line intersecting the Imperial and Emily Mines. The fault extends farther into the east face of the Emily than the Imperial's western face."

"Can the water be redirected in some way?"

"I advised Mr. Sandusky not to attempt it. The financial cost to SMC would be prohibitive with no guarantee of success unless the investment costs and engineering risks are shared with TJ&M. Mr. Sandusky approached Mr. LaTrobe with such a proposal only to be rebuffed. It is my suspicion because of that refusal Mr. Sandusky may have resorted to other and, shall I say, less honorable methods to accomplish his objective."

"Are you saying Sandusky had something to do with the flooding and damage to the Emily?"

"It's entirely possible. You may not know this, but the Emily is accessible through the Imperial by way of two ventilation shafts."

"I am aware of it, and I've seen at least one of them. The water pouring down through it was the cause for the three-day shutdown of the Emily. I'm still confused as to what any of this has to do with the murdered miner. While I understand the possibility of Sandusky trying to sabotage a competitor, I have difficulty believing he would go so far as to have one of LaTrobe's drillers killed as part of his plan to take over TJ&M."

"I learned that a driller by the name of Merrick working for TJ&M had previously been in the employ of Sandusky. It occurred to me this driller might still be employed by Sandusky to exploit the dangerous fault condition along the eastern face of the Emily."

"That is highly speculative, Mr. Markham."

"Indeed it is, and yet Sandusky's words and aggressive business methods are such to prompt me to suggest it."

Morgan thought if what Markham said was true, the motive for Hardesty's death might have something to do with the drill holes in the east face. Something wasn't adding up right. If Merrick was secretly working for Sandusky and drilled the holes, why was Hardesty killed? It seemed highly unlikely Hardesty was also working for Sandusky. On the other hand, perhaps they were, and that was why Frank heard two voices. Based on the angle of Hardesty's wounds, Dr. Chambliss believed two men committed the crime. Either Chambliss was wrong or two other men besides Hardesty came into the drift. Did Tate Cardwell have an accomplice, and if so, was it Merrick? Just as likely it could have been Cardwell alone. He was big enough and equally skillful with both hands to wield the candle pick with one hand and a drill bit in the other. The way Cardwell had used both hammers simultaneously to pound the shoring timber into place made the shift boss a potential suspect. Stockwell said Cardwell was ambitious. Was his ambition incentive enough for him to take any action he believed would advance his standing with LaTrobe? By virtue of his duties, he had a legitimate reason to move about within the mine and to do so quickly using the bicycle-cart.

The Englishman interrupted Morgan's thoughts. "Mr. Westphal, you may be unable to do anything with what I told you, but I feel better for having talked to you."

"Thank you, Mr. Markham. What you've told me is certainly enough for me to talk to Sandusky. Good luck to you and a safe return to England." The faint chugging of the taxi grew louder as it rounded the corner and came toward the boarding house.

"Goodbye, Mr. Westphal. I wish you and your brother a successful outcome."

Chapter Twenty

Behind the TJ&M office building, Morgan looked up and down the alley to see if he was alone. Satisfied a Sunday afternoon and the presence of strikers around town would reduce the probability of being discovered, he began gently working the slender tool back and forth inside the door lock. The lock was a conventional one, and it didn't take long before he was rewarded with a soft click. With a last look around, Morgan quickly opened the door and ducked inside.

Markham had unintentionally given him the notion of searching LaTrobe's office. By suggesting Hardesty's death may have been part of a larger conspiracy to sabotage the Emily, it raised the possibility the driller may have been discovered in the act and was killed for it. If Sandusky was behind sabotaging the TJ&M mines, he didn't expect him to admit it. He also needed to consider the possibility Markham had made the wrong assumption about who was really behind the sabotage. Cady said TJ&M was in financial trouble and facing considerable loss and made worse should the encroachment lawsuit be settled in favor of SMC. Was LaTrobe prepared to go to any lengths to get back at SMC for the legal fight over encroachment? Victor LaTrobe was no less unscrupulous than Sandusky; consequently, he may have devised a plan to cut company losses by damaging the Emily and then suing, SMC for doing it. No more than Sandusky, LaTrobe would deny any knowledge or a role concerning the circumstances of Hardesty's death and the recent damage to the Emily. He needed to learn when TJ&M discovered the problem with the east face and what LaTrobe intended to do about it.

Inside the building, Morgan found he was in a small furnace room dimly illuminated by a small barred window next to the door. At the opposite end of the room a door opened to a stairway to the floor above. After reaching the top of the stairs, he stopped and listened carefully before slowly opening the door. He walked down the corridor in the direction he thought LaTrobe's office might be located. He was oriented after reaching the main reception area where Cady had greeted him. He turned left and walked quickly toward LaTrobe's private office. He was surprised to find the door was ajar.

In marked contrast to his visit a few days before, the office was a shambles. Papers were strewn about, desk drawers were either half open or upended on the floor, and the room had an unpleasant odor that became stronger as he neared the desk. He looked at the wastebasket and floor around it and saw where someone had recently vomited into it with only limited success. Partly obscured under the mess was an empty bottle of laudanum that made him think of Adele Belden. It occurred to him if the mystery man who had been visiting Adele was Victor LaTrobe. Both had been in Telluride at the same time, and LaTrobe was financially well enough off to afford an expensive mistress like her. The fact LaTrobe's wife was so beautiful made such a theory somewhat improbable until he considered how emotionally cold she was. The thought made him all the more convinced his hunch might have some merit. If so, LaTrobe may have been with Adele before she died or even have been the one who killed her.

After a cursory examination of the scattered papers, he concluded he was wasting his time sifting through routine company correspondence and private letters with no obvious connection to Phillip Hardesty. He sat down at the desk and probed through the few drawers that had not been emptied on the floor. There seemed to be nothing of interest. He was about to give up and abandon the effort when he noticed a small leather-bound ledger toward the back of the center drawer with LaTrobe's name embossed in gold on the front.

It proved to be LaTrobe's personal checkbook. Only a few checks had been written during the past year. He was about to put it back when he noticed the entry on the stub for a check written a few days ago. Opposite the date, the amount $100 had been entered and underneath was the name T. Cardwell. The date was the day after Hardesty died.

Morgan stared at the entry and wondered what Cardwell or LaTrobe would have to say if he asked them why the shift boss had been paid out of LaTrobe's personal bank account. The difficulty would be in asking the question without revealing how he knew about it. He replaced the slim leather book and was about to stand up when he noticed a wooden box smashed on the floor next to the desk. It appeared as if someone had intentionally crushed it. Curious he picked up the broken lid and saw a black-bordered label with the name '*Salvorsan*' in large letters with '*arsphenamine*' in smaller letters next to it. At the bottom right where it said '*Physician,*' the name P. Chambliss appeared. The next time he saw the doctor he intended to ask what the medication was prescribed for.

Morgan thought the next likely place to search was the office occupied LaTrobe's executive secretary. Warren's position would give him access and knowledge of company matters including the most sensitive files.

In keeping with the secretary's fussy manner, the office was meticulously neat down to the centered writing tablet on the blotter, the row of pencils lined up according to length, and the perfectly aligned photographs of the Emily, Dorothy, and Pearl head frames hanging on the wall above the desk. The desk drawers proved to contain nothing of interest.

The locked filing cabinet located in one corner of the small office was more challenging than the lock on the alley door. Morgan groaned when he found the top drawer completely filled with bulging folders. After scanning the meticulous notations at the top of each folder identifying the contents, he was reassured the task might not be quite as daunting as he first thought. The top drawer held primarily correspondence responding to requests from local charities seeking contributions, monthly output reports to an address in Virginia, and invoices for supplies and equipment. The last folder in back contained written warnings to supervisors for some failure to meet production objectives. He found three such letters addressed to Tate Cardwell. The third letter dated in late April was worded considerably stronger than the previous two. Contrary to what Stockwell had said about Cardwell being in good standing with LaTrobe and bucking for a promotion, the letters gave more evidence Cardwell was struggling to hold on to his job. He was about ready to close the file when a handwritten note apparently written by Mr. Warren indicated Cardwell was to meet with 'VL' on May 10. Morgan recalled the entry on the check to Cardwell dated the same day. If Cardwell was not performing as expected, it made little sense that LaTrobe would be giving him a check for $100.

The second drawer contained nothing but weekly shift reports recording the progress of each tunnel. The third drawer was full of cardboard tubes with the name of one of the TJ&M mines labeled and dated on the side. He opened a recently dated tube for the Emily and spread the diagram found inside on top of the desk. It looked to be the same as the one Cardwell had shown him underground. The contents of the bottom drawer filled only half the space but looked more promising. The top of each folder was stamped with "Confidential: VL Personal Correspondence", "Sensitive", and "Most Sensitive". He took all the folders and stacked them on the desk for closer examination.

Many of the letters to and from Victor LaTrobe were handwritten undoubtedly to assure internal confidentiality. The contents mainly consisted of exchanges between senior personnel involving issues and problems LaTrobe would not wish auditors and stockholders to know about. It didn't take long to confirm Victor LaTrobe and TJ&M in general was in serious trouble. Early correspondence took LaTrobe to task for the outcome of the sale of company holdings in Telluride. More recent letters warned of overextending company resources in Adobe Wells brought about by the purchase of the rail line to Mesquite Flats. Cady's information about TJ&M's potential insolvency appeared to be grounded in fact. Other letters indicated senior TJ&M management was fully well aware of the problems concerning the east face according to the reference to a geological study conducted by M. Thomas Morris, senior hydrology engineer for Binschoff & Myers completed in September, 1914.

In the folder marked "Most Sensitive" was the Binschoff & Myers geological survey Skipping rapidly through it, he found much of the material was too technical for him to get anything more than a general idea of what he was reading. From what he did understand, it seemed to follow what Markham had told him about the hydrological challenges facing the Emily and to a lesser extent the Dorothy and Pearl. The survey concluded with recommendations listed in priority and all focused on mitigating the instability of the overburden and reducing the risk of flooding.

The first recommendation unambiguously warned against any drilling or blasting to the east along a north-south measurement marked as a dotted line on a fold-out diagram. The dotted line was located a hundred feet west of the surveyed boundary between the Emily and Imperial Mines. The diagram bore the date September 5, 1914. Morgan retrieved the recent diagram of Tunnel 3 and compared it to the one in the survey. It was obvious there was considerable disparity. The latest diagram showed the eastern drift virtually running along the Imperial/Emily boundary. The proximity to the boundary was also close enough to give Sandusky a legitimate concern TJ&M was encroaching although, assuming the diagram was accurate, there appeared to be no clear intent to do so.

Morgan put the survey to one side and picked up the next document. It was a handwritten note from the Emily's foreman advising of the results of exploratory holes drilled into the east face to further assess the extent of flooding. The note concluded with an urgent recommendation to stop all further work in the easternmost drift and permanently seal it. If seepage persisted after sealing the drift, then it might be necessary to seal the adjacent drift as well. The note was dated April 2, 1915. Morgan had no doubt the drifts cited were those Hardesty and Frank had been working the night the murder took place. He speculated why LaTrobe would ignore the foreman's warning unless LaTrobe wanted the mine to flood, which made no sense at all. He assumed LaTrobe was willing to risk the chance of flooding to continue mining the richest ore veins in the Emily to offset losses in Telluride and from the rail line purchase. LaTrobe needed to restore confidence in his management of the company. No wonder LaTrobe was furious the day before, Morgan thought. He had probably seen his worst fear come true. He had gambled and lost.

The last document gave him a start. It was a copy of a typed letter signed by Victor LaTrobe to the senior engineer and staff of the Emily. The letter dated April 5 ordered an immediate halt to further mining in the easternmost drifts in both Tunnels 2 and 3. Efforts to permanently seal the drifts were to begin immediately and to be completed by April 10, the same day Hardesty had been murdered. If the drift was to be sealed on that day, why was Hardesty still mining it?

Morgan leaned back in the chair, ran his fingers through his hair, and pondered whether he had enough circumstantial evidence to confront Cardwell and LaTrobe. He concluded he did not. Suspicions were not proof. Merrick was the one individual who may hold the key.

Morgan took a last look around to see if the office was exactly the way it was when he came in. Satisfied nothing looked out of place, he retraced his steps to the basement entrance. After carefully locking the outer door behind him, he set off down the alley. He hadn't gone far when Kincy Blaylock, emerged from a narrow alley wearing a sardonic smile.

The shotgun on his shoulder was bad enough. That two other men were with him made it a lot worse.

Chapter Twenty-One

"I don't think this is your lucky day, Westphal. I've had some bad luck today myself, but it's nothing compared to yours."

"What happened, Blaylock, did you wake up this morning and find you pissed in the bed or did you just fall out?" gesturing to the purplish bruise on Blaylock's right cheek. One of the men snickered.

"Shut-up, Parker," Blaylock said in a low voice then to Morgan. "In a few minutes you're gonna be sorry you got me fired this morning."

"So Truesdale finally realized how worthless you are. It took him long enough."

"I figured I might as well settle a little score before the other deputies found out I didn't have a badge anymore. I'll give your brother one thing, he takes a lickin' pretty good. He managed to get in a couple of good ones. Right now, he ain't feeling too good, although I 'spect in a few minutes he'll be better off than you." Blaylock dropped the shotgun off his shoulder and leveled it at Morgan.

With effort, Morgan controlled himself. He felt the weight of the Colt under his arm and considered the odds of being able to draw it before Blaylock could use the shotgun.

"I know what you've got inside your coat, but I wouldn't try it unless you want to die right now."

"You'll have a lot of explaining to do if you fire that scatter-gun."

"I ain't too concerned. By the time the Stokes brothers are through with you, I won't need to use it. Besides, there's more than one way to use a shotgun than pulling the trigger–your brother sure found that out."

"How did you know where to find me?"

"Parker lives right up the alley here. He saw you passing by and watched you go in. He went and got Jesse and they came and got me. Kind of strange you going in the back way of the TJ&M office on a Sunday when everything is all closed down, particularly when you're a deputy. If I was still wearing a badge, I'd be askin' what you've been up to. Instead, I believe I'll just mention it to Mr. LaTrobe. I'm certain he'll be obliged to know you've been visiting through the back door on a Sunday when the office is closed."

"Gesturing to the two brothers, Morgan said, "Why don't you boys leave now. So far, you haven't done anything to break the law. If you stay here, you're going to be in more trouble than you bargained for. Do you boys know I'm wearing a badge?" Jesse gave Parker a questioning look. Morgan had a brief moment of hope that quickly faded when he saw the stubborn expression on Parker's face.

Parker Stokes shook his head and responded, "I reckin' we'll be stayin' here."

Directing his attention to Blaylock, Morgan said, "I don't suppose you'd consider putting the shotgun down so we can settle this by ourselves?"

"Afraid not, although I'm tempted."

"And what's your real interest in all this, Blaylock? There's more to this than what I told Truesdale about you."

"You're smart, Westphal. It makes me think you're maybe too smart for your own good, and certain people might not appreciate that. Now instead of just beating the shit out of you, I'm going to have to take care of things in a more permanent way."

"Before you do, how about answering a few questions?"

"Depends on the questions. There's things the Stokes don't know and don't need to know."

"Did you know Adele Belden was lying when she came to see you claiming she was Willard Merrick's wife?"

"Sure did."

"How did you know?"

"On account Tate Cardwell came in and asked me to find Merrick. He told me he was livin' over at Ballinger's. That ain't no place for married people so I knew the woman was lying, although I didn't know why. I was curious and started checking around. Unfortunately, about the time I found out who she was, she ended up dead. Too bad because I figured she knew where Merrick was."

"Why did Cardwell want to find Merrick?"

"Don't know and didn't care. I figured it was something personal between Cardwell and Merrick."

"Do you always do what Cardwell says?"

"Yep, and especially when he said TJ&M would really appreciate any help I give. LaTrobe is gonna be grateful enough he'll make me marshal of Adobe Wells"

"Didn't it cross your mind Merrick might have had something to say about who killed Hardesty?"

"Nope. Your brother killed Hardesty and he's sitting— well, he's probably layin' down—over yonder in the jail where he's gonna stay until he gets his neck stretched."

Morgan realized if Blaylock really believed Frank was guilty, that could only mean his involvement in whatever was going on with TJ&M was incidental at best. To reinforce his supposition, he asked, "Who are you really working for? Is it Victor LaTrobe?"

"In a way, I suppose it is. You see, he doesn't much like Truesdale and hasn't made any secret of it. The way I see it, when I find Merrick, LaTrobe is going to be real grateful. I figure his influence is enough to get Truesdale fired and me appointed marshal." Blaylock's comment further confirmed Blaylock's involvement was tangential, motivated solely to gain LaTrobe's support for the marshal's job.

"So you haven't found Merrick yet? How do you know he didn't leave town the night Hardesty was killed?"

"I don't think so. If he was going to leave, he wouldn't have stayed with the whore who was pretendin' to be his wife."

"How did you learn he was staying with her?"

"I didn't know for sure, but considering she was a whore and where she lived, it seemed the most likely place to hole up. A crib would be the last place anyone would expect to look for him." Morgan had to give Blaylock credit for an idea that until now hadn't occurred to him. "I'm betting he's still around here somewhere, and I'll find him. Hell, he might've been the one that killed her." Morgan couldn't discount the possibility Blaylock was right. Merrick was a more likely suspect than LaTrobe who he had yet to prove he even knew Adele Belden. "I think that's enough questions, Westphal. Parker, you and Jesse get on with it."

Grinning in anticipation, Parker Stokes drew a thin-bladed knife from a sheath in his boot. "Mister, first I'm going to gut you like a fish."

Blaylock laughed. "Go to it, Parker, but leave a little for Jesse."

Morgan watched the Stokes brothers walking slowly toward him. His chances began to improve slightly when the two men gradually converged as they came closer. A few more steps more, and they would block Blaylock's view and force Blaylock to step to one side or the other to get a clear shot. Evidently, Blaylock had noticed the same thing and shouted a warning.

"Damn it, you fools, come at him from both sides."

The two brothers quickened their pace and began to move apart. He wasn't going to get a better chance. He drew the Colt and fired as Blaylock went to the left. There was a loud explosion, and Morgan felt a sudden pain in his left leg and arm. Parker Stokes screamed, threw up his hands, and collapsed facedown where he lay groaning, his back a bloody mess. Jesse Stokes stood frozen in shock then half-turned toward Blaylock as he looked down at the blood dripping down his right shoulder. Blaylock's face registered only annoyance as he cocked the shotgun's other hammer and prepared to fire again. Morgan's second and third shots took Blaylock in the chest and stomach. Blaylock fell backward.

Morgan pointed the Colt at Jesse Stokes and said, "Drop the club, Jesse. The fun's all over. See to your brother." Morgan watched as Jesse Stokes bent over to examine his brother and noticed the younger brother was also badly wounded.

"Parker's dead." He moaned after dropping to his knees beside his brother.

Ignoring Jesse and the throbbing in his arm and leg, Morgan limped toward Blaylock and verified the former deputy was also dead. He quickly examined his arm and leg and was satisfied the painful buckshot wounds were not serious. He heard an automobile engine, shouts, and the sound of running feet. Morgan saw Truesdale and two other men coming down the alley toward him. While he waited for them, he looked over at the Stokes brothers and saw Jesse was on his side next to his brother. Morgan went over to him and found he was more dead than alive.

"Jesus, Morgan, it looks like a goddamn battlefield!" the marshal exclaimed. "What the hell happened?" as the other two deputies gaped silently at the dead men.

"These three jumped me. I guess Blaylock was looking for a chance to work me over with help from those two," pointing toward the Stokes brothers. "Fortunately for me, but not so good for them, when Blaylock let go with the shotgun, they got in the way. Parker Stokes is dead and his brother doesn't look like he's going to make it either. I shot Blaylock before he could use the second barrel on me. I guess that about sums it up."

Truesdale spat and looked dubiously at Morgan, glancing briefly at his blood-soaked shirt and trousers. "All right, we'll leave it at that for now. Wilson, you come along with me. After you drop me, Mr. Westphal, and Jesse Stokes off at the hospital, you're gonna swing past the jail and get the tarp on the back shelf of the storeroom. Then you come back and help Telford take the two bodies on over to the morgue. Be sure and use that tarp so's you don't mess up the truck."

The man identified as Telford stood up after taking a close look at Jesse Stokes and said, "Marshall, this one's dead too."

The marshal nodded. "No loss. He was workin' hard to be as bad and worthless as his brother."

As the three men walked toward the truck, Truesdale cleared his throat and said, "Morgan, I'm not sure how to tell you this and make it sound better'n it is...."

"If it's about Frank, Blaylock told me. How bad is it?"

"Real bad. The doc ain't sure he's gonna make it. He's pretty busted up, broken ribs, maybe a punctured lung. If he pulls through, Frank ain't ever gonna be pretty no more. What Blaylock done to that boy's face is worse than I ever saw done to anybody, and I've seen my share of bar fights. What I can't figure is why."

"It wasn't about Frank. It was me he was after, and he did it so I'd come after him."

"Why?"

"Blaylock didn't say except someone may have been depending on him to get me out of the way."

"I don't follow," Truesdale said with a puzzled frown. "You ain't been in town long enough to rile anybody that much."

"It may be somebody thinks I'm getting too close to finding out who killed Hardesty. Strange thing is, I'm not too sure I am."

"Got any notion who it might be?"

"I've got a couple of candidates in mind. One of them is Willard Merrick. Blaylock thought he's still somewhere in town."

"Who's the other?"

"I'd rather not say right until I do some more checking."

"Considering what you just told me, you'd best not keep me in the dark too long else you could end up with a bullet or knife in your back."

"All right, when we get to the hospital, I'll tell you what I know and who I think killed Hardesty"

Chapter Twenty-Two

Morgan looked down at Frank and wished Blaylock had taken longer to die. The only way he knew it was Frank was the nurse told him so. Bandages covered most of his brother's face. What little that was free of the bandages was severely swollen and discolored or covered in stitches. The chart indicated head contusions, facial cuts, a broken finger, and two broken ribs. Heavily sedated and immobilized as Frank was, the guard Truesdale had placed in the room seemed superfluous. The nurse was cheerfully optimistic and said the wounds, while serious, were not life-threatening. He wished Chambliss was available to confirm the nurse's prognosis; however, the doctor had been called away suddenly leaving another doctor to dig the buckshot out of his arm and leg. He started to reject the order to remain in the hospital overnight for observation then realized he had little choice when the nurse refused to return his clothes or the Colt .

Morgan limped back down the hall to his room and reached it just as Truesdale came up the steps carrying his holstered Colt . "Here, put this under your pillow just in case. Morgan, I'm real sorry about Frank. I reckin' it was my fault. Blaylock and I had words last night. It started after I warned him about what you told me about the way he was treating Frank. Got to thinkin' about it early this mornin' and then did what I shoulda done a long time ago. Anyways, I went over to where Blaylock was livin' and took his badge. Never come to mind he'd go back to the jail. Myron found Frank and then called me. I was out looking for Blaylock when I heard the shots."

"What's done is done, and there's no reason to blame yourself."

Truesdale drew up the one chair in the room and pulled it closer to the bed on which Morgan was sitting. "Maybe this is as good a time as any to tell me what you know and what you don't know."

"I think either Willard Merrick or Tate Cardwell killed Hardesty. It's also possible they were working together. Why Hardesty was killed is something I'm still trying to work out."

"What makes you think it was Cardwell?"

"Cardwell is the one man on level three who is able to go anywhere in the tunnel when he wants to. His job requires it. The other miners are pretty much restricted when and where they can go. A man seen away from his assigned worksite would be noticed. Merrick was working close enough to get to the drift Hardesty was working with little risk of being seen. Chambliss said the results of his autopsy indicated two men may have committed the murder; one struck Hardesty on the head, and the other stabbed him in the back with a candle pick and that makes Cardwell and Merrick principal suspects. There's another possibility. Tate Cardwell is a big man and is equally skilful using either hand. I saw an example of that during my visit to the Emily Mine. The murderer or murderers may have surprised Hardesty who would likely be standing with his back to the drift tunnel. The noise of the drill would have masked the sound of anyone coming up behind him."

Morgan wasn't surprised to see a skeptical expression on Truesdale's face, "Can you give me one good reason why Cardwell or Merrick, or both, had any reason to kill Hardesty and especially down in a mine? Hell, if either of 'em wanted to kill him it would've made more sense to do it on the surface."

"I admit I haven't figured out why; however, where he was killed makes a lot of sense. If I'm right, the plan was to make the murder look like an accident. Whoever did it finished drilling the last one or two holes of Hardesty's round. Tate Cardwell knows how to use a drill and Merrick was a driller. Either one or both would have been able to finish the job. Frank said he heard voices when he stopped to change a drill bit. The voices could have been the killers talking to each other or the one murderer talking to Hardesty. Later, after the drilling resumed, Frank heard who he thought was Hardesty call out a warning he was about to light the fuses. When Frank looked at his watch, it was a few minutes past eleven o'clock. Working backward from that time, the voices Frank heard suggests Hardesty was hit and stabbed around ten that night based on the time it would have taken to finish the one or two holes left. Frank told me he estimated Hardesty was five minutes ahead of him when he lit his fuses and went back to the tunnel. Frank then claimed his charges went off before Hardesty, and it was at least a full minute before they did. Dan, the five to six minute delay would have given the murderer more than an enough time to leave the tunnel and get back to a location where he would be above suspicion in case anything went wrong. And maybe something did go wrong."

"What do you mean something went wrong?"

"I think it was intended Hardesty would be buried under the ore blasted from the working face. He, or they, left Hardesty thinking he was dead. He wasn't and revived in time to see the fuses burning. He may have managed to crawl back through the crosscut and into the drift to get Frank's help, but by then Frank had already gone back to the tunnel to wait for his charges to go off. Frank's charges went off and hit Hardesty. It's possible Hardesty may have already been dead before the round went off. If not, the resulting explosion was enough to dislodge the overburden above him that crushed his face. Understandably, Frank thought he was responsible for not clearing the drift. At that point, Frank and everyone else thought it was an accident. It wasn't until Chambliss found the puncture wound in Hardesty's back that the death became a murder and not an accident. Frank looked like a logical choice since he was the closest to the scene and presumably had a reason to kill Hardesty based on the rumors and exaggerated beliefs they were bitter rivals."

"It's a good theory, I'll give you that. But it still don't point a finger at Cardwell. Mebbe to Merrick, since he skedaddled, but not Cardwell."

"It's quite possible the murder wasn't premeditated. Cardwell may have caught Hardesty in the act of trying to sabotage the Emily and there was a fight. Cardwell then went on to cover it up by making it look like an accident."

"Hold on, you're way ahead of me on this sabotage thing. Morgan, back up and take it slower."

"Before what happened to TJ&M yesterday, I had reason to believe the company was the target of external or internal attempts to sabotage the mine. I believe I found evidence of it on the east face of Hardesty's drift. A number of drill holes were there where they shouldn't have been."

Morgan summarized the results of what Markham had told him and his study of the geological report he had read. He omitted telling the marshal how or when he had access to the report.

"TJ&M management was fully aware of the dangers in mining toward the TJ&M eastern boundary. LaTrobe had taken steps to cease mining along the east face after apparently becoming convinced there was too much risk of a catastrophic flood if excavation there continued. He had already risked drilling for eight months following an independent survey that recommended stopping all further drilling at the end of Tunnel 3."

"Why did LaTrobe keep on drillin' when he knew it was risky?"

"Because he couldn't afford not to. TJ&M is in financial trouble, don't ask how I know. LaTrobe needed the profits from the richest deposits in the Emily which happen to be along the mine's eastern boundary. It looks as if TJ&M is way over extended and ripe for takeover. Louis Sandusky would be in a position to profit most if TJ&M assets here in Adobe Wells went into receivership."

"You think Cardwell or Merrick may have been workin' for Sandusky?"

"I can't rule it out. Before Merrick was hired by TJ&M, he worked for Sandusky. It wouldn't be the first time something like that happened. Maybe Merrick was still working for Sandusky by hiring out to work in the Emily."

"Any chance the union is behind any of this?"

"I still believe Stockwell when he says the union is doing its best to avoid anything like what happened yesterday. You heard LaTrobe threatening to bring in the army. Stockwell knows it would be Cripple Creek and Ludlow all over again. The union's chances for getting what they want would be set back for years if it was found they were responsible for what happened in the Emily and to the other two TJ&M mines."

"What if LaTrobe was behind the trouble? He's facing a lawsuit from Sandusky. Mebbe he's getting' ready to put the blame on Sandusky."

"That's possible too, but I don't think so. LaTrobe is in too much financial trouble to take a long shot by making up losses through a long and protracted lawsuit accusing Sandusky for sabotage he can't prove. If someone working for TJ&M is responsible for the explosions, I'm betting LaTrobe doesn't know it. His reaction yesterday was no act. He's angry and knows he's facing ruin because of it."

"You gonna be talkin' to Louis Sandusky?"

"I will first thing tomorrow just as soon as I can get out of here."

"You reckin' there's any connection to any of this and the whore you found dead?"

"I can't be sure there is, although I wouldn't be surprised. Since Adele Belden was posing as Willard Merrick's wife, it's obvious there's at least a link, but it doesn't necessarily prove she even knew Merrick much less had anything to do with Hardesty's murder. She was a whore, and whores do things for money. Adele Belden had a mystery benefactor who arranged to visit her every Thursday night. There's a good chance the mystery man is Victor LaTrobe, and if so, he would be a logical suspect. That is if it can be proven he visited her the night she died."

"Are you suggesting LaTrobe had something to do with Merrick's disappearance?"

"I have no reason to say one way or the other. I do believe Adele Belden was hired or persuaded to play the role of Merrick's wife, perhaps by Merrick to give him time to get out of Adobe Wells. The act didn't fool Blaylock. Blaylock told me he knew from the start Adele was lying about being Merrick's wife since the night Merrick disappeared, because. Blaylock had already been looking for Merrick at Ballinger's boarding house. Ballinger doesn't allow women boarders. Why he was looking for Merrick, Blaylock didn't say. I think it was Tate Cardwell who put Blaylock on to Merrick for whatever reason only Cardwell can give."

"You shore are tryin' hard to make a case against Cardwell, maybe a little too hard."

"I uncovered something else that keeps me thinking Cardwell may have been paid to kill Hardesty."

"Damn, where you comin' up with all this shit, Morgan?"

"For the time being, I'd rather not answer."

Truesdale's eyes narrowed as he looked toward the back door of the TJ&M building. "So what did you find in LaTrobe's office?"

Morgan acknowledged Truesdale's pointed question with a smile. "LaTrobe gave Cardwell a personal check for $100. I don't know why, but I have a hunch it's connected in some way to Hardesty."

Truesdale raised both hands in protest. "I can't believe LaTrobe is involved in killing one of his own drillers."

"I agree it sounds farfetched; however, Olivia LaTrobe gave me the impression without admitting it in so many words she was having an affair with Hardesty. She said she met Hardesty and my brother in Telluride. She claimed they did some personal work for LaTrobe. Everyone says Hardesty was well-favored. If Olivia LaTrobe was having an affair, it's entirely possible Victor LaTrobe paid Cardwell to take care of him. Frankly, at the time she told me, I didn't give any credit to what she said. Now I see it as a possible motive for LaTrobe to have Hardesty killed."

"Jesus Christ, if that don't beat all," Truesdale said. "How you gonna prove any of this? I don't 'spect Cardwell and LaTrobe are going to admit anything even if it is true. And Morgan, I'm not convinced it is."

"I agree. What's important to me is for Samuel Spencer to lay out a case strong enough to convince a jury Frank didn't do it, and that's enough for me. Merrick is still the key. He's either one of the killers, or he may know who the killer is. Whether he's also involved in sabotaging the TJ&M mines remains only an unsubstantiated possibility."

It had grown dark outside when Truesdale stood up to leave. "After what you told me, best keep that Colt real handy. I'm wondering if the guard I put on Frank might better be outside your room."

"Don't worry, Dan, I sleep light, and I'm safer in here than walking around on the street—this afternoon is proof of that. And thanks to you, I've got safe company," gesturing to the Colt beside him. "Dan, do me a favor and bring me some clean clothes; the shirt and trousers I was wearing when I came in here are blood-soaked." Truesdale nodded and closed the door behind him.

The next morning Morgan donned the fresh clothes Truesdale had dropped off and went down the hall to see Frank. He was encouraged to find his brother sleeping peacefully. He sat down in the chair next to the bed and considered how best to approach Lewis Sandusky.

Before leaving the hospital, he went down to the basement and was able to locate one of the men who had been with Dr. Chambliss the day he had gone to the morgue. At first, the orderly was adamant in his refusal to show him the box with Hardesty's effects without the personal order of Dr. Chambliss. Morgan produced his badge and issued an order of his own. The reluctant orderly brought the box and Morgan retrieved the small key from the change purse. After signing for the key, Morgan pocketed it and left the hospital. He ran into the marshal in front who told him Will Cosgrove had left a message at the jail to call him.

Chapter Twenty-Three

During the taxi ride to Sandusky's office, Morgan considered the telephone conversation with Will Cosgrove and hoped the meeting with Sandusky would produce more results than his partner had been able to find about Hardesty and Adele Belden.

Apparently what the part-time whore had said about Adele Belden being a former nurse was true. She was born and raised in Syracuse, New York where she remained until she left for a Baltimore hospital at the age of eighteen to enter a two-year nurse's training program. After successfully completing the program, she was employed in two different hospitals in Baltimore before relocating to Pittsburgh. An addiction to laudanum had eventually ended her brief and socially acceptable career a few years later. In 1905, she was discharged from Presbyterian Mercy Hospital in Pittsburgh for stealing narcotics. The only record after that was in police files in St. Louis and Kansas City for prostitution. There were no further records of her whereabouts until she surfaced in Denver in 1912, where she was registered as a prostitute working in a bordello on Tandy Street for two years until she moved to Telluride. In Telluride, she lived alone at 112 Elm Street; the house was rented under the name David Anderson.

There was even less information to report concerning Phillip Hardesty. Apart from an address for a boarding house on Wilmont Street in Telluride where he lived from July, 1914 until relocating to Adobe Wells eight months later, his partner had found nothing else about Phillip Hardesty. He recalled Cosgrove's comment that it was as if Hardesty had arrived in Telluride out of thin air. There seemed to be as much mystery surrounding Hardesty's lack of a past as the circumstances of his death. Perhaps the absence of any background was the most significant thing about Hardesty. Whoever it was killed in the Emily Mine, Morgan was willing to bet his name wasn't Phillip Hardesty. If his hunch was right about the small key he obtained from the victim's personal effects, there would be a good chance of revealing who Phillip Hardesty really was.

The administrative office for the Sandusky Mining Company was located on the edge of town where the road from Mesquite Flats entered Adobe Wells. From its drab, functional appearance, size and location by a spur line, the large rectangular, single-story building must have originally been a warehouse. In any case, it was in sharp contrast to the elaborate, multi-story office building occupied by TJ&M.

Morgan climbed gingerly out of the taxi, careful to avoid bumping his leg or arm. Both limbs were sore but not particularly painful as long as he remembered not to make any sudden moves. He was surprised to see Elias Stockwell coming out of the entrance and walk down the street in the opposite direction, his usual dour expression lightened by a broad smile.

The building's interior matched the utilitarian exterior. From the scarred and stained wooden floor, open rough-hewn rafters, and musty smell, Louis Sandusky's interest and capital were focused entirely on mining and not on an elaborate corporate office. Rows of desks filled one side of the cavernous room. There was a low hum as men and women worked sitting hunched over desks or standing in small groups poring over charts and diagrams. The other side of the building was partitioned off with an unpainted wall constructed of wood planks. Morgan assumed behind the plank wall was where the more senior managers and administrative personnel were located. He asked a harried young woman seated at a desk nearest the door where he

231

could find Louis Sandusky. She stopped typing long enough to point toward a door in the center of the wood partition.

Morgan was reaching for the door handle when it suddenly burst open, and a stocky man with tousled red hair shot with gray bumped into him. Morgan grimaced in pain and quickly grabbed the door to keep from falling.

"You all right, mister?" the man asked with what seemed like genuine concern.

"I'll be fine, thanks. Can you direct me to Mr. Sandusky's office?"

"I'm Lou Sandusky. What can I do for you?" Morgan was surprised. Dressed in denim trousers, wool shirt, suspenders, and heavy work boots, Sandusky looked like any other miner working underground. Short and clean-shaven, Sandusky radiated the bluff confidence of a man used to authority and accustomed to getting his own way.

"The name is Westphal, and I'd appreciate a few minutes of your time concerning a private matter."

"I'm sorry this is not a good time. I'm just on my way out...." Sandusky stopped abruptly. "Wait a minute. You say your name's Westphal? Yes, of course, you're the man I read about in the paper this morning, the one involved in the shooting behind the TJ&M building."

Embarrassed, Morgan nodded. "It would be helpful if you delay your departure. I'll try not to take up anymore of your time than I have to."

"It's out of the question. You'll have to come back this evening, I suggest around six tonight. I should be available then although I can't promise it."

"I'm afraid that won't do. I'm going to have to insist."

"Insist all you want, but the answer is the same. I really must be going."

Morgan's voice was low and conversational as he pulled aside his coat and revealed the badge. "Mr. Sandusky, you can talk to me now here in your office, or I'll arrest you and take you down to the jail and ask my questions there. It's your choice."

Sandusky frowned, and his friendly manner quickly disappeared. He regarded Morgan with a calculating look. "I've half a mind to call your bluff. I can't imagine on what charge you can possibly arrest me." He hesitated and glanced at his wristwatch and relented. "All right follow me, I'll give you a few minutes. I'm curious to see what this about."

Morgan followed the older man through the door and down a central hallway with small offices on each side. Through open doors, the same degree of concentration on the faces of the occupants mirrored those on the other side of the partition.

Louis Sandusky's office was small, sparsely furnished, and devoid of the personal items which might have been expected in the office of an owner and senior manager. The desk was piled high with papers and rolled charts. Diagrams of the Sandusky mines were tacked on the walls; more charts were propped on easels in one corner.

Without offering a chair, Louis Sandusky perched on the edge of his desk, folded his arms across his chest, and gave Morgan a cold look. "You said you'd be brief so get on with it."

"What can you tell me about what happened to the Emily mine on Saturday?"

"Not a goddamned thing. Next question?"

"Do the recent problems TJ&M are experiencing benefit you?"

"Now I see where you're going with this. You think I'm responsible for LaTrobe's current problems." Sandusky's eyes narrowed and his mouth tightened. "What I should do is call my lawyer, and you can put the rest of your questions to him. Well, I'm not going to do that for the simple reason I have absolutely nothing to hide, so I'll answer your question. Of course, there's no doubt the misfortune LaTrobe is having benefits my company. I might add the same is true for the other independents. Do you intend to interrogate them as well?"

"I will if I think it's necessary. I'm told a driller employed by TJ&M by the name of Willard Merrick who once worked for SMC may still be working for you."

"I'm not familiar with the name; however, I can have our personnel records checked to see if that's true. I'm a little unclear why I would want to employ this man if he's already working for LaTrobe."

"Let's not play games, Mr. Sandusky. Willard Merrick is wanted for questioning concerning the murder of Phillip Hardesty who was killed in the Emily Mine last week. Merrick is also a suspect in the sabotage of the Emily Mine on Saturday."

"So, if it can be established there is a connection between SMC and this missing driller, it can be rightly assumed I am responsible for the explosions that damaged the TJ&M mines. Naturally, I deny any such connection with this man or anyone else who may be responsible for what happened on Saturday afternoon."

"Did you ever have a conversation about flooding in the Emily?"

"I wonder how you happened to learn of this. Yes, I had several such conversations with my senior engineers. All but one were hypothetical and based on the consequences to the Imperial if catastrophic flooding ever occur in the Emily. One of my engineers had the nerve and stupidity to suggest we should create the conditions whereby the Emily would be more vulnerable by excavating the Imperial's western face. I fired that man on the spot. And that, Mr. Westphal, happens to be a matter of record. By any chance, is Mr. Markham the source of your information?"

"He is one source; there's another."

"I'm afraid whatever your sources heard or thought they heard was either taken out of context or a misunderstanding of what was actually said. Mr. Markham provided invaluable service to this company. I had hoped he would remain with us longer, but I was unable to persuade him. Since you and Mr. Markham have apparently discussed the hydrological problems affecting the mines in and around the Emily, I need to make several very important points. As you seem aware, Mr. Markham provided geological evidence confirming what I most feared."

"Did you ever discuss the consequences of flooding in the Emily with Mr. LaTrobe?"

"Indeed, I did. I went to his office and showed him a copy of Markham's report. I wanted a mutual agreement to restrict mining along the Imperial and Emily boundary to prevent irreversible damage if a rupture of the weak fault between the two claims ever occurred."

"And what was LaTrobe's reaction?"

"The sanctimonious son of bitch all but threw me out of his office right after I refused his offer to buy the Imperial."

"Did he perceive how dangerous the fault was?"

"I'm not certain he did. LaTrobe is more of a manager than engineer. It's conceivable he saw my request as nothing more than an attempt to reduce the Emily's output."

"What did you plan to do when he turned you down?"

"I filed an injunction against further drilling. Regrettably, the judge ruled against it."

"Is that why you sued for encroachment?"

"I had no other choice even though I realized it was going to take longer to stop LaTrobe from continuing to drill along my western boundary. It was also a lawsuit I knew I could win."

"How can you be so certain?"

Sandusky smiled. "Let me show you something," and directed Morgan's attention to a surface diagram of the south slope tacked to the wall. Dotted lines clearly delineated the boundaries of each mining claim on the slope. Sandusky pointed to the area where Morgan saw the name of each mine inscribed within the square or rectangular boxes.

"Notice the boundary between the Imperial and the Emily. Now, Mr. Westphal, I want you to look closely at the red dotted line slightly west of the marked boundary between the Imperial and Emily. That red line indicates the actual boundary. I took the trouble of having the claims resurveyed. I admit I didn't really expect anything except a confirmation of the existing boundary. I suspected LaTrobe was getting close to his eastern boundary, and I simply wanted to be sure he wouldn't cross it intentionally or unintentionally. To my surprise, the actual boundary was off by as much as 20 feet along the northern end of the boundary. Note the diagram next to it." Morgan saw the diagram was in three parts and depicted each level of the Emily. "These diagrams are several weeks old; however, notice the third level. The eastern drift is east of the red line by, I would guess, anywhere from 12-18 feet."

"How can you be so sure about the measurement?"

"My surveyors went down through the ventilation shaft and measured from inside the Emily. I'm quite convinced the survey is accurate within a few feet. I only need to prove LaTrobe is only a foot over to win the lawsuit and make the bastard pay for it. With anyone but LaTrobe, the matter of encroachment and flooding could have been settled with a handshake and mutual efforts to solve the flooding problem."

Morgan took a closer look at the diagram and realized the eastern-most drift was actually the one Frank had been drilling; the one Hardesty was working was well over the red line. "Mr. Sandusky, I've been down in the Emily, and I can tell you this diagram is no longer accurate. There's another drift farther east of the one shown here."

"Christ, I can't believe the fool actually kept on digging," exclaimed Sandusky shaking his head in disbelief. "If what you're telling me is true, he made it easy for whoever wanted to flood the Emily. A damned shame," he added bitterly.

"I'm surprised, Mr. Sandusky, to hear you say that. I'd think you would be pleased with LaTrobe's misfortune."

"Don't misunderstand. I want LaTrobe to fail, and he will and a lot sooner than he realizes. You see, Mr. Westphal, it isn't in my interests to see the Emily flooded, at least not to the extent it can no longer be worked. TJ&M here in Adobe Wells is finished even if LaTrobe doesn't realize it yet. In my opinion, the company is leveraged beyond any possibility of saving it. The loss of the Emily will push it over the financial edge, and when that happens, I'll pick up the pieces including ownership of the Emily, Pearl, and Dorothy. The destruction of the Emily and the strike will finish LaTrobe within a month."

"What makes you so sure?"

"I too have my sources of information, so we'll leave it at that. The strike is the final blow. LaTrobe won't settle with the union out of principle. Fortunately, I'm not so burdened."

Morgan now understood why Stockwell was smiling when he left. "You've just struck a bargain with Stockwell."

"That's right. Now you know why I'm in a hurry. I need to get my mines back into full operation. In a week or so when LaTrobe's balance sheet shows a steep decline, I'll make my first offer and he'll refuse. I hope he does, because a couple of weeks later, I'll make a second offer and lower than the first—he'll have to take it because by then his stockholders will be ready to string him to the nearest streetlamp. In the end, LaTrobe will fail I'll take over TJ&M's assets here in Adobe Wells for less than half of what the company is worth."

"You make it sound personal."

"Not all Mr. Westphal. I admit I don't like him, but I have nothing personal against Victor LaTrobe. I don't respect him because he's a poor manager, and even worse he's a bad engineer. For those reasons alone, he deserves to fail, and as sure as I'm standing here, he surely will and very soon." Sandusky gave Morgan a searching look. "Why do I get the idea there's more to all this than what happened Saturday to the three TJ&M mines."

"What happened to the TJ&M mines is only the latest of a series of related incidents beginning with the death of the miner I mentioned. Since then four other people have been killed who either had a direct or indirect link to Phillip Hardesty's murder."

"Is the shooting incident yesterday part of it?"

"I believe so. I have a personal stake in finding the man or men who killed Hardesty. The man now in jail accused of murdering him is my brother. He's also innocent."

"I see. I've told you the truth Mr. Westphal, but I don't see how I can help you further."

"I believe you, Mr. Sandusky. I also believe Hardesty's murder is incidental to the reason those holes were drilled in the east face of Tunnel 3. You've convinced me it was never in your interests to see the fault between the Imperial and Emily ruptured, and I don't think LaTrobe ever intended to sabotage his own mine. I'm betting he took a risk by mining as far as he did strictly because the richest ore veins were along the eastern boundary. If I can find out why someone wanted to sabotage the Emily, I'll have a lot of the answers including who killed Hardesty."

"Then, Mr. Westphal, if there's nothing else, I really must be on my way."

"Perhaps there is one more thing. I'd like to see the personnel file you have for Willard Merrick, that is if it's still in the company records."

"Of course. As I said before, I don't recall the name; however, I'll put you in touch with Mr. Hernshaw; he's responsible for all employee records. He'll know if we ever hired a man by that name." Sandusky walked to the door with Morgan and then paused. "Tell me, Mr. Westphal, did you kill all three of those men yesterday?"

"No, only one of them."

Sandusky's brow wrinkled, "What's it like to...? Never mind, it's a stupid question." Morgan silently agreed.

Mr. Hernshaw produced Willard Merrick's employment file consisting of an employment application, a pay record of weekly wage payments, and a cryptic handwritten note saying:

> "W. Merrick gave notice Feb 11, 1915; all assigned
> equipment inventoried and accounted for on Feb 12
> and final wages paid."

Morgan scanned Merrick's employment application, which was filled out in a barely legible scrawl and dated September 21, 1914. Employment as a master driller was to commence on October 1 at $2.50 per hour in addition to company script worth .25 cents per day to be tendered for each 12-hour workday. Employee is entitled to medical assistance only for injuries sustained while actively working above or below ground during a scheduled workday in the amount of $2.00 for each day missed not to exceed 5 days.

The questionnaire indicated Merrick had then been thirty-seven years old. In the space requesting prior experience, he identified mines in West Virginia, Arkansas, and Colorado. Merrick gave a post office address in Trinidad, Colorado, care of the Hercules Mine for his last residence listed; the current local address Ballinger's boarding house. The final space was reserved for the names of family members. In the space provided, a name had been partially written and then blackened out. The word 'none' had been printed instead.

Morgan regarded the entry and the name of the mine listed in the Colorado address and it occurred to him he may have found one of the answers he was looking for.

Chapter Twenty-Four

It was the Trinidad address in care of the Hercules Mine on Merrick's application that had given him the clue why the Emily had been damaged so badly. The editor of the Adobe Wells *Citizen Gazette* had obligingly brought Morgan the back issues for April 20 through April 30, 1914. He found what he was looking for on the first page of the April 23 issue.

"MASSACRE IN COLORADO"

Death Toll Continues to Mount

Unrest continues in the town of Ludlow, Colorado, following months of conflict between striking coal miners and state militia struggling to regain control of the town and nearby coal mines. The number of deaths attributed to the strike including all parties to the strike is now 160.

The mines and property of Thurlowe, Jansen & McCormick have been particularly affected and under siege since the strike was called by the Western Federation of Miners on September 13, 1913.

A senior representative of TJ&M Corporation was quoted as saying "However regrettable the recent deaths outside the town of Ludlow, they result from the efforts by union agitators to disrupt free commercial enterprise and can no longer be tolerated. It is the union who must bear responsibility and held accountable for the violence and unnecessary deaths that have occurred."

The reference was to the latest and calamitous deaths of four women and eleven children who perished on September 20 as a result of a devastating fire deliberately started by members of the local militia. The fire destroyed a tent city near the town of Ludlow where striking miners and their families had been living following their eviction from company housing soon after the strike commenced. The charred remains of the victims were found later in a pit beneath the burned tent under which they had been hiding.

Morgan continued to read through the lengthy article; it ended on page three with the names of the fifteen victims listed. Toward the bottom of the list he found why Willard Merrick tried to destroy the Emily and damage the other two TJ&M mines. There were two reasons: the first was Elspeth Merrick, aged twenty-nine, and the second was Arabella Merrick, aged five. Morgan wondered how he would have reacted had he lost his wife and child in such circumstances. He supposed the deliberate manner he killed the man in Las Cruces who shot Lydia was not all that different. He doubted Merrick had any more regret for his action than he did. It had taken him a long time to face the truth. When he had gone to the brothel looking for the cowhand who killed Lydia, he had every intention of killing him. The only difference between him and Merrick was he had been wearing a badge at the time, and that made his action legal even if questionable.

He was still left perplexed over the circumstances of Hardesty's murder, that is, if he was murdered at all. Merrick and Hardesty were known to be friends; therefore, what reason would Merrick have for killing him? If Merrick had a vendetta against TJ&M, why wouldn't he have gone after someone like LaTrobe or the company's senior management instead of a fellow miner? More unanswered questions.

Morgan's next stop at the post office was a brief one. It didn't take long to find out the small key with the number 149 was not compatible to any issued by the postal service in Adobe Wells or in Mesquite Flats.

The teller at the First Citizens Bank of Arizona took one look at the key and directed Morgan's attention to the assistant manager sitting at a desk on the far side of the lobby. Morgan identified himself to the florid-faced man and explained why he was there. Mr. Napier took the key, gave it a quick glance, and frowned before handing it back.

"I'm afraid that's impossible. I can't allow access to the deposit box because it would violate bank policy. If what you say is true about the owner of this key, the matter will have to be settled in probate before the box can be opened by a second party."

"Mr. Napier, I understand and fully appreciate the bank's position. I can only hope you can understand the position the marshal's office is in as well. Whatever is in that box may do much to help us in solving a murder." The banker's eyebrows lifted in surprise. "This key was found in the possession of a miner killed while working underground last week. The coroner concluded the circumstances of this man's death were not accidental. The contents of the box may tell us why this individual was killed and who may have done it. I don't believe it would violate bank policy if the contents were inventoried and nothing is removed. Of course, I would insist on you or another person representing the bank be present to attest in writing as to the contents of the box including the fact nothing was removed."

"Mr. Westphal, this is highly irregular...."

Morgan sensed the banker was starting to waiver. "If you feel uncomfortable, I'll certainly be happy to wait until you've checked with the manager. Perhaps my request exceeds your authority," he added, blatantly insinuating the assistant manager was afraid to show any initiative.

"I believe under the circumstances, the bank can authorize an exception under the conditions you've described."

Mr. Napier led the way to a small room located in the rear of the bank and told Morgan to wait. The room was bare except for a high table positioned in the center of the room. The assistant manager returned a few minutes later cradling a small, rectangular metal box. On top of the box was a single piece of paper. He laid the box on the table then withdrew a fountain pen from his coat pocket and waited expectantly while Morgan inserted the key into the lock.

Morgan unlocked the box and lifted the lid. The 25-caliber Colt automatic pistol inside was clearly a surprise to Mr. Napier who drew an audible breath when he saw it. He opened a small leather case beside the pistol and found a badge identifying the Pinkerton National Detective Agency. Morgan put the badge and weapon aside and began removing the remainder of the contents as Mr. Napier catalogued each item including the three hundred dollars in large bills found inside an envelope. The documents and correspondence revealed Phillip Hardesty's identity as John R. Simmons, a senior investigator whose assignment was defined in a letter from Victor LaTrobe dated in late January, 1914, to Jefferson L. Daniels, Agent in Charge Western Division, Pinkerton National Detective Agency.

Dear Mr. Daniels,

Thank you for your prompt response to my letter of 10 January. I shall look forward to hearing from Mr. Simmons in the near future.

I assure you I am most grateful for the rapid response shown by your agency to my request for assistance. As I indicated in my initial request, I am convinced the incidents of sabotage and labor unrest TJ&M is now experiencing are caused or inspired by union sympathizers who are seeking to promote the cause of socialism. I believe the WFM is specifically targeting TJ&M because of our firm's historic resolve to maintain a work place free of socialist intervention and influence.

I think it advisable for Mr. Simmons to have access to another person within TJ&M other than myself should it be necessary to communicate with me. As Mr. Simmons's identity includes his occupation as a driller, it seems only practical to have a contact underground in the event Mr. Simmons may require assistance. One of my shift managers, Mr. Tate Cardwell, will be entrusted with the knowledge of Mr. Simmons's true identity and purpose. I have also arranged for the use of a residence in the town of Telluride occupied by Miss Adele Belden and rented under the name David Anderson where Mr. Simmons and I can meet in private. I expect Mr. Simmons to keep me personally and confidentially informed concerning his progress .

Sincerely,

Victor LaTrobe
Superintendent, TJ&M Enterprises

The last paragraph seemed to rule out the likelihood of Tate Cardwell being Phillip Hardesty's—John Simmons'— murderer. It also explained Adele Belden's relationship to Hardesty and to Victor LaTrobe. It was a clever idea to hold private meetings in a place suited to keeping visits discreet and confidential. If there was anything more than a business relationship between Hardesty and Adele as intimated by Stockwell, there was no way to know. It looked just as likely Victor LaTrobe was taking comfort from Adele Belden to compensate for a loveless marriage while using her houses in Telluride and an Adobe Wells as convenient places to meet.

Morgan briefly considered the possibility Stockwell may have been responsible for Hardesty's murder. Stockwell hated the Pinkertons for what had happened in Cripple Creek. Had the tough union representative known Hardesty's identity, he would have been more apt to take care of Hardesty himself rather than depend on someone else to do it, assuming he would have been able to gain access to the Emily Mine, a remote possibility at best considering how the miners were logged in and out. Nor would Stockwell try to make the murder look like an accident. On the contrary, Stockwell would go out of his way to make Hardesty's death both a statement and a warning. He also didn't believe Stockwell had the capability to dissemble; he was simply too blunt and explosive to conceal his feelings. The moment he suspected Hardesty worked for the Pinkerton Agency, he would have more likely dealt with him on the spot. That left Willard Merrick as a likely suspect. He supposed the conclusion was logical if not yet provable. A circumstantial case implicating Merrick was at least as strong as the one facing Frank in the event the missing driller couldn't be found alive or dead which was becoming a definite possibility.

Morgan left the bank still considering the contents of the deposit box as he made his way to the jail to inform Truesdale what he'd found. He took a shortcut past the Arabian Club. The club made him think the identity of the mystery benefactor Josephine Dylan, the sometime whore, had mentioned was Victor LaTrobe. More out of curiosity than from conviction he would learn anything more, he entered the Arabian Club to find Nat Hoskins whom he was certain had lied to him about not knowing the identity of Adele Belden's Thursday night visitor.

Morgan found the card-playing pimp sprawled in the same chair he had occupied the previous week. This time Hoskins was fast asleep, head thrown back, mouth wide open, and snoring loud enough to be heard over a noisy group of men clustered around the roulette wheel. Morgan picked up the half empty glass of beer on the table in front of Hoskins and standing to one side, poured a generous amount down the sleeping man's open mouth.

Red-faced and choking, Hoskins finally managed to say, "You bastard!" as he reached for a derringer tucked in his left boot.

Morgan calmly sat down on the other side of the table and pulled his coat aside displaying the badge and Colt revolver. "I wouldn't do that."

Hoskins eyed the badge and revolver and slowly lowered the small pistol. "Jesus Christ, I could've choked to death. Why in hell did you do that?"

"Because you held out on me."

"What are you talking about?"

"The last time we talked, you said you didn't know who Adele Belden was seeing every Thursday night. You lied to me Hoskins. I'm going to give you one more chance to tell the truth."

"I told you then I didn't know and I still don't."

"I think we'll take a walk on over to the jail. I expect a little time in a cell might jar your memory."

"On what charge? You can't arrest me, 'cause I ain't done nothin'."

"I'll think of something, how about lying to a peace officer, obstructing the investigation of a murder—well I've got time to think of a few more things."

"What do you think I been lyin' about?"

"Let's start with why you didn't tell me Victor LaTrobe was the one paying for Adele Belden's time and the rent on the house she was living in."

"How do you know that?" Hoskins said in surprise.

"The truth usually comes out, and I'm giving you one more chance to tell me what you know about it."

"All right, all right, you've made your point. About eight months or so, some skinny guy comes in here looking like he's got a corn cob up his ass." Morgan thought it was an apt description of LaTrobe's executive assistant. "He said he wanted to rent the house on behalf of Victor LaTrobe. It was to be a confidential matter, and I was to say nothing about who would use the house and when. He said a woman by the name of Adele Belden was going to be the sole occupant. She'd be available for privately arranged engagements only except on Thursday when she was supposed to be off. I'd be paid an amount for each client I arranged for her to see. Hell, it was the best goddamned deal I ever had in all the years I been runnin' whores."

"Did you ever see Victor LaTrobe meet there with anyone besides Adele Belden?"

"Mister, I never laid eyes on Victor LaTrobe. If he went there, it must've been at night on account that was the one night Adele wasn't available. The rent was always on time, and she never held back on me as far as I know. She treated me right, and I did the same to her. I didn't figure it was in my interests to ask any questions as long as I was getting paid."

"Did she ever have any visitors who weren't paying customers?"

"Well, now you mention it, there was one. I went over there once on a Sunday afternoon to ask if she was gonna work Monday night. There were a couple of fellas there eatin' dinner. From the looks of them, they was miners. I remember one of them was a real handsome feller. I figured maybe Adele was probably letting him have it for free."

Morgan was certain the individual described was Hardesty. "Adele told me off later, 'cause I came over unannounced."

"What did the two men do when you saw them?"

"The good lookin' one with the blonde hair kinda turned away like he didn't want me to get a good look at him, but the other darker haired fella, he just looked like he didn't care."

"Did you ever see either man around there again?"

"Yeah, the dark-haired man used to come in the Arabian now and then. I don't know if he went back to see Adele. If he did, he was one of her private arrangements."

Morgan described Elias Stockwell and asked if he had ever been seen in the Arabian or visiting Adele. Hoskins vigorously denied seeing him or knowing who he was.

Morgan stood up satisfied Hoskins had told him what he knew. "If you think of anything else you've forgotten to tell me you better look me up. If I find out you haven't been straight, I'll be back and take a hard look around in case there's anything wrong with the tables or cards, if you catch my drift."

"I told you what I know, and that's all I got to say. Maybe since you're here you might find out who broke into Adele's place. Whoever did it must've cut himself pretty bad on the broken glass. There's blood on the door and some bloody bandages on the floor. Didn't see anything missing except some cans of food that used to be on a shelf next to the stove."

Morgan stared at the card player and wondered how he could have been so blind.

Morgan saw blood stains on the porch and door below the broken pane, on the kitchen floor, and in the hall leading to the bedroom. Inside the bedroom, there was a large pool of dried blood next to the bed. One of the bed sheets had been ripped apart presumably for bandages.

Morgan drew the revolver and left the house through the back door for the partially covered mine entrance. The kerosene lantern which he had noticed before near the entrance was gone. Cautiously, he bent down and squeezed through the narrow opening, pausing long enough for his eyes to become accustomed to the dark interior. The air coming out of the mine was cool as it fanned his face; it also carried the faint odor of sweat and human feces. He heard a rustling noise farther down the tunnel and was acutely aware he was silhouetted against the entrance. Gradually his eyes became adjusted to the gloom. He saw a flicker of light ahead, and heard the sound of labored breathing growing louder as he slowly walked toward the lantern.

"Willard Merrick, my name is Morgan Westphal, and I'm armed. Don't make it worse by doing anything foolish." The only response was an audible groan.

Morgan found Merrick lying on a dirty makeshift pallet next to the lantern. Empty cans were piled up nearby. Even in the dim light cast by the lantern, it was easy to see Willard Merrick was in bad shape. Holstering the Colt, Morgan lifted the lantern and turned up the wick to better examine the prone man's condition. Merrick's lower left forearm cradled on his chest was abnormally short. Where his hand had once been, there was now only a crude blood-soaked bandage. The arm visible above the bandage was badly swollen. Morgan knelt down for a closer look and saw Merrick was staring at him through half-open eyes.

"Merrick, I've got to get you to a hospital. Are you able to stand?" The injured man shook his head without saying anything. "Then I'm going to have to leave you and get help."

In a voice soft but surprisingly steady, Merrick said, "Don't bother. After what I done, I might as well finish it here, and I figure it ain't gonna be much longer at that. Been layin' here waitin' and wonderin' if I'll go out before the lantern. But I ain't sorry for nothin' except what LaTrobe did to me and mine."

"You want to tell me about it?"

"Not much to tell. They killed my wife and daughter the same as if they had shot them down." Morgan knew Merrick was focused on Ludlow and not on the Emily Mine. "Hell, worse than the scabs dressed up in army uniforms were them bastards from one of them detective agencies. They had this goddamned truck with a machine gun mounted on it they called the 'Death Special.' They come around mainly at night and shot at the tents. We dug pits under the tents and slept there to keep from getting gunned down in our sleep. The militia had machine guns up on the ridges, too. We never had no chance a'tall. Then they set fire to the tents;

Elspeth and Arabella didn't make it out. That was the end of the strike, and we was the ones who lost. Some of us lost more'n the others."

In spite of what Merrick had done, Morgan felt sympathy for the loss of his wife and daughter. Merrick closed his eyes, and Morgan thought the injured man had drifted off. When he opened them again, Merrick gave Morgan a hard look. "Who the hell are you, mister?"

"I'm Frank Shaw's brother. You remember Frank?"

"Yeah, I knowed Frank. Sure don't make no sense why he up and killed Hardesty. Must had somethin' to do with that woman is all I can figure."

Morgan was incredulous as he realized Merrick thought Frank had killed Hardesty. Could he have been so wrong about Frank? He refused to believe it. "Are you talking about Adele Belden? "

"Nah, not her, I'm talkin' about LaTrobe's wife, you know he's the superintendent of TJ&M."

"Olivia LaTrobe!" exclaimed Morgan, hardly able to believe what he had heard. "How do you know about her?"

"'Cause I knew Hardesty was sweet on her, and so was Frank. That was the reason they had a falling out. What the hell does it matter anyhow?"

"It matters a lot since I don't think Frank killed Hardesty. What happened between you and Hardesty?"

"We had an argument. I thought he was gonna help me flood the Emily. When I went down to the drift I'd been workin' before and where Hardesty was when Frank killed him, I expected to find him finishing the holes in the east wall like we planned. Everybody knew the east wall was weak and likely to go anytime on account of the water problem in that part of the mine. I figured blowin' the wall would finish the Emily. When I got there, Hardesty told me he changed his mind and was backin' out of the whole thing. He was supposed to have finished drillin' the holes I'd started the day before. He said he don't want no part of it. I got mad and hit him. I hit him harder than I intended. He fell back and hit his head on the jack-leg. It must've knocked him out 'cause he didn't move. I thought I might as well go back to where I'd been workin' since by then, it was too late to do any drillin' on the east face. I started to leave, but then I got to feelin' bad about what I done to Hardesty. Even if he did back out on me, he was good man and a friend of mine. I didn't want him to get in no trouble with Cardwell, so I figured I'd make up for what I done by finishing his round. The holes were mostly drilled so all's I had to do was drill a couple of holes and set the charges. When I finished setting the charges, I dragged Hardesty back into the crosscut where he'd be safe from the blastin'. He was just comin' around when I told him to stay where he was until after the charges went off. I left him to go back and light the fuses."

"He was alive when you left him?"

"Yeah, but he didn't look so good. He was sittin' up and had his head down like he might be gettin' ready to puke. I told him to stay where he was 'cause I was gettin' ready to light the charges. He nodded like he understood, but I wasn't certain he understood what I was tellin' him. Finally, he nodded and seemed to understand, and that's when I left him."

"You didn't stab him in the back with a candle pick?"

"Why the hell would I do that?" Merrick asked in genuine astonishment. "I didn't have anything against Hardesty. Sure, I was sore and mad enough to hit him, but I ain't no killer. My argument was with TJ&M, and them's the ones I was after."

"Where was Hardesty's candle pick when you came into the drift?"

"I don't rightly remember. I remember where it was when I went back to light the fuses. It was layin' there on the tunnel floor about ten feet or so from the jack-leg." Morgan breathed a sigh of relief. Hardesty must have fallen on the candle pick, and Merrick never knew it anymore than he had

251

any idea who Hardesty really was. The irony was Hardesty had died an accidental death after all.

"How did you know who I was and where to find me?"

"I thought the damage to the Emily and the TJ&M equipment yard was done by someone with a grudge against the company. I was trying to find you after you disappeared the night Hardesty died. I looked at your employment file with Sandusky Mining and saw where you had started to write the name of your wife. The Trinidad address was the giveaway. I knew the Hercules mine was near Ludlow."

"After I left Colorado, I come here and went to work for Sandusky. I wanted to forget what happened in Ludlow. Then TJ&M come down here, and I knowed it was a sign I was meant to do somethin' for Elspeth and Arabella."

"Why didn't you go after Victor LaTrobe or some of the other company managers?"

"I told you before, I ain't no killer. I wanted to see TJ&M pay for what they done. I shoulda stopped after floodin' the Emily and shuttin' down them other two mines, but I went after the equipment yard," Merrick added in disgust. "That's how I got this. Goddamn fuse was bad on the last charge I lit. Too bad it warn't more'n my hand, then I'd a gone quick-like instead of goin' slow like this."

Morgan didn't bother to waste time with false cheer. He'd seen enough death in Cuba to know Merrick was lucky to have survived this long. Instead, he continued to probe the dying man.

"Tell me about Adele Belden. Why did you have her posing as your wife?"

"After Hardesty was found dead in Frank's drift, I got scared and panicked. I thought maybe it was somehow my fault for hittin' him on the head then leavin' him like that. I figured I'd better get out of there while I could. Damn fool mistake 'cause it just made doin' what I needed to do that much harder. I told Adele what happened to Hardesty, and that I might be the one to get the blame. It was her come up

with the idea to make it look like I left town. I been hidin'
out in here ever since."

"Did you see who killed her?"

"No. After LaTrobe left—"

Surprised, Morgan interrupted. "You saw LaTrobe visit
Adele?"

"Yeah, I guess he was a regular visitor. No accounting for
that, considering how good lookin' his wife is. As I was
sayin,' after he left, I went back some time later to talk to
her. She was on the bed and pretty well done in from the
laudanum she was always takin.' She was undressing and
gettin' ready for bed. She said she was too tired to talk and
could it wait until tomorrow."

"Did you leave?"

"Yeah."

"And did you come back the next morning?"

"Yeah, just before sunup. Found her dead with one of her
stockings around her neck. I left damn quick and come back
in here. I got real scared I was gonna get blamed for killing
her. Shit, Phillip and Adele were the only two people I cared
about."

"Do you have any idea who killed her?"

"Mister, I got no idea a'tall."

Chapter Twenty-Five

"That was the doc," Truesdale said to Morgan after putting down the phone. "He said Merrick is awake and maybe we should come over to the hospital and see about gettin' a formal statement. He said we'd better be real quick. The doc's gonna have to operate again to take more of the arm off. He says he ain't real confident he'll make it through the operation on account of all the blood he's lost. But he also said he can't afford to wait until he's stronger; there's already signs of blood poison. If Merrick is able to repeat what he told you, it'll probably be enough to convince Judge Breen to drop the charges against Frank."

The two men walked out of the jail toward the roadster and heard a low rumble. Truesdale looked up and saw clouds rapidly gathering above. "Reckin' I'd best get the canvas on, sure looks like it's gonna be a doozy." Morgan helped the marshal pull up and fasten the canvas top on the roadster. "What about Adele Belden?" Truesdale said as he started the car and eased the throttle forward. "You got any idea who killed her?"

Morgan shook his head. "Not really, although Victor LaTrobe is still a possible suspect. He could have come back and killed her sometime after Merrick saw him leave. I can't think of a reason why he would. I'll do some more checking in the time I've got left here. Now that the strike appears to be pretty much over, if I don't come up with anything, you may have to finish the investigation yourself."

"You think it coulda been Blaylock?"

"I don't think so. He had no reason to, and if he had, my guess is he probably would have told me. Since he planned on killing me it wouldn't have mattered what he told me. I suspect he didn't even know who Hardesty really was or his connection to LaTrobe and Adele Belden. There's also the difficulty he would have had getting inside the Emily."

"Why was Blaylock looking for Merrick if he already knew the whore was lyin' 'bout him being her husband?"

"Cardwell was suspicious when he came up to the surface and found Merrick gone. Cardwell knew he was going to have to answer to LaTrobe for the holes I told him I'd found in the drift. Until then, he claims he didn't know they were there. Since Merrick was the one working the drift until that night, he had every reason to believe Merrick was the one responsible. It's even conceivable Hardesty had already told LaTrobe and probably Cardwell too that Merrick was up to something. Perhaps the reason Cardwell assigned Hardesty to the east drift was to protect the Emily from precisely what happened later. Cardwell never suspected Merrick had anything to do with Hardesty's death. The night it happened, he and everyone else thought the death was accidental. When Chambliss found the puncture wound on Hardesty's back, Cardwell had reason enough to think Frank was responsible. Cardwell went to Blaylock because he knew Blaylock would keep his mouth shut about his reason for finding Merrick. It was also no secret to you or LaTrobe that Blaylock wanted your job. Blaylock was willing to look for Merrick since he figured if he found him, LaTrobe would be appreciative enough to back him when he ran for marshal."

"Why did LaTrobe want an autopsy done?"

"Could be LaTrobe wasn't convinced the circumstances of Hardesty's death were entirely accidental. He probably thought someone had discovered who Hardesty really was. And like Cardwell, he suspected Frank was the culprit."

"Morgan, you ever figure why Hardesty had his bags packed?"

"I've got a notion he was planning to leave town. He was ready to point a finger at Merrick for his plan to flood the Emily, and maybe a few others he knew or suspected were union men. He also may have thought his cover had been or was about to be exposed. I'm sure it was Adele Belden that packed his bag."

"Mebbe she was leavin' with him."

"It's possible. She had a picture of him, and Stockwell even said they seemed at least respectful of each other when he saw them together. More likely, Adele Belden was simply doing a job she was being paid to do. It was a job that paid well and kept her in the one thing she cared most about, laudanum. Her murder may have had nothing to do with Hardesty or Merrick."

"When are you going back to Albuquerque?"

"As soon as Frank is released, and that could be as early as tomorrow."

At first it was a just fitful rain without any indication of the fury that would follow. Lightning flashes, the crack of thunder, and brief torrential downpours lashed the hospital window with a furious intensity. The nurse came in the room where Morgan was sitting with Frank and whispered to him Willard Merrick had died in the operating room. She also told him Dr. Chambliss wanted to see him right away.

Morgan considered waking Frank to tell him about Merrick and just as quickly decided against it. There was no point. Frank would know soon enough, and after all, he already knew Merrick had given a statement repeating what he had said in the tunnel. Once the judge saw the statement, Frank would be a free man, and he could leave Adobe Wells, or least after fulfilling his promise to help Truesdale find out who killed Adele Belden. Privately, he wasn't optimistic in finding the murderer. There was a better chance the case would never be solved. Whores were vulnerable by the very nature of their trade. She wouldn't be the last one to die by the hand of a customer, or for that matter, another prostitute jealous of an arrangement Adele had she didn't. Josephine Dylan said Adele wasn't popular with the other prostitutes. Perhaps for one particular individual, envy or dislike, or both was the motivation to kill her. The idea was at least worth exploring.

Wearing a hat and slicker, Chambliss was carrying a medical bag. "Mr. Westphal, I think it might be a good idea if you were to come with me. I tried to reach the marshal; however, I was unsuccessful."

"I don't understand."

"I just received a call from Victor LaTrobe's chauffeur. It seems I'm needed most urgently. I'm very much concerned there may be a need for a peace officer as well."

"What makes you think so?"

"Let us say for the moment I have my reasons. I sincerely hope they are unfounded. If not, then your presence will be important. If I'm wrong, you will have taken a drive in the rain for nothing. My obligation to my patients and their privacy prevents me from saying more."

"Your patients?" Morgan said.

"Yes, Mr. Westphal, Olivia and Victor LaTrobe are both my patients."

Fortunately, the doctor proved to be a skillful driver who confidently negotiated the rain-washed streets now covered in viscous mud or running water. In several low areas, debris had collected to form makeshift dams creating pools deep enough to wash over the automobile's running boards.

"Doctor, I came across something the other day I've been meaning to ask you about. What is *Salvorsan?*"

The doctor abruptly braked the automobile to a stop and gave Morgan a long searching look, his expression reflecting a mix of surprise and suspicion. "Mr. Westphal, I find your question most curious both for why you've asked and why now."

The reaction was more than Morgan expected. "No particular reason. I was merely curious what ailment it would be prescribed for, and since you're the one who wrote the prescription for Victor LaTrobe."

The doctor's sudden flash of anger slowly disappeared, replaced by calm resignation. "I'll not ask how you came to know I prescribed the drug for Victor LaTrobe. At this point, I doubt it hardly matters. Mr. Westphal, *arsphenamine*, or *Salvorsan* as it is commercially known, is used to treat syphilis."

In spite of the driving rain, the chauffeur was standing anxiously with the door open waiting for Morgan and the doctor to climb the steps to the veranda.

"Fletcher, this is Deputy Marshal Westphal." Fletcher acknowledged the introduction with a nod. "Where is he?" Chambliss said.

"He's in the study, Doctor. I'm afraid this time it's very bad."

"Quite so, it was to be expected. I'm only surprised it's taken this long."

Mystified, Morgan followed the doctor and chauffeur down the hallway. He heard a woman sobbing somewhere upstairs. The two men entered the study and found the room a shambles with books and broken vases littering the floor. Victor LaTrobe sat rigidly at his desk, hands gripping the framed wedding photograph so tight his knuckles were white. Morgan was shocked at what he saw. In sharp contrast to his usual neat appearance, LaTrobe was disheveled, in need of a shave, and his hair was uncombed. His unbuttoned shirt revealed an angry red lesion on his chest.

"Victor, how are you today?" Chambliss spoke in a soothing voice while extracting a small case and glass vial from the medical bag. LaTrobe did not answer and instead threw his head back and laughed shrilly. Making no further effort at conversation, the doctor opened the small case and took out a syringe and proceeded to fill it from the vial. LaTrobe never moved when Chambliss pulled up his patient's sleeve and plunged the needle into his arm. When he finished the injection, the doctor calmly turned to Morgan and said, "I've given him a sedative. In a few minutes, he will be much more relaxed, possibly even lucid. In the meantime, Mr. Westphal, you are observing the ugly effects of tertiary syphilis."

"Will he get better?"

"No, he will only get worse than he is now. The tragedy is that he may continue to live a few more years. Increasingly, he will understand less and less what is wrong with him or control his actions. Eventually, he will dwell in a world where he is the only inhabitant. He has gone there now for a brief visit. It would be better for him not to come back to this one. Regrettably, Victor LaTrobe is not alone. The disease has reached epidemic levels in many countries, and we are no exception and among the worst. Conservative estimates suggest between 10-15% of our men, women, and yes, even children suffer from various stages of the disease. Strangely, men seem more severely afflicted than women. I conjecture this is because women are more likely to seek treatment than men. We have an absurd belief in our society any discussion or publication of sexually transmitted diseases cannot be tolerated. Because of that, a disease that can be successfully treated in its early stages is kept locked away behind closed doors. Those infected are treated as social lepers inspiring too many to avoid seeking the assistance of a physician for fear their shame will be revealed."

"How long has he had the disease?"

"He's probably had it for at least fifteen years. When I first saw him soon after his arrival and questioned him, he wasn't sure. He claimed he contracted it when he was in Europe as a young man. He was treated with applications of mercury, which was then the accepted and reasonably effective treatment. At least, it was until recently when *Salvorsan* was proven to be a more effective treatment. He said his symptoms disappeared in time, and he believed erroneously that he was cured. Syphilis is a pernicious disease. It can lie dormant for years then suddenly it will be revealed sometimes masquerading as something else that is incorrectly diagnosed. I'm afraid such was the case with Victor LaTrobe who eventually transitioned to a latent and secondary stage of the disease. During this stage, he had no idea he was still infected. One-third of those with secondary syphilis will contract tertiary syphilis. The tertiary stage is characterized by serious arterial and neurological damage along with severe lesions of the skin, bones, and the brain. Note the lesions on Mr. LaTrobe's chest. They are the visible ones; the lesions in his brain are not, but they are there."

Morgan now understood LaTrobe's partial paralysis, the uncontrollable anger he displayed at the Emily Mine, and the condition of his office where he must have gone right after Truesdale ordered him to leave the mine. He was struck by a sudden and alarming thought. He turned to Fletcher and asked, "Where is Mrs. LaTrobe?" The chauffeur glanced at Chambliss in surprise.

"No, Fletcher, I haven't told Mr. Westphal. I suggest you take him to see her." Fletcher nodded, and Morgan followed him upstairs. The sound of a woman crying grew louder the farther they went toward the back of the house. Morgan was surprised. He didn't think Olivia LaTrobe was the type to cry over anything.

Fletcher finally stopped in the hallway and gestured silently to an open door. By now it was apparent the room was the source of the weeping. Morgan entered and saw the woman crying was not Olivia LaTrobe; it was Celia. The grief-stricken housekeeper was sitting on a divan with her face in her hands. Olivia LaTrobe was lying on the bed covered in a blanket to her chin. Her porcelain features, somewhat frozen in life, now seemed oddly relaxed, almost serene, lips curving upward slightly in the barest suggestion of a smile. Morgan saw there was more resemblance now to the woman in the wedding photograph on Victor LaTrobe's desk. She seemed happy in the photograph, her expression one of contented satisfaction not unlike the way she appeared now.

Morgan walked toward the bed and smelled the sweetish odor of blood. He pulled back the blanket and saw a large dark stain spreading across the front of her white satin gown. He also found the pistol that had taken her life toward the foot of the bed. It was obvious from the position of the weapon she had not taken her own life.

"What happened, Fletcher?"

"Last night around eleven o'clock, I heard them arguing. It was worse and went on longer than usual. Mr. LaTrobe was very angry. It seemed the madder he got, the more she laughed. She often said things just to provoke him, and yet this time it was different. In the past, he would go back to his room and close the door. Instead, he went to the study. Soon I heard crashes and the sound of breaking glass. I put my robe on and went into the hall. I met Celia in the hall. She was on her way upstairs to see if Mrs. La Trobe needed anything. When I got to the study, Mr. LaTrobe was quiet and drinking a glass of brandy. He told me everything was all right and apologized for the noise and the mess he had made. He told me to go back to bed. On the way back to my room, I met Celia coming down the stairs. She told me Mrs. LaTrobe was preparing for bed and was in very good spirits. Celia even said it had been a long time since she had seen the missus smile as much. I was getting ready for bed when I heard the sound of a loud noise upstairs that sounded like it might be a gunshot. I put my robe on and ran up to the second floor. I met Mr. LaTrobe in the hallway. He looked the way he does now. I asked him what was the matter and if Mrs. LaTrobe was all right. He wouldn't answer me and just laughed. I ran to Mrs. LaTrobe's room and found her lying on the bed. I knew right away she was dead before I saw the gun at the foot of the bed. I covered her with a blanket and went to tell Celia and to call Doctor Chambliss. The doctor told Celia and me to call him if Mr. LaTrobe ever got worse.

They told me he was in surgery and wasn't available, so I left a message for him to call me."

"Why didn't you call the marshal's office?"

"I tried, but the operator said she couldn't get through. She thought the line must be down."

"You said the LaTrobes argued frequently. Do you know why they argued?"

"Yes, it was always about the child."

"What child?"

"A year after they were married, Mrs. LaTrobe gave birth to a baby boy they named Christopher. Mrs. LaTrobe had a difficult time and nearly died. It would have been better had the baby died at birth. It was badly deformed and lived for almost two years before it finally passed away. From the time of the birth, the troubles began between them. Outside the house, they carried on as usual; inside, it was a different matter. Mrs. LaTrobe blamed her husband for the baby's condition and for the reason she couldn't have another child. From that time on, she made his life unbearable. He never argued with her and would simply let her say awful things to him. He tolerated it because he blamed himself. Over the past several years, he began to resent her verbal attacks when they changed from angry accusations to taunts and laughter for his impotence. She told him she had affairs with other men. He would get angry and leave the room. Later he would buy her expensive gifts to make amends. Most of the time, she would give or throw the gifts away."

"Did Mrs. LaTrobe have affairs?"

Fletcher nodded slowly, "In a way I suppose she did. She was beautiful, and men found her attractive. I would say she flirted more than anything else. Celia and I think she never went beyond that. I believe she couldn't or didn't want to love anyone. She merely made it look as if she did simply to torment Mr. LaTrobe."

"You said Mr. LaTrobe was impotent. How do you know this?"

"Mrs. LaTrobe used to tell him they deserved each other; she was barren, he was impotent, and neither one of them had any further value."

"Did you know he was paying to see a woman in Telluride and here in Adobe Wells?"

"Yes. I drove him there. I would drop him off a few streets away and pick him up afterward."

"Did Mrs. LaTrobe know about the arrangement?"

"Yes, she did."

"Did she resent it?"

"No, she laughed about it. It was another way to taunt him. She would tell him he was wasting his money since he wasn't able to do anything with her."

"I'm curious, Fletcher, why did you and Celia stay with the LaTrobes? This must not have been a pleasant place to work."

"They may have been unkind to each other, but they were never so to us. Celia had been with the Thurlowe family for many years before Mr. and Mrs. LaTrobe got married. She loved Mrs. LaTrobe as if she had been her own daughter."

Doctor Chambliss was standing next to Victor LaTrobe taking his pulse when Morgan re-entered the study. The sedative had taken effect, and there was an almost miraculous difference in LaTrobe's demeanor. His face showing only faint interest. LaTrobe watched Morgan approach the desk. The photograph LaTrobe had been clutching was laying face-up on the desk.

"Good morning, Mr. Westphal. Are deputy marshals now obliged to make house calls with Dr. Chambliss? I'm surprised to see you, and for that matter, the doctor as well. I don't recall sending for him, and I'm not altogether certain why he's here."

"How are you feeling, Victor?"

"Fine, I've never felt better. I don't know who did this," he added, gesturing to the condition of the room. "I'll have to speak to Fletcher to be more careful locking up at night. I've no doubt some of those union wretches are responsible."

"Mr. LaTrobe, why did you kill your wife?" Morgan asked quietly.

"Oh, you found Olivia then, did you? Doesn't she look beautiful? I'll always love her no matter what she said to me. That's why I put up with her hatred all these years. I deserved it. She was right, you know, what happened to Christopher was my fault. I didn't know anything was wrong with me when we married. She never believed me. I saw her abuse as the punishment I deserved."

"Then why kill her?

"She told me last night she strangled Adele Belden." Morgan and the doctor exchanged startled looks.

Astonished, Morgan asked, "Why would she do that?"

"It was another way to strike at me. I also think she was jealous. It wasn't that she resented Adele, rather, it was in seeing me come home happier than when I left—for achieving something she was unable to have even with her occasional affairs. Oh, yes, I knew all about them. She never missed an opportunity to tell me about them.

But killing Adele was unforgivable. I couldn't let that pass. I know what you're thinking. Adele was just a whore who would do what you paid her to do. To me she was more than that. Adele was my friend. She was the companion Olivia no longer was. For a few hours, I pretended she was Olivia. We talked and played cards. She would hold me in her arms and tell me she loved me. I knew she didn't really, but I was lonely and didn't mind she was pretending. The hours I spent with Adele were the only happy moments I've had for many years. I suppose in some way the visits only caused me to miss even more what I once shared with Olivia for such a short time."

Morgan thought Victor LaTrobe's admission was about the saddest thing he'd ever heard.

Doctor Chambliss said, "Mr. Westphal, when you've lived as long as I have, you make the mistake of thinking you've seen and heard all there is to see and hear. Once again I'm proven wrong."

"I suppose by telling him she killed Adele, she anticipated what he would do. If true, perhaps it was her way of ending her own misery in addition to committing a final act of revenge by goading him into killing her."

Chambliss nodded and gazed thoughtfully out the window at the rain still beating against the window pane. "I wonder if Victor LaTrobe is in some way the latest example of the human tragedy."

Morgan was only half-listening to the doctor and chose not to respond even though he privately thought Victor LaTrobe was anything but a tragic figure. He was distracted by the disquieting feeling he had somehow missed something. It was like a missing piece in a jigsaw puzzle that without it the final picture was still incomplete. He was still thinking about it when Truesdale arrived a few minutes later and arrested Vincent LaTrobe.

Chapter Twenty-Six

Morgan found his brother looking much better than he expected. Frank was sitting in a wheelchair on the back porch of the hospital chatting with a young, attractive nurse. He thought the nurse's company was doing as much for him as any pills he was taking. Although his face was badly discolored, the swelling had gone down considerably. The sutures on his cheeks and forehead reminded Morgan of railroad tracks. If Frank was concerned about how he was going to look when he healed, he didn't show it with his cheerful, welcome smile. Morgan noticed the way the nurse was looking at Frank and concluded she didn't seem to mind either. His brother had never needed to depend solely on his good looks; he had a personality and way about him women gravitated to. He had always envied Frank for this quality, something he didn't seem to have.

"Morg, how're you doing? This is Cora. Cora this is my brother, Morgan. I owe this man more than I'll ever be able to repay." Morgan was touched by the comment.

The nurse smiled and made her exit, citing duties she had to perform. Frank watched her go and sighed, "Wonderful little girl. I'll miss her when I leave."

Morgan asked in surprise, "Where are you going?"

"I heard they're hiring down in Bisbee. Soon as I get better, I believe I'll try my luck there. I've had my fill of Adobe Wells. Reckon this town ain't been too good for me. When are you leaving?"

"This morning. I just dropped in to say goodbye."

"Hell, Morg, I was hoping you'd stick around a little longer so's we could spend a little time together." He saw Frank was genuinely disappointed and felt guilty.

"I wish I could, Frank. I've got a business to run in Albuquerque, and my partner is probably wondering when I'm coming back. I wired him yesterday the judge dropped the charges."

"I meant what I said to Cora. You've been good to me and always stood by me, helpin' me when I needed it. I've cost you a few bucks, too, and I ain't forgettin' that neither. One day I'm gonna pay you back, yes, siree, every penny of it, I promise." Morgan knew Frank was just as sincere in promising as he was in his capability to forget all about it.

"Never mind that. You can pay me back by staying out of trouble."

Frank laughed. "Well, you know me. I never go lookin' for trouble. Shit, it just finds me like a hog findin' an acorn."

This time Morgan merely smiled instead of giving the same lecture he'd delivered before after one of Frank's escapades. He accepted the fact his brother would never change. There would undoubtedly be another time when he would be obliged to come to his brother's rescue, financial or otherwise and usually both. The conversation was getting too personal, and he changed the subject. "Frank, something's been bothering me. The night you went to see Hardesty, what did you go to see him about?"

Frank hesitated before replying reluctantly. "Phillip was havin' an affair with Olivia LaTrobe. Leastways, he thought he was. Claimed they was gonna get married or some such foolishness as that. I tried to reason with him."

"Why did you feel like you had to do that?"

Again Frank hesitated clearly reluctant to explain. "'Cause I knew what kinda woman she was. You see, I sorta got involved with her in Telluride. Now, I swear it wasn't what you're thinkin' a'tall. It never amounted to much. By and by, I got the impression that was all it was ever gonna be. I'd also heard rumors she'd carried on with others even though if she did, I never heard anyone admit it. Phillip and I had been friends, and I thought I should tell him what I thought she was up to. That's all there was to it. We shook hands on it, and I left."

"So Olivia LaTrobe was the reason you two had a falling out?"

"Yep, I guess that's about the size of it."

"Why didn't you tell me when I asked what was between you?"

"It was embarrassing, and I didn't want to cause Olivia. LaTrobe any trouble. And besides, I didn't figure it really mattered anyhow."

Morgan nodded. "I suppose you're right. No harm done." Morgan held out his hand. "I've got a train to catch, so I'd best be leaving."

Instead of taking the outstretched hand, Frank stood up and enfolded Morgan in a hug that must have caused a twinge to his bandaged ribs. At first, Morgan was startled and almost drew back, unprepared for the spontaneous affection. He stepped back and took a close look at Frank. It occurred to him he had spent too many years resenting Frank for things he couldn't help. It was more his fault than Frank's they weren't close and maybe never would be. He resolved to try and see things different in the future the next time he got a telegram, letter, or phone call from Frank. And he knew he would. If he had to help Frank in the future, perhaps he would do it because Frank was his brother and not because he'd promised ma. It was a revelation that would take time to get used to.

Morgan left the hospital and joined Dan Truesdale waiting to drive him down to Mesquite Flats. Most of the way down the steep and winding road, Morgan remained silent and oblivious of the number of times the marshal came perilously close to going over the edge. It was what Frank had said concerning his reason for going to see Hardesty that had got him thinking again about the entire sequence of events.

"Dan, do you recall what the chauffeur told me about

Olivia LaTrobe's affairs?" The marshal nodded and kept his attention on the road ahead. "He referred to them as being flirtations."

"You mean bluffing you're gonna play the hand then pull out of the game when the stakes get too high?"

"Yeah, something like that, but what if Victor LaTrobe thought otherwise? When I talked to Olivia LaTrobe in the park, she said she told her husband about Hardesty. LaTrobe admitted to me and Doctor Chambliss he knew all about her affairs. I assume the admission included both Frank and Hardesty."

"I don't know where you're headin' with this Morgan," the marshal responded with more irritation than curiosity.

"Perhaps LaTrobe thought the affairs with Hardesty and Frank were becoming more serious than the ones she had before. If so, maybe he intended to do something about it. Remember the notation I found in LaTrobe's check book indicating a payment to Cardwell of a $100 without any notation what it was for? What doesn't make sense is I also found correspondence indicating Cardwell was being put on notice for non-performance. If he was not performing on the job, why would LaTrobe pay him $100 out of his own pocket?"

"Jesus, what the hell does it matter now, Morgan?"

"Dan, I don't like loose ends. Consider Hardesty's bags were packed to leave Adobe Wells and concealing the fact he was. It's entirely possible Olivia was going with him, or at least Hardesty believed she was. More significant is that maybe LaTrobe believed it." Truesdale glanced at Morgan with interest.

"Are you suggesting maybe LaTrobe was payin' Cardwell to take care of Hardesty?"

"That's exactly what I'm proposing, and Frank was part of the plan as well. Cardwell arranged for Hardesty to be there in that particular drift at that specific time not for the purpose of protecting the east wall but rather to put Hardesty in a place where he could be killed with the least chance of being discovered. Cardwell assigned Frank to the adjacent drift to put the blame on him for Hardesty's assumed affair with Olivia. That was why LaTrobe wanted the autopsy done in order to show Hardesty did not die accidentally but was really murdered as he paid Cardwell to do. If Olivia told her husband about Hardesty, she probably confessed to the one she had with Frank."

"Are you sayin' your brother was having an affair with Latrobe's wife?" The marshal asked in astonishment.

"Frank admitted to me he did in Telluride, although he said it never went very far. Perhaps she made more of it when she told her husband. If she did, LaTrobe would get revenge on Frank by seeing him convicted and hanged for Hardesty's murder."

"I thought Hardesty fell back on the candle pick?"

"So did I, at least until now."

"What makes you think now he didn't?"

"I asked Merrick if he stabbed Hardesty, and he said he didn't. I believed him then and still do. Merrick knew he was dying; therefore, he had no reason to lie. I asked where he saw the candle pick, and he said the candle-pick was close to the jack-leg Hardesty hit his head on. The position near and low to the jack-leg was where it would have been logically placed to have been any use as a warning to Hardesty in the event of mine gas. I made the assumption Hardesty fell on it by accident. The mistake I made was I didn't consider where I found the candle-pick. It was too far past the crosscut to have fallen out of Hardesty's back when Merrick dragged him into the crosscut."

"Merrick said after he got Hardesty into the crosscut, Hardesty was groggy but conscious and sitting up with his head down. I think that's where Cardwell found him. He hit Hardesty with the drill bit I saw in the crosscut. That explains the position of the head wound at the back of his head Doctor Chambliss described to me. Until now, I thought Hardesty had been struck from behind but in reality Cardwell was standing over and facing Hardesty when Cardwell struck him. When Hardesty fell forward, Cardwell stabbed him in the back to make sure he was dead. Cardwell then pushed Hardesty into Frank's drift. Then he went back through the crosscut into Hardesty's drift to make his way to the main tunnel. He dropped the candle pick on the way back to the main tunnel. Cardwell probably thought he got lucky when he found Hardesty barely conscious. It made the job a lot easier to do what LaTrobe paid him for."

"Why did Cardwell go looking for Merrick?" Truesdale said.

"I think Cardwell passed Merrick when he was heading for Hardesty's drift. He probably didn't think much about it until Merrick disappeared after he helped take Hardesty's body up out of the mine. When Merrick wasn't with the body, Cardwell got worried and began to wonder if Merrick had seen or suspected what had happened. That's when Cardwell contacted Blaylock and told him to find Merrick."

"Well, I'll be damned! How you gonna prove any of this?" he asked as they drove into Mesquite Flats.

"Me? The way I see it, the reason I came to Adobe Wells was to get Frank's neck out of a noose, and that's been done. Since I gave you back my badge, I no longer have any legal authority in Adobe Wells. Dan, the real question is how are *you* going to prove it?"

"Jesus Christ, Morgan, I don't have any notion how I'm gonna nail Cardwell. You said LaTrobe wasn't lookin' too good when you last saw him and unless he's gonna admit he hired Cardwell to kill Hardesty, I got no way to prove Cardwell did anything but do his job the night it happened."

There was a shrill shriek of the steam whistle as the engineer signaled the train was about to depart. Morgan reached out to shake Truesdale's hand and said, "Dan, LaTrobe is still rational enough at times to ask him about Hardesty. If I'm right about him hiring Cardwell, my guess he'll probably admit it. After all he's already confessed to killing his wife, so he has nothing more to lose. With a confession from LaTrobe, there's a good chance Cardwell will fold, particularly if you suggest to him Merrick saw him leaving Hardesty's drift."

"Well it might work at that," the marshal conceded somewhat doubtfully, watching Morgan board the train. "I'll let you know how it turns out," he yelled above the chuffing engine and grinding wheels as the train began to pull slowly away.

Morgan turned around on the top step and gave a final wave to Truesdale, but the marshal was already walking away. He looked up at the distant escarpment above the town of Adobe Wells and saw the skeletal silhouettes of some of the mine head frames against the blue sky. He thought the one farthest to the right and leaning at an angle was the Emily, but he wasn't sure

.

Historical Note

The labor wars at Cripple Creek and the Ludlow Massacre during the Colorado Coalfield War are a matter of historical record. Ludlow today is a ghost town; however, a statue erected by the United Mine Workers of America in 1918 commemorating the massacre continues to be maintained. The role of the Pinkerton National Detective Agency and other detective firms is well documented during these conflicts. My research suggests these agencies were responsible for inciting much of the trouble. The Baldwin–Felts Detective Agency was responsible for the 'Death Special' employed at Ludlow.

THE MYSTERY CONTINUES

A TROUBLESOME AFFAIR

The next Morgan Westphal Historical Mystery

Rueben LeCroix, a highly decorated Negro sergeant, is in the guardhouse at Fort Huachuca, Arizona, accused of the robbery, rape, and attempted murder of a white woman. The victim is Sophia Parmenter, wife of an army major. Morgan Westphal is a civilian private investigator who is surprisingly asked to investigate the crime. Against the historic backdrop of the U.S. Punitive Expedition into Mexico in 1916, *A Troublesome Affair* is a mystery with intricately connected characters caught up in a turbulent current of racial and military conflict.

WATCH FOR
A TROUBLESOME AFFAIR
Coming from Moonshine Cove
in 2014

Prologue

Office of the Commanding General
Southern Department, Fort Sam Houston, Texas

March 2, 1916

Colonel Wallace F. Broadmore
Commanding Officer
10th U.S. Cavalry, Colored
Fort Huachuca, Arizona

Colonel Broadmore,

General Funston has read your report describing the assault on the wife of Major Benjamin D. Parmenter with great concern. That the accused is colored and charged with the assault of a woman who is both white and the wife of a senior regimental officer requires this matter be handled expeditiously and with great sensitivity for the good of the United States Army. Every effort must be taken to ensure the pending court martial of Sergeant LeCroix does not receive undue public attention. To further minimize the latter, General Funston directs the trial be convened at Fort Apache instead of locally at Fort Huachuca.

The commanding general is also concerned about the potential adverse effect this troublesome affair may have on regimental morale at a time when the civil unrest in Mexico is threatening the lives and property of U.S. citizens along the border. Punitive action by the U.S. military against Mexican rebel forces may yet be necessary, and if so, any such effort will require participation by the 10th Cavalry Regiment.

A copy of this letter has been sent to Col E. F. Delaney, Commanding Officer, Fort Apache.

E.G. Ritter, Colonel
Adjutant General

Chapter 1
March 8, 1916

Sergeant Major Isaiah Washington, 10th Cavalry, Colored, looked at the prisoner and said, "Reuben, your only chance is to tell them what you told me."

Stable Sergeant Reuben LeCroix gripped the metal slats of the cell and responded, "I can't do that, and you swore you wouldn't repeat what I said. I'm holdin' you to it."

"Better think real hard on changing your mind 'cause the least you'll get if they find you guilty is 20 years, maybe more, at Fort Leavenworth."

"You know damn well, it don't matter how many years they give me. If I do get there, the guards will look the other way, and I'll be one dead nigger. Before a week goes by, they'll be throwin' dirt on my face."

The sergeant major knew LeCroix was right. Rape and attempted murder of a white woman was a death sentence. He gave up and changed the subject. "What did you want to see me about?"

"Might be there's somebody could help me prove I didn't do it. You know Corporal Jasko Smith would say anything to get back at me, and Gandy will swear to anythin' Smith tells him to."

"What're you talkin' about?"

"There's a man by the name of Westphal–he was a corporal in Roosevelt's regiment I met in Cuba back in '98. Now he's some kind of private investigator. I saw in the paper this mornin' he's in Bisbee visitin' his brother. He owes me."

"What for?"

I saved his ass, killed the Spanish soldier 'bout to shoot him in the back. Weren't for me, he never would've left Cuba except in a box.

"That was a long time ago, how do you know he's gonna remember you?"

"He'll remember when you tell him we met down by a creek the night before we took Kettle Hill."

The sergeant major frowned, waiting for LeCroix to tell him why he was so sure. When LeCroix didn't elaborate, he said, "I can't see the colonel agreein' to a civilian pokin' his nose in army business no matter what he did for you."

"Talk to the colonel. You and him go way back, he'll listen to you. The way I figure it, he owes me too–made him and the regiment look pretty good in Cuba. Least he can do is give me a chance, better'n the one I got now with Lieutenant Patterson," referring to the officer appointed to defend him.

"All right, I'll ask him but don't get your hopes up."

LeCroix looked out the barred window as the sergeant major walked out of the guardhouse. He knew what he'd asked the sergeant major to do was a long shot, but it was worth trying. If it didn't work out, he had no intention of staying around long enough for them to put him on a train to Leavenworth. He could afford to wait a few days to see how things worked out, and if they didn't, well he had a plan that didn't include going to Kansas.

"Pardon me, Mr. Westphal, but there's a soldier in the lobby who'd like to see you. Shall I tell him to wait while you finish your dinner?"

Morgan put down his knife and fork and looked up at the hotel clerk. "That isn't necessary. Tell him to join me here."

The clerk hesitated then said in a low voice, "I'm afraid that won't be possible."

Irritated at the clerk's refusal, Morgan asked, "Why not?"

"He's colored, and the hotel policy is Mexican and Negroes aren't permitted in the hotel dining room. Shall I tell him to wait until you're finished?"

Curiosity overcoming his irritation, Morgan put his napkin on the table and pushed his chair back. "No, I'll see him now."

Morgan followed the clerk into the lobby and saw a tall, rangy Negro in a khaki uniform wearing the chevrons of a regimental sergeant major on his sleeve standing expressionless by the front desk. His face was deeply lined, close-cropped hair streaked with gray.

Without offering to shake hands, Morgan asked, "You wanted to see me?"

In a deep baritone voice at odds with his spare frame, the soldier replied, "Sir, I'm Sergeant Major Isaiah Washington, 10th Cavalry. I'd appreciate a few minutes of your time. Is there somewhere where we can talk in private?"

"There's a waiting room over there," The clerk offered, pointing across the lobby.

Once inside the room and the door closed, the sergeant major didn't waste time in preliminaries. "Mr. Westphal, do you remember a colored soldier by the name of Rueben LeCroix?"

Morgan shook his head. "I don't recognize the name?"

Expressionless, the sergeant major prompted, "How about in Cuba? He says he saved your life down by a creek the night before the attack on Kettle Hill."

"I'll be damned, so that was his name. If that was LeCroix, he's right. Before he saved my life, he came close to killing me. I thought when he picked up the rifle he was going to finish the job he started with his fists. Instead, he shot a Spanish soldier who came out of the bushes behind me."

"What were you fighting about?"

"Just before dark, I was at a creek filling my squad's canteens when LeCroix showed up and started doing the same upstream. I asked him to wait or go farther upstream, because he was getting the water muddy. He acted like he didn't hear me. The next time I didn't ask, I told him. He

277

said a few things I didn't like. The result was two young men with more sap than brains went at it. It didn't take long for me to wish I'd kept my mouth shut and moved instead of being dumb enough to argue the point. After he shot the Spaniard, I introduced myself and tried to thank him, but he said saving me was an accident. He said a few other things, too, but by then I knew enough to keep my mouth shut. Frankly, he was one of the most unlikable men I ever met."

Washington nodded, "I reckon we're talkin' about the same man."

"Sergeant Major, you didn't come to see me about something that happened eighteen years ago, what's this all about?"

"LeCroix wants you to help him."

"What for?"

"He's in the guardhouse at Fort Huachuca charged with robbery, rape, and attempted murder. The victim is Mrs. Sophia Parmenter, the wife of Major Benjamin Parmenter, Post Commander at Fort Huachuca. His court martial will take place in a couple of weeks. If they find him guilty, they'll lock him up and throw away the key."

"Did he do it?"

"He says he didn't, and I believe him."

"What makes you think he's innocent?"

"I've known LeCroix from the time he joined my squad back in '94. He's one of the best soldiers I've ever known. He's not easy to get along with, but he ain't the kind of man to do what he's accused of."

"Does anyone else believe he's innocent?"

The sergeant major hesitated and looked Morgan in the eye, "No, I'm about the only one."

"What kind of evidence is there?"

Shrugging, brow creased in a worried frown, Washington replied, "A couple of worthless troopers who'd say anything to see LeCroix lose his chevrons and get locked up for life."

"What makes you think I can do anything to help him?"

"LeCroix read about you in the Bisbee paper this morning. He remembered your name–it's unusual. The newspaper said you're a private investigator with a good reputation. He wants your help to prove he's innocent. He says you owe him and asked me to come here and tell you that."

"Where did the assault take place?"

"In Major Parmenter's quarters at the fort."

"Sergeant Major, even if I were to agree to look into this matter, which at this point I'm not inclined to do, I can't believe the army would allow a civilian to get involved in a purely army offense."

Morgan was astonished at the other's quick, assured response. "It's already been arranged. You have an appointment to see Colonel Broadmore, the regimental commander, tomorrow morning."

"Why would Colonel Broadmore be willing to have a civilian investigate something I assume has already been thoroughly looked into by the provost marshal?"

"Because I asked him."

Morgan looked away as he considered how he was going to frame a refusal. After only a few moments, he realized he couldn't say no without first making a reasonable effort to find out more about the case.

"In that case, I'll see Colonel Broadmore, but I won't promise anything more than that. I owe LeCroix at least that much."

"I'll have transportation waiting for you at Huachuca Siding tomorrow morning at 8:30. The first train leaves here at 7:45."

Morgan nodded, "Tell me, Sergeant Major, has LeCroix's attitude improved any over the years?"

The sergeant major's mouth curved in a smile, "Reckon not. He's still the same sunnuva bitch he's always been."

About the Author

Preston Holtry is an avid traveler, reader, alpine ski instructor, VA hospital volunteer, and novelist. He has a BA degree in English from the Virginia Military Institute and a graduate degree from Boston University. A career army officer, he served twice in Vietnam in addition to a variety of other infantry and intelligence-related assignments in Germany, England, and the United States. Introducing Morgan Westphal, *Death in Emily 3* is the first in a series of Westphal mysteries. *A Troublesome Affair* and *Seal of Confession* are completed drafts; a fourth novel, working title, *Murder at Cockcrow* is underway. He is also the author of four other unpublished novels: The *Arrius* trilogy are historical novels about a battle-hardened Roman centurion serving in Judea and Britannia in the second century Roman Empire. *Looking for Steiner* is a contemporary mystery with an international setting. Now retired, he lives with his wife, Judith, in Oro Valley, Arizona.

To keep up with what's new with the author, visit his web page: presholtry.webs.com)

CPSIA information can be obtained at www.ICGtesting.com
Printed in the USA
LVOW08s0240061113

360198LV00002B/91/P